Brutal Ice

Ice Breakers Cold Case Romance
Book 11

Cynthia Eden

He was never meant to be anyone's savior...and then he found her.

Royal Boudreaux isn't interested in being a hero. Quite the opposite. Darkness clings to him, and he lets that darkness out by hunting and catching the most dangerous killers who roam the streets. Everyone needs a hobby, right? During his latest hunt, Royal expects to take down his prey. He doesn't expect to find a beautiful woman trapped in the trunk of a car.

Save the woman. Then walk away...

He intends to drop the gorgeous victim at the nearest police station and then get the hell away from her. Only walking away isn't an option for Royal. Not this time. Because there is something about dancer Violet Murphy that calls to him. A driving, primitive pull. Royal finds that he can't stay away from her. Scratch that--he doesn't *want* to be away from Violet. What he does want? *Her*.

Determined, fierce, and unwilling to give in to the fear that he sees in her eyes, Violet slides right past Royal's guard. Fragile on the outside, but with a core of steel in her soul, Violet is a fighter. But she can't fight this battle alone.

She needs protection. Lucky for her, Royal has experience at playing bodyguard.

When Royal saved Violet, the killer escaped. Somewhere in the hot Savannah night, the killer still lurks. Royal intends to protect Violet and take out his prey. But Violet has uncovered the dark truth about Royal, and instead of being repelled, she's determined to be at his side in order to get the justice she seeks. Being a victim again? *Not* on her agenda, thanks.

An unlikely alliance. A desire that can't be contained.

Danger. Lust. Need. Desire burns brutally hot on a Savannah night. But the killer isn't the only one closing in... because a very unexpected ghost from Royal's own past is heading to town. Everything Royal knew about himself is about to be completely upended. Hero, monster...which one is he? With chaos reigning, there is only one certainty for Royal...*protect Violet.*

Save the woman. Then never, ever walk away.

Because you don't walk away from the woman who holds your battered heart in the palm of her hand.

Author's Note: Royal's hobby is dangerous, diabolical, and definitely not ordinary. But then again, he's all of those things, too. When he discovers Violet, his entire world shifts focus. She matches him, she scares him, and...she just damn well might complete him. But in order to have a life with Violet, Royal has to first hunt down and stop the man who abducted her—and killed three other women. Lucky for Royal, he's not hunting alone. The Ice Breakers are back. Passion, twists, and hot romance are coming your way.

Chapter One

Everyone needed a hobby, and Royal Boudreaux's hobby? It just happened to be the little matter of murder. Or, rather, the matter of stopping murderers.

Someone had to hunt the bastards, after all. When the cops failed, when the blood kept flowing, and the families were grieving, someone had to step in and do the dirty work. He was good at getting his hands dirty. And bloody. In fact, he excelled at the task.

So he crept through the dark Savannah night, his body tense and alert because he knew that danger waited up ahead. But he wasn't afraid. Royal didn't fear much in this world. He made it a point to be the one that others feared. And his prey tonight? By the time Royal was done with him, he'd be teaching the SOB a whole new meaning to the term *terror*.

You'll be begging me to stop.

His steps were silent. His body moved easily to blend with the stretching shadows all around him. The insects chirped, and the old, forgotten and failed vineyard and its hollowed out winery waited in dead silence around him like the graveyard that the place was.

His gaze slid to his prey's vehicle. A faded sedan. It was the kind of vehicle most people wouldn't look at twice. That was why the predator had chosen it. To blend. To slip right past everyone's guard. To appear ever so harmless.

Often, the most harmful things could look innocent.

He eased past the sedan. His eyes were on the main building to the right. His gloved fingers stayed loose at his sides. He was so close.

Thud.

Royal stopped. Tensed. His head turned—the barest of movements—as he glanced back at that sedan.

Thud.

His eyes narrowed. The faint moonlight and starlight spilled onto the car. No driver. Because the driver had gone inside one of the buildings. Or into the stretching, barren fields of the vineyard. *But I'll be finding you soon.* And giving the guy the punishment he deserved.

Thud.

Royal took a step toward the vehicle. Was that sound seriously coming from the trunk of the sedan?

Thud.

It *was* coming from the trunk. The closed trunk. Still with silent steps, he hurried to the driver's side. The window had been left half-down, so he shoved his gloved hand inside. Yanked up the old lock and opened the door. Then it just took him a few seconds to find the little lever that would pop the trunk.

Even as the lid of the trunk rose up, he ran back to the rear of the sedan. He yanked the pen flashlight from his pocket and shone it inside.

Holy shit.

It took a lot to surprise Royal. He'd seen so much—done so much—during the days and nights of his life that he was rarely ever caught off-guard. But he did not expect to see a bound woman staring back at him.

Royal blinked once. His light fell straight on her face. Her beautiful, terrified, tear-stained face. Gray duct tape covered her mouth. Her raised hands were bound together with the same rough, gray tape. Her wide, desperate eyes—glimmering with tears—stared up at him. Fear and hope fought in those gorgeous eyes.

A beautiful woman who was trapped in the trunk of a killer's car.

Sonofabitch. His prey wasn't still scouting for victims as Royal had believed. Time had run out. The bastard had taken another woman.

With his free hand, Royal reached out and carefully removed the tape. Even though he was trying to be gentle—and gentle was not often a word associated with him—she winced. Shuddered.

His chest tightened. He balled up the tape. Tossed it into the trunk.

"Are you...are you going to kill me?" A low whisper from the woman. Husky. Absolutely terrified.

Fuck. The night was not going according to plan at all. His gaze darted away from her. Toward the stretching old vineyard. Somewhere out there, his prey waited. Prey—a killer who had already murdered three other women.

His gaze returned to the bound woman in the trunk. A woman who was meant to be victim number four.

In his mind, he had a flash of the other victims. The brutal torture that had been inflicted on their bodies. The way they'd been found. Broken. Tossed away.

A tear leaked down her cheek.

She thought he was the killer.

Royal shook his head. "No." He scooped her out of the trunk. Into his arms. Heard her gasp. Barely felt the slight weight of her in his arms. Then, staring down at her, Royal said something that he had never, ever expected to say, "I'm going to save you."

He'd learned long ago that you couldn't save the world. Sometimes, it was just better to watch the world fucking burn. But, this one time, he could save this one woman.

Can't leave her behind. Don't know where he is on the property. If I leave her and hunt for him, he could circle back. Could kill her while I'm searching for him.

With his teeth grinding together, Royal hurriedly made his way back through the darkness. He'd stashed his ride about a mile away. He hadn't wanted to alert his prey, so he'd gone in silently. She didn't struggle against him during that mile-long walk. Didn't move at all. Hell, the woman barely seemed to breathe. He'd turned off his light, but he still gripped it on one hand even as he carried her. Royal kept his body battle-ready. If the prick who'd taken her came at him with an attack...

I'll be vulnerable with her. She'll make me weak.

He couldn't afford weakness. Actually, he freaking hated weakness. Better to just eliminate the weakness as soon as possible.

The insects had gone quiet. The fact registered even as Royal froze. Very, very slowly, his head turned to look back at the path he'd just taken.

Only darkness stared back at him.

"If...if you cut the tape from my ankles, I can walk." A breathless whisper. "You don't have to carry me. I-I can—"

"Run from me?" he rasped. "Sweetheart, you're shaking like a leaf. You're obviously scared as hell of me." Royal kept walking. "I cut that tape now, and you'll run, and you'll probably run straight into *him*. He'll shove his knife in your gut, and then my Good Samaritan efforts will be for jack and shit."

She shuddered even harder in his arms. She also, he noted, *didn't* deny that she'd run. As if he hadn't been able to figure that out.

"I'm not the one who took you," he said, voice barely a breath. "I'm saving your sweet ass."

Then there were no more words because every instinct he had was screaming at him. Royal was used to being the predator. But with her in his arms, with the hair on the nape of his neck rising, he swore in that instance...

Prey.

Hell, no. He never wanted to be prey.

His black Lexus waited up ahead. He eased the mystery woman to her feet—she nearly fell so he kept a grasp on her waist—and he opened the passenger door to ease her inside. "Don't try to get away," he ordered softly when he had her settled on the seat.

He heard the click of her swallow. Right. Probably the wrong thing to say.

Royal rushed around the car. Slid inside. Shut his own door and turned to face her.

"Who are you?" she whispered.

"I'm your hero for the night."

"That's..." A slow exhale. "Not a name."

Indeed, it wasn't. "This is how we're going to play things...I'll drop you off at the nearest police station, and, in return for me saving your life, you will forget my face completely." He pulled out his knife. "Deal?"

Her eyes were on the knife.

Hell. "I suck at the saving business." Because he was

clearly just terrifying her more when he'd actually meant to be semi-reassuring. "Hands."

"Wh-what?"

"Give me your hands, sweetheart." The endearment just sort of rolled out. Another vague effort to be reassuring? Gruffly, Royal added, "Give me your hands unless you want to ride all the way to the police station with them still bound."

She shoved her hands toward him.

Carefully, because he did not want to so much as nick her, Royal eased the blade between her bound wrists. One quick slice, and he had the tape open. He pulled it off her wrists, then rubbed her skin. The tape had been tight as hell, so she had to be experiencing some pain as feeling rushed back to her fingers.

"Thank you." Soft.

He grunted. Then leaned down to free her feet. No shoes. Another reason why it had been better to carry her through the night. She would have just sliced the soles of her feet on the rocks and old twigs and who the hell knew what else in the dark. His hand curled around her bare calf as he maneuvered toward her bound ankles. Hard to bend down that far in the tight confines of the car—especially with his big size.

She had on a black skirt that ended above her knees— and the skirt had risen even more when he settled her in the car. Her skin was soft, silken, and she was absolutely shaking with terror as he touched her.

Trying to be fast—but still careful—Royal sliced with his knife. He hauled back into his seat. "I'm not going to hurt—"

And she was gone. She'd shoved open the door and run back into the night.

Dammit. Was this what it was like for heroes? No wonder he didn't want to be one. Saving someone was a total pain in the ass. Maybe he should just let her run.

But what if she runs right back into her abductor?

There was truly no rest for the freaking wicked. He threw open his door and lunged out of the car. She hadn't gone far—she'd fallen about four feet from the Lexus. Probably because her ankles had been bound too tightly and the feeling and pain had rushed back to her feet and sent her stumbling. But the woman was trying to crawl forward. She'd made it onto her knees. He rushed up behind her. "Would you just—"

She threw a handful of dirt in his eyes.

Something that absolutely pissed him off, but damn if it didn't impress him, too. He blinked rapidly and growled even as she staggered to her feet again. She took a step forward.

Still blinking and ignoring the burn in his eyes, Royal locked an arm around her waist. "Hey, pain in my ass," he breathed against her ear. "Here's some helpful info for you. Going back that way will lead to death. A violent, pain-filled death."

She shuddered against him.

"I get that I'm no prince charming," Royal continued, voice grim and low, "but I'm also not a sadistic prick who is going to carve you up and kill you, so...there's that."

She clawed at his arms. He was wearing long sleeves. Still had on his gloves. She didn't touch his skin. He did haul her back to the car. The passenger side door was open. The interior light from the vehicle freaking lit up the scene. He plunked her down in the seat, then leaned in toward her. "You trying to get *me* killed?"

Her chest heaved.

"Because you're shining a damn spotlight on us both. He could shoot me in the back right now and take you again. Then what the hell do you think your odds of survival would be?" And, since he didn't want to get shot in the back, Royal needed to move. Fast. "You run again, and I won't come after your ass. You can face him on your own. I'm not dying for you." Cold. Savage. He rose and stared down at her. *But I will follow you. Might even use you as bait. And I will kill the asshole.* Those words, though, he didn't say. No sense in adding to her fear.

The choice would be hers.

Then, deliberately, he stalked back around the car and got in the driver's seat.

She didn't run again. She did haul the door closed.

He tossed his gloves into the backseat and cranked the engine. "Good choice," he growled. And he shifted to drive and shoved his foot down on the gas pedal. But his gaze darted to the rear-view mirror.

I'll be back for you, bastard. Because his prey never got away from him.

* * *

SOMETHING WAS WRONG.

He knew it as soon as he saw the sedan's trunk lid rising up in the air. *No, no, no!* He raced forward with a snarl cutting from his lips. The trunk should *never* have been opened. He used the damn car specifically because there was no emergency release latch inside the trunk. The ride was too old to have one. The other women hadn't been able to get out.

She shouldn't have, either.

But as his hands slammed down on the edges of the

open trunk, he saw that his beautiful prey was gone. His breath heaved in and out. Rage twisted and snarled within him. He grabbed the balled-up duct tape that had been left behind.

She got out. She found a way to escape me.

He whirled, stared at the night, and screamed her name, "*Violet!*"

* * *

"Violet..." Soft. She swallowed. Her mouth was so dry, and her lips and the skin around her mouth ached from the tape. "My name is Violet Murphy."

He grunted.

Her fingers inched toward the door handle.

"Seriously, if you open that door and jump out while I'm driving sixty miles an hour, you will be a dead woman."

Her fingers stopped inching.

How had he even realized what she was doing? His gaze seemed to be staring straight ahead.

"And if you go killing yourself, you'll undo all of my good work."

Was it her imagination? Or had there been mockery in his voice when he said "good" just then? "I'm not jumping out."

"Excellent to know." A deep, dark rumble of sound.

She licked her lips. "I'm Violet," she said again. "And you are...?"

"The man driving you to the police station."

"Promise?" The word just slipped from her. And it cracked with both fear and hope.

She saw his fingers—broad and strong—tighten around

the steering wheel. "Promise." Still growled but somehow less harsh.

Not that there seemed to be a lot about her savior that wasn't harsh. When he'd opened the trunk and shone his flashlight on her, she'd been sure that she was doomed.

Too big. Too strong. She'd stared up at his shadowy form and known that he'd overpower her in an instant. Fear had nearly choked her. All she'd wanted was to escape and she'd asked him...*Are you going to kill me?*

His answer had sent shock rolling through her. Before she'd fully recovered from that shock, he'd been carrying her through the darkness at double-time speed. He hadn't even seemed winded by what had seemed like at least a mile traveling with her cradled in his arms.

She'd just told him her name because—even though he said he was there to save her, and even though he *said* he was taking her to the cops—she was still afraid to trust him. So she'd been trying to humanize herself. Not just be some random victim. *In case he is the bad guy, and this is some psychological BS game that he's playing with me.* A game where he gave her hope, only to snatch it away.

By offering him her name, she wasn't just some faceless woman to kill. She was Violet Murphy. And she had a life. "I have two brothers. Both older. Parker is deployed, and I haven't heard from him in six months." Her words tumbled out. "But my other brother Dawson lives in town. He runs a real estate company. I, um, I'm a dancer."

"Why in the hell are you telling me this?"

"So you won't kill me." An immediate response.

His head turned toward her.

She automatically squeezed her eyes shut.

"And why are you closing your eyes?" he gritted.

"Because I'm scared this is some sick game. You're

making me think I'm going to leave, that I'm going to get away and go home, but it's just a trick so you can rip the hope away from me."

The car braked. Hard. Hard enough that she shoved forward, and the seatbelt cut into her shoulder. And then...

His fingers curled around her chin.

"I promise I won't play sick games...with you."

She could feel the rough texture of his callused fingers against her skin.

"I can't say the same about the sonofabitch who took you."

Her eyes flew open.

His face was close to hers. The light from the instrument panel spilled into the front of the car. She'd seen his features under the moonlight as he carried her. She glimpsed them now and again had the same thought...

Dangerous. Deadly.

"I'm not mind-fucking you, sweetheart. I'm saving your life. Though I can see where you might get confused. Good deeds are new for me."

His face was so close to hers. His mouth close. And she was seriously screwed up because she was staring into his eyes and thinking...

Fallen angel. He looks like a fallen angel. Sculpted cheeks. High forehead. Beautiful, but in a savage and dark way. His thick hair tumbled over his forehead. He wore all black. A thick shirt with sleeves that stretched down to his wrists.

"How did you wind up in the trunk of that car?" he asked her.

She blinked. Her eyes had been on his mouth. A mouth that was slightly cruel. Oddly...sexy.

What is wrong with you? You can't find anything about him attractive. Not the time. Not the place. Not the man.

Except...

Hero?

"Violet," he said her name as if he were tasting it—and he liked the taste. "How did you wind up in the trunk of that car?" His thumb brushed lightly over her lower lip.

"I was...dancing. I have a show coming up. I-I'm playing Snow White, and I stayed late because I was working on the finale. Everyone else left. I came out. The stage was dark. The whole theater was dark, as if everyone had forgotten me. I went out the back. I pushed open the theater's rear door and then..." Her voice trailed away. She could recall shoving open the door. Going out into the night. Her breath caught.

"Remembering details, are you? Something that scares you?"

Everything about the night scared her. "I went out the back." Her voice was a whisper. "Didn't look behind me as I hurried for my car. S-someone grabbed me. Slapped a hand over my mouth."

His thumb brushed over her lips once more. An ever-so-careful caress.

"And another hand grabbed my waist. I didn't have time to scream." The memories poured out as if a dam had burst. Fear poured through her. "I kicked back at him. Fought at his hold. I got free, stumbled forward, and—" Violet stopped.

Because the memory stopped.

"Violet?"

"He slammed into me. Twisted me and threw me to the ground. I think I hit my head." Maybe?

His hand freed her chin. Rose to lightly slide over her

temple. Then, higher, to her forehead. His long fingers dipped under the thick curtain of her hair, and she winced when pain shot through her head.

"Bastard," he breathed.

"Then I was in the trunk. It was dark, and I couldn't get out."

He let her go. Eased back fully into his seat. "You didn't see him. His face?"

She pushed at the memories but found darkness. "I don't remember seeing him."

He started driving once again.

"I'm not a big fan of the dark," she confessed. She was rambling and didn't care. Still trying to humanize herself in case he was the bad guy?

He doesn't feel bad. He touches me so carefully. And when he'd said *bastard* in that low, lethal snarl, she'd heard the rage. A rage that had been directed at her attacker, not at her.

"When I was seven, my older brother Dawson locked me in a closet." Violet gasped after her confession. Why, *why* had that spilled out? Now she just needed to stop. Only she couldn't seem to do that.

"Why the fuck would he do that?"

"He thought it was funny. A joke. We were playing hide and seek, and he locked me in, and he meant to get me right out—that's what he said—but, the lock got jammed. I was stuck in there." Shivers spread over her arms. "My mom wasn't home, and Dawson didn't know how to get me out. It was so dark in there, and I stayed in that closet—"

"How. Long?"

"Five hours. Until she got back. Dawson got tired of hearing me crying, so he went into the other room. He turned his radio up as loud as he could. I think it drowned out my cries."

"Want me to kill your brother?"

"*What?*"

He turned the vehicle. Headed down another long, dark stretch of road. "I'll take that as a no."

"*Who are you?*" And he hadn't been serious. Right? *Right?*

"Savior. Get-away driver. Ass kicker."

"That's...still not your name."

"A name doesn't mean anything."

"It does to me."

She saw his jaw harden. "If I give you a name, you'll have to give it to the cops."

"I..." Okay, she might. Quite likely.

"You're an oversharer. Kinda cute, in an odd way."

Her brows shot up. "I'm riding a whole lot of adrenaline right now, so just excuse me if I talk too much." *It's been a killer night, all right?* "I am not normally like this. In fact, I don't normally share personal details at all. Even with close friends."

Soft laughter. Deep. Warm. *Sexy.*

Nope. There it was again. The descriptor that should not be there. *Sexy.* "How did you find me?"

"Would you believe I was just out for a stroll and happened upon you?"

She shook her head. Then realized he couldn't see the movement because he was looking at the road while she was looking at him. "No, I don't think I would believe that."

"Good. Because that would be a total bullshit lie."

She peered down at her fingers. "Why won't they stop shaking?" Though it wasn't just her fingers that shook. Her whole body trembled.

"You're in shock. Probably have a concussion. Adrenaline and fear are tearing you apart on the inside, but you are doing a damn fine job of holding your shit together. Really. Bravo."

She jerked.

"So talk to me if you want," he invited, voice almost lazy. "Tell me your secrets. Tell me your fears. Tell me anything you want. But don't expect the same from me. I'm a shadow in your life, and that is all I will ever be. When I leave you at the police station, forget me."

I don't think I could forget you if I tried. Tears slid down her cheeks.

"Talk to me, Violet."

"He was going to kill me, wasn't he?"

"I won't let that happen." A vow.

But...

He hadn't denied it. I was supposed to die.

Her hands balled into fists. "I've been dancing since I was six years old. My dad died that year, and my mom was trying to distract me, I think. She signed me up for lessons. Signed my brothers up for taekwondo. Baseball. Had us all so busy we didn't have a minute to let the tears take us." Tears were taking her right then. "My first show was *The Nutcracker*, and I was a mouse." Dawson had called her a rat. Parker had told her she was a cute mouse.

"Bet you were fucking fantastic."

A startled laugh escaped her. *How can I laugh now?* "I was terrible. I fell off the stage."

A rumble came from him. Laughter that was deep and warm.

Without thinking, she reached out and her hand touched his arm. The surge hit her without warning. An electric charge that pulsed up her arm and throughout her whole body. Scared, she snatched her hand back.

"I kept dancing," she heard herself whisper. "My brothers gave up baseball. Stopped taekwondo. They moved on to football. A thousand other things. But I kept dancing."

"Why?"

"Because I had learned that you could escape any pain when you went onto a stage. When you dance, you become someone else." *And I'll get on the stage again, and I'll escape this, too. I'll be someone else again.*

She could pretend that she hadn't been taken. That she hadn't been a victim. That this nightmare wasn't real. Act as if it had all happened to someone else. *Just a role. Not me.*

"I'm good at pretending," she heard herself say. "I'll blend in, and I'll become someone new, and this won't hurt me anymore. I'll wake up, and this will all feel like a bad dream. Everything..." Her gaze flickered over him once more. "Except you."

"Oh, Violet, don't fool yourself." Rough. Low. "I'm the baddest dream there is."

* * *

He braked the Lexus near the police station. Not right in front of it, but in the lot about fifty feet from the entrance. Close enough, Violet supposed. She stared at the bright lights of the station. A beacon in the night.

Beyond the glass doors and windows, she could spy uniformed cops milling around.

"You're safe."

His warm, deep voice washed over her.

"Just put one foot in front of the other and go inside."

He wasn't the bad guy. He hadn't been, uh, mind-fucking her, as she'd feared. He really had saved her life.

"You're not getting out of the car," he noted.

Her head swung away from the police station and those bright lights, and she looked back at him. "Thank you." How did you repay a man who had just saved you from hell?

"You don't need to thank me."

Yes, she did.

She unhooked her seat belt. And lunged toward him. Her hands curled around him, and she held him tightly in a fierce hug. "You saved me."

His fingers pressed lightly to her back. "Not like I could leave you in the trunk."

A shiver chased down her spine.

"You have to go inside, Violet. Tell the cops what happened. Just leave out as much about me as possible."

Her head tilted back. "Why?"

"Because not everyone will think I'm a hero." His eyes were on her mouth. "And because they won't be wrong. I'm not a hero."

Was his head lowering toward hers? Did he...wait, did he want to kiss her?

Did *she* want to kiss him?

Her heart shoved hard in her chest, and she knew a million reasons why she should not do this...

Kidnapped. Nearly killed. Concussion. Wrong place. Wrong time.

But Violet didn't care. Maybe because she was beyond control and rational thought. Maybe because she just was reacting based on pure animal instinct. Her hands lifted to curl around the back of his head, and she dragged him toward her. Their mouths met in a too-hard crash. No finesse. No care. She crashed her lips into his and squeezed her eyes closed.

He laughed lightly against her lips.

She jerked back.

"You are unexpected," he murmured. "But let's try it this way..." His thumb slid over her lower lip. Her mouth parted for him.

This time, he kissed her. Soft. Careful. His tongue dipped between her parted lips, and she was absolutely lost. No other word for it. Animal instinct took over again as a driving, primitive need swept through her. Lust. Hunger. Desire.

He kissed her with care and a tender savagery that called to something deep inside of her. He tasted her as if he had all the time in the world. She tasted him as if she'd been dying of thirst and he was truly the best drink she'd ever been offered. Her first sip of wine.

And...

He pulled away. "Go." Gruff. "Before I decide to keep you."

A joke, of course. Wait, wasn't it? She scrambled toward the door even as one hand rose to her lips. She could still taste him.

She wanted more.

Her fingers fumbled and opened the door. "I won't forget you."

"I'd rather you did. As soon as you walk into the station, please do forget all important descriptors when it comes to me."

She wanted to look at him again, but she didn't. She opened the door. Stood. Felt the pavement bite into her bare feet. Violet started to take a step forward but found she couldn't move.

"I won't leave until you get inside the station." Low. "I'll have my eyes on you the whole time. You're safe when I'm watching you."

You're safe when I'm watching you.

Her head moved in a slow nod. One foot lifted. Then the other. Jerky movements. Like she was one of those old wind-up robots that lurched and staggered its way forward.

Step by step, she got closer to the lights of the station. Even though the urge was strong, Violet didn't glance back over her shoulder. One step. Another.

Inside the station, the officer behind the counter looked up. Frowned.

She kept advancing. Lurching. Creeping. Violet grabbed for the door. Her fingers curled around the handle, and she wrenched it open. "Help..." Too soft. She swallowed. "Help me!"

The uniformed cop ran from behind the counter. "Ma'am? Ma'am, what happened?"

"I was...kidnapped. Taken..."

His hands curled around her arms.

She did look back. In that last moment, she did.

She saw the Lexus's taillights as her savior drove away.

Chapter Two

Being a hero absolutely freaking sucked. Royal didn't care what BS the books and movies shouted to the world. Heroes didn't win. They didn't always stop the villain. And they damn well did not get the girl.

Instead, the villain got away. Got to slink off into the night in order to kill again another day, and, as for the girl...

She walked away. She didn't look back. She went back to her world. The bright lights. The fans. Snow White went right back to dancing on her stage to the roar of the crowd.

And the hero went right back to hell.

And, in this particular instance, hell was the fundraising party where the rich and obnoxious of Savannah, Georgia, were currently milling around in their bright jewels, gossiping about everything under the sun, and truly destroying the last bit of patience that he possessed.

What in the hell am I doing here?

Two weeks had passed since Royal had dropped Violet's gorgeous ass off at the Savannah PD. Two weeks since the press had gotten wind of her story. Two weeks since half the town started thinking she was a victim, and half the town became convinced she was a publicity whore trying to drum up more attendance for the upcoming production of her ballet.

The evidence said she'd been taken. Real evidence that the cops had uncovered. A surveillance video from the back of the theater that clearly showed a ski-mask-wearing prick tackling Violet to the ground before he carried her limp body off the screen. And doctors had examined her. Her concussion had been very real.

Violet had even remembered where she'd been taken. She'd been able to describe the vineyard and old winery that she saw. *When I carried her sweet ass out of there.*

The cops had gone to the scene. Searched it. So far, they'd turned up nothing useful.

I don't think they looked hard enough.

So, sure, yes, there were parts of Violet's story that absolutely, one hundred percent had been substantiated but...

"How did she escape?" The question came from a woman to the right of Royal. Blond. Breasts spilling from her skin-tight, sky-blue dress. Diamonds glittered at her ears. "That's the part I don't get." She raised a flute of champagne to her lips. "Isn't that suspicious? That she can't remember exactly what happened from the time she got out of the trunk until she showed up at the police station?"

"Concussions are funny things," the man next to her replied with a sage nod as if he had all the wisdom in the world.

From his position against the wall, Royal quirked a brow.

"She was probably drifting in and out of consciousness," the man continued. "Whoever saved her—well, she may never remember his face."

"Dr. Barnes." The blond put down her empty flute so that she could grasp his arm. "You are so knowledgeable."

Was he, though?

Her blood-red nails stroked up toward the doctor's shoulder. "And I'm so sorry about your wife. I heard she passed away—how long has it been? Two years ago now? I hope you are—"

"There's Violet," the doctor cut through her words. "There she is."

And that same proclamation was echoed multiple times by people who'd been waiting for the star of the show to make her appearance.

There. She. Is.

Yeah, fuck it, even Royal shoved away from the wall as interest spiked through him. He'd shelled out the two hundred bucks for the ticket to the fundraiser just because he knew she would be there. *And I wanted to see her again. Up close. Personal.*

Hell, he hadn't just paid two hundred bucks to get inside.

He'd dropped ten grand in order to buy the privilege of the first and only dance with the star of the show.

She hadn't seen him yet. She was slowly walking down the stairs. Violet wore red. A silky dress with tiny, spaghetti straps that clung lightly to her delicate shoulders. His eyes narrowed on her. She seemed...smaller. Even more fragile than she'd been before. Makeup had been skillfully applied, but he still caught the hint of dark shadows under her eyes.

Have you been sleeping, sweetheart? Or do nightmares keep you up?

Her lips were painted a bold red to match her dress. Long, dangling earrings hung from her lobes, and those earrings slid in and out of her thick, dark hair.

As she drew closer to the landing, conversation stopped. All eyes were on her.

Royal knew that he sure as hell couldn't look away. He wasn't even sure if he was breathing.

Not the first time I've seen her since that night. Get a fucking grip, man.

Because...he had gone back to check on her. To stay close to the theater when he knew she was rehearsing late. To make sure that she got home safely.

To make sure *she* was safe.

Bullshit. Don't lie to yourself.

He'd returned to...see her.

"Thank you all for coming!" It was the pompous ass beside Violet who'd just made that announcement. Micah Wright. The artistic director for the show. The man who basically was in charge of the ballet when it came to Savannah. His hand curled around Violet's shoulder. A proprietary touch that had Royal's gaze sharpening.

She gave a small flinch.

Royal's back teeth ground together.

"It's a big night for our show!" Micah called out. "The premiere will be next week, and I can't wait for you all to see our Snow White take the stage!"

Applause spilt the air.

Micah—one of those pretty boys with capped, perfect teeth—smiled. "Your fundraising efforts mean so much to our group. And, as the band strikes up the first dance, I want to personally thank the winner of our dance auction. This individual donated ten thousand dollars for the privilege of dancing with our star!"

More applause. Heads turned as speculation mounted about just who had dropped that ten grand.

Violet didn't glance around, though. Her gaze seemed focused on the marble floor. *Too delicate. Too afraid.*

But she was still being paraded around in front of the gawking crowd. Royal didn't like that shit, not at all.

"I'd like to thank Royal Boudreaux for the generous donation. Mr. Boudreaux?" Micah's voice rose. "Are you ready for your dance? Mr. Boudreaux?"

Royal didn't answer. Instead, he started walking forward. People instinctively got the fuck out of his way. They'd always done that. He smiled grimly at the onlookers. He'd made sure to wear the right tux so he'd blend with this crowd. No one staring at him now would ever guess he'd started life by being abandoned on the streets by his family. No one would guess he'd fought and clawed for survival in gang life. And no one would sure ever know...

That for fun, he hunted down serial killers and became their worst nightmares.

Violet wasn't looking at him. She showed zero curiosity about her dance partner.

But Micah was looking. The man's big smile dimmed a bit when he got a good view of Royal. "Uh, Mr. Boudreaux?"

Royal nodded. "That'd be me." He stopped right in front of Violet. He extended his hand toward her.

Very, very slowly, her gaze began to drift over his body. Started at his feet. Her gaze darted up. Her head rose. Lifted as she looked at his legs. His chest. His neck.

His chin.

A light beard covered his jaw. It had been fourteen days, after all. So he wasn't clean shaven like he'd been the night they met. He waited to see recognition in her eyes—those amazing, golden eyes. But there was no recognition.

Not so much as a flicker of emotion crossed her face.

"Thank you," she whispered as her fingers curled around his.

Desire knifed through him.

"My pleasure," he murmured.

Her body jolted. The eyes that had started to lower once more flew to meet his.

He smiled at her. For her. A real smile. "I believe the dance is mine." *And so are you.*

Her tongue snaked over those lush, red lips, but before she could speak again, the band began to play. He pulled her against him, into his arms, and took her onto the dance floor while everyone else watched.

Every single eye was on them. And as for Violet...

"Sweetheart, you look like you've just seen a ghost." Low words. Meant for her alone.

She stumbled.

He made a quick tut-tut with his tongue. "I expected more, especially from such an accomplished dancer as yourself. Shall I slow down? Will that help?" And he did. But just so he could pull her closer. Hold her tighter. He towered over her.

Be careful. She's breakable.

"You...paid ten thousand dollars to dance with me?"

Dammit, her voice was too sexy. Husky and sensual and it stroked over him with way too much force. "A bargain, don't you think?"

Her head shook. "I would have danced with you for free."

He was the one who almost stumbled. "Hardly the way to raise money, now, is it?"

One of her hands curled around his upper arm. The other gripped his hand. "It's *you.*"

"My name's Royal. Royal Boudreaux. But then, I think you heard that handsy prick when he introduced me."

Her breath came faster and faster.

His left hand slid down to curl around her waist. "Pull in a deeper breath. Nice and slow." He inhaled. "What is that scent?"

"L-lilacs."

"Violet smells like lilacs." Soft laughter escaped from him.

She stopped. Tried to pull away. To retreat. He just spun her back into his arms. And held her ever closer. "Easy," he whispered against her ear. "So many people are watching us. I think you are supposed to look as if you're fascinated by me. Not as if you're afraid." He didn't want her fear.

Violet shivered against him.

"I am not here to hurt you."

Her head turned. She peered up at him with truly the deepest, most golden eyes he'd ever seen. "Then why are you here?"

So many eyes were on them. Too many. *I only care about her eyes.* "The cops think the perp was a crazed fan."

"I-I'd done a national tour of *Swan Lake* before coming here. So many cities. The detectives think he followed me."

"The detectives are dead wrong. The man who took you isn't some obsessed fan. He's a fucking serial killer."

This time when she stumbled, he kept a steady grip on her. Carefully, he steered her toward the doors that led out onto the balcony.

"How do you know that?" she asked.

"Because I know all about the monsters who hide in the dark."

The band kept playing.

"You didn't tell the cops about me," Royal noted.

Her gaze slid over his face. As if memorizing every feature.

"Did you even recognize me," Royal pushed, truly curious, "until I spoke?"

"I hear your voice in my dreams."

"Nightmares." He nodded.

"*Dreams*," she corrected flatly. "I know the difference between a nightmare and a dream. In my dream, I'm safe and I'm with you."

"You'll always be safe with me." Now why in the sweet hell had he just said those words to her?

She licked her lips again. Damn. She really needed to stop tempting him. "Why didn't you want the cops to know about what you'd done?" Violet asked. "You saved me."

He smiled at her. "You shouldn't ask questions that you don't want answered."

"I really, really want that answer."

He supposed she did. Didn't mean he was going to give it to her, though. "You moved out of your brother's house. You went back to your place." A move she'd made earlier that day.

Her eyes widened. "How did you know that?"

They were almost at the balcony doors. And the song was nearly at an end.

"Were you *watching* me?" Violet's voice rose a little too much.

"Protecting you," he corrected. "Seems I developed a taste for it." And to think, he'd once mocked his brother for doing something very similar once upon a not too long-ago time. Oh, but if Beau found out about Royal's current situation...

The asshole would never let me hear the end of things. For a variety of reasons.

For now, he was keeping secrets from his brother. Better for them both that way. And, since they were on the subject of brothers... "You should return to your brother's place," Royal told Violet. "Go back and stay with Dawson. It's not wise for you to be alone."

The band slowly trailed away as the music ended. The crowd applauded. Violet glanced around the ballroom and offered a shaky smile to everyone.

Micah motioned toward her. She took a step in his direction.

"Nope, I want you with me." Royal kept one hand on her wrist and with the other, he pushed open the balcony door.

She peered down at his hand, then back up at him. "Bossy, aren't you?"

"Absolutely. I'm Arrogant. Demanding. Vengeful. Obsessive. I could go on about my bad qualities for days." He shrugged. "Can't say you weren't warned."

"Are you *trying* to warn me away from you?" Her head cocked. The earrings caught the light and threw it back at him. A glimmer in the darkness of her hair. Not completely black hair, though. He could see red highlights hidden in that darkness.

"Maybe I am," he heard himself say.

"Then why come to see me in the first place? Why pay for the dance?"

"Because I think the killer is going to come after you again. The cops don't need to be blowing smoke and saying it's some obsessed fan." The words were low. Meant only for her. "You have to be on your guard. Always."

Violet swallowed. "You're scaring me."

"Good. Then my brilliant plan is working."

"Violet!" Micah called.

Royal spared him an annoyed glance. The other man was rushing across the dance floor and torpedoing straight toward them. "Tell him to fuck off," he advised.

"That's my boss. I can't say that to him!"

"Your boss wants to fuck you. Guy has a reputation for fucking all his leading ladies." Royal had been doing some digging on the people in Violet's world.

"I'm not interested in fucking him." Prim.

Fucking prim and adorable. "Stop it," Royal told her as his gaze flew back to her.

"Stop what?" Violet's brows arched. "Are you having an episode right now? Is there someone you need me to call?"

"You're being damn cute. You shouldn't do that with me."

"Uh, okay." She backed up a step. "Definitely an episode."

"Violet!" Micah was almost on top of them.

He did not have the patience to deal with that prick. "Come with me onto the balcony. I want to talk with you. Without eyes on us and ears straining to hear every word we say."

She bit her lip.

And Micah was there. "Violet." He reached out toward her. "Violet, there are other donors you need to—"

Royal stepped into his path. "Ten thousand dollars is buying me ten more minutes." It had better. Royal gave the man a hard grin. "Violet and I have a little more talking to do. Privately. You'll excuse us?" And Royal thought that was the nicest way he'd ever said *fuck off* to someone before. Violet wouldn't know it, but he'd just showed pretty insane restraint.

Micah blinked. "What?" He blinked three times in fast succession. "You...you didn't buy Violet. I mean, not time with her. You have to—"

"I'll be there in ten minutes," Violet broke through his words to say. "Mr. Boudreaux is considering additional donations, and I'd like to speak with him privately about those."

Well, again, not the official *fuck off* that he'd wanted, but the jerk was her boss. Maybe she was being tactful.

Micah's brows beetled. He craned his head to see her around Royal's form. "Violet?"

"Ten minutes," she repeated. "I'll be right outside. And I'll be perfectly safe with Mr. Boudreaux."

Micah's suspicious eyes returned to Royal.

"I do so love the ballet," Royal murmured. "Just want to see if I'm making my contributions in the right way."

Micah pulled up a smile. "I'll be happy to answer any questions you have."

"Thank you so much." *You prick. Stop cutting your gaze at Violet. And keep your hands off her in the future.* "If you'll excuse us?" He didn't wait for a response. Royal edged toward the open balcony door. Violet exited first.

And he followed right on her heels.

* * *

THE BALLROOM WAS full of beautiful victims. But he only wanted her.

The red dress had made Violet look as if she were covered in blood. At least, to his eyes. She'd spun and glided on the floor, held too close by the hulking asshole who'd bid too high on the dance with her.

Violet had looked at her partner with fear in her lovely eyes.

These days, she looked at most people that way.

A new change, seeing prey in this light. Knowing that he'd been the one to instill the fear in her. Sweet, somehow. Poignant.

It made Violet different. Special.

Not special enough that she would actually get to escape. Oh, no, never that. But still, her end would be particularly meaningful for him.

You won't get away. The cops had been watching her. Paying a bit too much attention. So he'd waited. He'd bided his time.

But the cops couldn't stick close forever. There were other cases. Other crimes. Other victims. Violet wouldn't be protected forever.

Eventually, she'd go back to her old routine. Her old life.

And when she lowered her guard...

I'll be here, Violet. Waiting. And we'll finish what we started.

Chapter Three

He'd come back.

Violet sucked in the fresh air and tipped back her head as she stared up at the starry night. So many stars. They glittered above her and reminded her of another night.

Another place.

The night she'd spent with him. Her mystery hero. The white knight who'd saved her. Kissed her like he was starving for her. Then told her to walk away and never look back. Only...

He'd come back for me.

He stood behind her now. She could feel the heat from his body stretching out to wrap around her. "Royal." Now she had a name for the shadow that was her savior.

His hand curled around her shoulder and slid down her arm.

A shiver chased over her.

"You don't need to be afraid of me." His voice was deep and dark, and it rumbled like a growl. Why on earth did she find it so sexy?

Maybe because she found everything about him to be sexy.

"I'm not afraid of you," Violet returned softly.

"You can lie to the rest of the world. In fact, I need you to lie to them. But you don't have to lie to me."

Her hands clamped around the top of the balcony railing. The river waited below. Lights gleamed in the water, reflections from the nearby buildings. "I don't know you."

"Sure, you do. I'm your own personal boogeyman."

She spun around. Found herself trapped between him and the railing.

"Boo," he murmured.

"Is that supposed to be funny?" she snapped even as her heart raced too hard in her chest.

"Ah. There she is." He smiled. "Thought she was in there, but you were a shell tonight. All glamour and cold facade. Had to break through to see the real you."

Her chin lifted. "What does that even mean?"

"It means fear is cloaking you. Don't let it. You let fear rule you, and you'll hate what you become."

"Easy for you to say. You weren't knocked out and locked in the back of some jerk's trunk." *A man who is still out there somewhere.* And if he was out there, he could come for her at any time. Her breath came faster, just as it had when they danced. Too quick. Almost panting.

His hand rose and pressed over her racing heart. "I scare you." Then, halting, "I don't...want to scare you."

Then don't be so shady and mysterious. "You're a criminal." A conclusion she'd had to reach.

Soft laughter. Mocking. "Is that what I am?"

"You have to be." She'd tried to put these pieces

together in the last two weeks. On the nights when she couldn't sleep, her mind had spun the possibilities over again and again. "Why else wouldn't you go in the police station with me? You're wanted by the cops, aren't you?" What crimes had he committed?

"There is currently no warrant out for my arrest. I give you my word on that." His hand fell away from her. He took a step back. "But I've certainly been called a criminal before. By plenty of people. Plenty of times. I've got to say, the label gets old."

Why did she feel like she'd just hurt him? Her hand flew out. This time, she was the one to touch his chest. Right over his heart. "I'm sorry."

He looked down at her hand. Back up at her. "You should know...I want you."

She blinked.

"Probably could have been more suave with that reveal, huh? Didn't feel like being suave. Thought I'd be honest with you instead. So you, touching me—that's probably not the best idea."

She didn't stop touching him. "I want you, too." Soft. He...

Backed up another step.

Her hand fell back to her side.

"You often want criminals?" Royal asked her. His voice was all mild. As if he'd just asked her what sort of ice cream she liked or who was her favorite musician.

"I don't typically fall for criminals, no." To be clear. And, so they could get back on topic, "You just paid ten thousand dollars to dance with me."

"I did. Charitable donation. Earning good karma and all of that."

Now he had distracted her. "Do you *need* good karma?"

"Hell, yes."

"You're *not* a criminal." She wanted to focus on this. She needed to know that her hero wasn't someone terrible. She didn't want to be lusting after a monster.

His head cocked. "If I'm not a criminal, what am I?"

"You're...a businessman. Rich. You have money to burn. Thus, the wasted ten grand on a dance with me." He was dressed in a tux that looked as if it had been created just for him. The coat hugged his broad shoulders. Fit perfectly along his powerful chest. She'd felt his power when they danced. Remembered the strength of his body as he'd carried her through the night.

"No one has money to burn. That's just a jackass investment."

"And spending the money to dance with me wasn't an, uh, jackass investment?"

His gaze swept over her. "It was money well spent."

Her arms wrapped around her body as a cold chill seemed to sweep over her.

"Nope." Immediate. "Can't have that." Royal shouldered out of his tux coat and put it around her shoulders. The coat wrapped her in his warmth and scent.

Her head tipped back as she stared up at him. "Why couldn't I tell the cops about you?" Their bodies were brushing.

"Because I have unfinished business. The cops would have gotten in my way." His hand rose. Skimmed over her cheek. "I did not expect you."

She could see that. "Most people don't expect to find a woman in a trunk."

Soft laughter. "How do you do that?"

His hand still pressed to her cheek. Was she tilting her

cheek into his touch? Dammit, she was. "Do what?" Breathless.

"I don't laugh easily. I don't…smile so quickly. Not usually. Not and actually mean it, anyway. But I feel differently with you."

He was going to kiss her. Her lips parted.

And he stepped back. Again. "Move back into your brother's house until I tell you that things are safe."

"The cops said I should be fine. There are additional security measures in place at the theater. More security guards have been hired. The cast members always walk out in groups. I actually have a guard who walks with me every night, per Micah's orders. I also got a top-of-the-line security system installed at my rental house. I *am* safe."

"No." Very definite. "You are not. The illusion of safety won't protect you if he comes for you again. You shouldn't be alone."

"I can't hide forever. That's not a way to live."

"At least you would be living."

Great. Now her knees were about to start knocking together. "You kick me out of your car at a police station—"

"I *dropped* you off—"

"You ghost me for two weeks—"

"I was keeping a low profile and keeping watch on you. I couldn't suddenly pop into your life. I needed a way for us to be introduced that wouldn't arouse suspicion from the cops."

Her brows beetled. "Buying the dance was your entrance into my life? I hate to tell you, but it's not subtle."

"No, it's not. But every single person in that ballroom tonight will leave knowing that I couldn't take my eyes off you. They'll think I'm some love-sick—lust-sick—fool who will do anything to possess you."

All of the moisture had dried from her mouth.

"If you won't go back to your brother's place, then I'll have no choice but to move in close to you. I will need a cover in order to do that."

That's what the dance was about? Him creating a cover to be in my life?

"I told you before, Violet, you attracted a very dangerous predator."

"A serial killer." He'd said those actual words. Her knees definitely knocked together.

"You will need protection."

She shook her head. "The cops said he won't come back for me. They didn't say *anything* about him being a serial killer." A stalker, yes. An obsessed fan, yes. A serial killer? No, that had not been mentioned by any of the cops.

Royal just stared down at her.

"*Royal.* If you know more, tell me."

"Go back to your brother—"

"No." A hard denial. "I am not cowering in fear any longer. I have a show to perform. A whole crew of dancers waiting on me. If fear controls me, I can't step foot on the stage. I can't do my job. And I *won't* spend the rest of my life looking over my shoulder. That's not happening."

His gaze swept over her. "Fair enough. Then I'll have to use my cover."

The cover of...lust-sick fool? Her temples pounded. She needed to go back inside. Get away from him. She couldn't think clearly this close to Royal. And she could feel the secrets oozing from him.

"Our time is nearly up," Royal announced. "I need to kiss you."

No. He needed to stop jerking her around. "Good night, Royal." She brushed past him.

He caught her wrist. His grip was so careful and yet so very unbreakable. "You need me."

She looked down at his fingers as they curled around her. "I need the truth."

The balcony door opened. "Violet?" Micah poked his head outside.

Royal tugged her closer. "Kiss me," he rasped.

For his cover? "I only kiss someone for show when I'm on a stage. Otherwise, I mean it." She pulled free. "Good night, Mr. Boudreaux." Violet walked toward Micah. His gaze wasn't on her face. Instead, he stared beyond her as he frowned hard at Royal.

But Micah extended a hand toward her.

She started to take his offered fingers.

"Violet!"

She froze at Royal's grated call.

"I will be seeing you again," Royal promised her. "And thank you for the dance. Hopefully, it will be the first of many."

She took Micah's hand.

* * *

JEALOUSY. It was new for Royal and fucking annoying. His hands fisted as Micah curled his arm around Violet and led her back inside the ballroom.

Royal didn't like the other man touching Violet.

He didn't like the prick near Violet.

Because...

I want her.

The desire he'd felt for her hadn't lessened. If only. Instead, as she'd stood on the balcony, tipping up her chin and facing off against him, Royal had been surprised by the force of the admiration and arousal that had surged through him. He'd truly intended to just warn her. The cops were screwing her case to hell and back, and he had to wonder if they were actually that incompetent or...

Or are they using her?

She shouldn't be on her own. Shouldn't be staying alone. She should stay with the prick brother who'd locked her in the closet when they were kids. *Yeah, right, like I'll be letting that one go. He'll get payback soon enough.*

But she'd refused to heed his warning.

Unfortunate.

Royal had tried to give her a choice. No, he *had* given her a choice. What came next...well, she couldn't say that he hadn't warned her.

He—

The balcony door opened again. His head whipped up.

Violet was there.

Fuck. *Violet was there.*

She rushed back toward him. "I—"

His hand curled around her waist. He didn't second guess. Didn't even think. He just pulled her against him, and his mouth locked on hers. And it was just as it had been at the police station. He'd half-convinced himself that he'd imagined the burst of desire that erupted when he took her lips. That she hadn't tasted like the only slice of heaven he'd ever know. That his whole body didn't ignite with need when their lips met and their tongues brushed.

But this kiss—it was even better than his memory. He felt the kiss in every cell of his body. Felt her. Her lilac scent engulfed him. Her soft body pressed against him. She tasted like peppermint. Fucking delicious. And he wanted to eat her up.

More, he wanted to fuck her. Right then. Right there.

On the balcony. He could shove up that silky dress. Lift her up. Hold her while he thrust deep and hard into her. The people on the other side of those balcony doors never needed to know what they were doing.

She'd told him that she would kiss only when she meant it. She'd ditched that prick Micah and come back to kiss Royal alone. *No show.*

Would she fuck him now that they were—

Violet shoved him back. Her breath heaved and she… she jerked off his coat. "I brought this back to you."

He looked at the coat. At her. At the coat again. His brain was having trouble processing the scene.

"Take it." She thrust it against his chest.

He caught it, automatically, but for just a moment, he also caught her fingers and held them pinned against his chest.

"Who are you?" Violet whispered.

Told you. Royal Boudreaux. The man of your nightmares.

No, he hadn't told her the nightmare part. Because he didn't want to be that. Not for her. For others, yes. Not her.

Never. Her.

"Why do I want you so much?" she asked with a shake of her head.

Before he could figure out any sort of response, she whirled and left him. He still clutched the coat. He could swear it smelled like her now. *A Violet who smelled of lilacs.*

And he could still taste her.

The door swung shut behind her.

His heart slammed into his chest, and his dick shoved against the front of his pants.

Run, sweetheart. But I'm just going to chase you.

She was too important to lose.

* * *

"I AM DYING," Simone Wilmont announced with a dramatic sigh as she looped her arm with Violet's. "Dying of absolute boredom." With her grip on Violet, she tugged her past the elaborate ice sculptures of two swans—sculptures that were still in surprisingly good shape considering that the fundraiser was now winding down. "Save me," Simone beseeched Violet.

Violet forced a smile. She'd been hyperaware all night. Too focused on Royal and where he might be. And on what he'd said.

A serial killer? Oh, God, seriously?

And the kiss…the kiss…

"The donors are leaving. The party here is over, but we look fabulous." Simone adjusted the already low bodice of her top to make it look a little lower. "Some of the dancers are going to hit that new club that opened last week—Punishment? Have you heard about the place?"

She'd heard some of the other dancers talk about it, yes.

"Supposed to be killer." Simone tilted her head. Her blond hair had been pulled back into a tight twist. The style just accentuated Simone's high cheekbones. "We're going to get wild and have some drinks and live a little. And you are coming with us. That's not a question. It's a statement of fact."

Violet had already started to shake her head. "No, I—" Her gaze darted over Simone's shoulder.

"Yeah, he's gone, sunshine," Simone told her flatly. "Left earlier."

Her stare flew back to Simone.

"And I am so curious about what went on when you were out with him on the balcony. Did Snow White get a kiss that made her jolt back to life?" Simone's eyes gleamed.

Violet cleared her throat. "I should get home."

"You should *get back to living*. You know you want to come. You know you want to cut loose with me." Simone exhaled. "This is me, your dancing best friend. Pretend to be Miss Perfect with someone else. I know you have a wild side, and she has been pinned up too long. You need this." Sympathy flashed in her blue eyes. "Don't let him kill this part of you. Dance. Have fun. *Live*."

Simone was her best friend. Not just her *dancing* best friend. They'd met years ago while they'd both been at a conservatory in New York. Roommates by chance. Friends because no one could be near Simone and not be her friend. Their careers had taken them in different directions—literally, in different directions across the country, but they'd been lucky enough to work together a few other times over the years. And now, they were both in the *Snow White* cast.

When Violet got shy, Simone became extra vibrant. Simone was always confident. Always grinning. Always looking for fun.

"Let that wild side out, girl," Simone ordered her. "Tell that freak who took you to fuck off."

Serial killer. Not so easy to tell him to fuck off. Or to get him out of her nightmares. If only it was so simple. If only she could take charge of her life again.

And kiss the fear goodbye.

Simone and Royal are alike. Both wanting to tell someone to fuck off.

She'd never done that. Being polite had always been her go-to. Being the good girl all the time. And what had that gotten her?

Locked in a freaking trunk. Was that what happened to good girls?

"Come with me," Simone half-ordered, half-cajoled. "Dance like you want. Drink until the fear is gone. And have fun with me." A wink. "Let's get some Punishment together."

She shouldn't. She absolutely shouldn't…

"I am not taking no for an answer," Simone told her.

Several of the other dancers—male and female—gathered around them. Violet's gaze searched through the crowd once more. *Yes, I'm looking for him.*

Royal Boudreaux.

Except…

He was gone.

"Punishment," Simone called out. "Here, we come!"

The dancers cheered. But fear twisted inside of Violet even more. She was sick of being afraid. Absolutely sick of it. So, yes, fine. Maybe she would go out and dance with her friends. Maybe she'd drink. Maybe she'd forget…

Maybe she would let her wild side out to play.

* * *

She rushed out of the historic building in a circle of her laughing friends. The others were all smiling. Their voices lifted and carried in the wind.

Violet didn't laugh.

She didn't smile.

She did look back. Nervously glancing over her shoulder before she hurried forward with the others, as if she feared being left behind.

He'd been waiting for her. Watching and waiting.

Needing that moment when he could get her all to himself again. But she wasn't alone.

She also clearly wasn't going home.

Where are you going, sweet Violet?

He would just follow her and find out. And he'd wait. Keep watching and waiting.

Until he had her again.

Chapter Four

"THIS PLACE IS *INSANE!*" SIMONE'S VOICE ROSE TO A high-pitched and delighted shriek that was almost immediately swept away by the pounding music. She stomped her high-heeled feet and tilted back her head as the lights swept over the heaving, gyrating crowd. "I love it!"

Punishment was packed. The new club was certainly a success. People danced and bounced and drank and laughed. Excitement seemed to pulse in the air. Savannah had its share of bars, no doubt. Hidden speakeasies. Elegant whiskey escapes. But this place...

It wasn't elegant.

It wasn't hidden.

It was in your face. Loud. Wild. Heated. Throbbing. The music beat over and over, and Violet had given herself up to that driving rhythm the moment she'd stepped onto the dance floor. She'd always escaped into dance. *Always.* And she escaped again tonight.

She'd had shots. Two? Yes, two of them. Chocolatey and delicious. Provided by Simone as the whole dance crew had downed them at the same time. And Violet wasn't afraid any longer. Would not let herself *be* afraid. For the first time since that terrible night, Violet felt like she was living again. She felt like she was just like everyone else again.

And she didn't want to stop feeling that way. She didn't want the night to end. She wanted to dance and dance and forget everything else.

"The owner is supposed to be some big mystery man." Simone closed her eyes and danced even harder. "A guy with more money than God but with a shady past that would give the devil pause. He bought this joint six months ago...and look at it now!" Her eyes flew open. "*Love* it!"

The lights raked over the crowd again. Revealing. Concealing. Revealing. Concealing.

"More shots!" One of the male dancers pushed closer. "Here we go...these *glow*. Aren't they freaking amazing?"

And they were glowing. And the other dancers were reaching for the shot glasses, and Violet reached for one, too. Her fingers curled around it, and she started to lift it to her lips.

A strong hand curled around her wrist. Heat pulsed through her at the touch. An unmistakable awareness, and she knew who owned that hand even before her head turned and she met his intense, burning eyes.

Royal.

"Don't drink any damn thing," he growled. "Unless you see the bartender pour it yourself." He took the shot from her hand and pushed it back at the other male. But Royal never glanced at him. "*You* should know better," he fired at her.

And suddenly she wasn't so free. The night wasn't so safe. *I'm not like everyone else.*

She tugged free of him and whirled on her heel. Violet began marching for the exit.

He stepped into her path.

The lights rolled over them. Concealing. Revealing. Concealing.

"You followed me!" she accused him. "That's called freaking *stalking*, Royal!"

The band played louder. Had he even heard her words? Probably not.

Royal leaned close to her. He put his mouth right at her left ear. "I own the place, Violet." She felt the lick of his tongue and the rasp of his breath against her. "You came to me."

She sucked in a sharp breath. No, no, no.

But...what had Simone just said about the owner?

"Violet!"

It was Simone.

"Violet, you good?"

No, she didn't feel good. Not even a single part of her felt *good* in that moment. The warmth from her two shots had faded rapidly.

"Dance with me," Royal murmured.

She should not.

"Violet?" Simone had pushed closer. Her expression was hard to read. Odd, because Simone was usually an open book. Her friend bit her lower lip. Hesitated.

"I'm good," Violet said.

Simone glanced at Royal.

The lights rolled overhead once more. Concealing. Revealing. Concealing.

Royal pulled Violet into his arms. Simone turned back to their group. The music pounded. Hot and hard. A throb that Violet could feel beneath her skin.

Everyone else was moving fast and hard. Royal wasn't. He'd ditched the tux coat. Wore a black shirt. Black pants.

The top few buttons on the shirt were undone. He looked big and dark and dangerous beneath those rolling lights.

Sexy. Undeniably so.

But...

Be careful with him.

"Someone has to keep you safe. Apparently, you take drinks from strange men." His jaw hardened.

"I know Roderick. He's not strange. He's one of the palace guards in the show."

"Do we ever really know anyone?" He curled one hand around her hip. The heat from his touch poured through her. "Take you, for example. You're going to tell me that they really know you?"

She could feel his arousal.

She could feel her own arousal.

Dammit. What is happening?

"I'm not like this," Violet breathed.

"Like what?"

"Out of control." That was how she felt. "Like I want to scream and rage and—" But she stopped.

He didn't. "Fuck?" Royal finished.

No. Yes. *I do want to fuck. But not with some random stranger. I want to fuck Royal.*

Only he was a stranger, wasn't he? So why did she want to fuck him so badly?

What is happening?

"Come with me." An order from Royal. Or maybe an invitation. Hard to say for sure with the roar of the music. But he was suddenly curling his body around hers. Shielding her from the crowd and hurrying her through the darkness. They went right past a man who looked like a bouncer, then Royal was leading her up a spiral staircase. Up, up and...

Into an office. He shut the door.

Silence.

No more pounding music. No more laughter or voices from downstairs. It was almost as if they were the only two people in the world.

He was in front of her. The closed door behind her. But he'd let her go. Not touching her at all.

"We'll pretend to be involved. That will get me access into your house. Access to the theater. Wherever you are, I can be." His eyes narrowed. Hazel eyes. She could see them very, very clearly. A deep, dark combination of brown, green, and gold. "I've got plenty of experience playing bodyguard, so I can do the job. Trust me."

"How can I?" Her head tilted to the right. Her hair slid over her shoulder. "I know nothing about you."

"Except that I saved you."

"The vineyard and its winery were in the middle of nowhere. *Why* were you there?" A question that haunted her.

He leaned toward her, put one hand on the door behind her head, and caged her. "Shouldn't you just be glad that I was there?"

She was. One hundred percent. But... "Tell me the truth. Or I will call the police and inform them that I suddenly remembered all about my drive to the police station. My drive and my driver." She had her phone tucked into the little bag that hung from her shoulder. Her phone. Mace. A taser. She always kept weapons close these days.

In the face of her threat, he laughed.

Damn him.

"They already think you're lying, Violet. And I think they're lying to you, too. Tell me, did you speak to any federal agents while you were at the police station?"

Yes, she had.

"But they never told you about the other three women who'd been taken? Women who look far, far too much like you."

Her head shook.

"Women with beautiful, long dark hair. Fragile builds. Roughly the same age as you."

No, she had not been told about other women.

"You need me. Because when the darkness grows around you, you need someone who isn't afraid of it." A muscle flexed along his jaw. "You shouldn't be fucking dancing with those assholes downstairs. The men who wanted to put their hands on you. You should never drink what they offer. You should—"

"Let some mysterious and dangerous stranger whisk me away and lock me in his office?" she finished sweetly.

That muscle jerked once more along his jaw. "The door isn't locked. You can leave anytime you want."

But she didn't move.

"You don't want to run, do you?" Royal rumbled.

"I want to scream." A whisper. "I want to rage." Even softer.

"And you want to fuck."

She just wanted the tension within her to release.

"You're wound so tight." A growl from him. "You can't sleep, can you? When it gets dark, do you think you're back in that car?"

"Yes," Violet hissed.

And when she did manage to sleep, in her nightmares, when the trunk opened...Royal wasn't the one there.

Someone else was.

A voice. Whispering. Taunting her.

I am going to make you scream.

A tear slipped from her right eye.

Royal cursed. He pulled her into his arms. Spun around. And in a few, fast steps, he had her at his desk. No, on it. He knocked the laptop out of the way and put her up on the desk. He shoved her legs apart so that he could stand between them. Her dress hiked up. Her small bag fell onto the desktop. Her high-heeled shoes dangled above the floor. A moment later, the heels fell off and *hit* the floor.

His fingers curled under her chin. "I do *anything* that you don't want, you stop me. Got it?"

She nodded.

"I can make you scream. I'll give you the release you need." His hand went to her thigh. He eased the silk up even higher. Rough calluses brushed against her skin. "I will give you everything you want."

This shouldn't be happening. *So why do I want it—him —so much?*

"Stop me," he said again.

Only she didn't. Instead, Violet grabbed his hand. The hand on her thigh. And she pushed it up higher.

His whole body shuddered. "Where have you been for my whole fucking life?" A guttural growl.

Then his fingers were sliding under the part of her dress that had bunched up. Under the dress, and under the edge of her panties. She hissed out a breath, but Violet didn't stop him. She was way past that point. Self-control was gone. Now she acted only on animal instinct, and the animal in her wanted this.

His fingers slid over her folds. Slid over her clit. Rubbed. Carefully. Then he dipped one long finger into her.

She clamped her inner muscles around him.

"So tight."

He pushed her back on the desk. Lowered her. He grabbed her panties and hauled them down. The thin fabric ripped, and the sound jolted her. But before she could say anything, his mouth was on her. His lips and tongue worked her clit. Fast. Intense. Merciless. He ate her up and didn't give her time to do anything but gasp out his name and shove her hips harder against his lips and tongue.

This wasn't her. She didn't hook up with strangers.

That's all he is. A stranger.

A hero. A stranger.

A savior.

Stranger...

His finger slid back inside her even as his tongue kept licking her clit. Over and over and over and she squirmed on the desk and her hands grabbed for his shoulders. Her legs curled around him, and she just *erupted*. The pleasure hit her like a detonation. Sudden. Shocking. No build-up. Just oblivion. It blasted through her, and she screamed with the release.

All of the tension, all of the fear—all of the control she'd had vanished in an instant as she came against his mouth. It was the most powerful orgasm of her life. It pulsed through every cell in her body. Left her quaking and shaking and utterly limp beneath him.

His tongue licked over her once more.

She gasped out his name.

Royal slowly rose. He leaned over her as she sprawled—basically boneless—on his desk. His hands slammed down on either side of her head. "Let me fuck you."

Uh, yes, let's do—

The door flew open. The unlocked door. Because he'd told her it was unlocked before, and she hadn't tested his words for truth. But, clearly, he hadn't been bullshitting her. The door flew open and banged against the wall. She realized in that stark instance as she stared up at Royal that whoever had just come storming into his office would have a perfect view of Royal...as he stood between her spread legs.

"You didn't quit your extracurriculars, did you—" An angry, male voice. Snarling. Only that voice broke off in shock. "Fuck, *Royal*."

"Out!" Royal thundered. "Get your ass out, now!"

"This is why you should knock on closed doors." A woman's voice. Much softer.

Two people had seen her sprawled out beneath Royal?

The door slammed closed. Humiliation burned through Violet. The humiliation replaced the pleasure she'd felt only moments before. Her hands shoved against his chest. "Off. Now."

He immediately pulled back. "I'm sorry. They shouldn't have come in. My brother can be an ass."

She sat up. Shoved down the skirt of her dress. His brother?

"I didn't lock the door because I was trying not to scare you. Don't actually try that shit a lot. It's new for me."

Not scaring people was new?

She jumped from the desk. Her bare feet hit the floor, and her jelly-like knees promptly decided they weren't going to help her stand upright. She would have slunk to the floor right then and there, but he grabbed her. His hands locked around her arms and held her up.

"I didn't realize things would go that far, that fast," Royal told her.

"I need to get out of here." Escape. That was her goal.

"No. No, we aren't done."

Her head whipped up. She stared into his eyes. Saw the

lust still burning. No, wait, did he seriously think they were going to finish? Now?

"Yeah, the mood is gone for you. I get that. But I meant *you* and I aren't done. We have to talk. Stay here. Let me get rid of that interfering prick, and I'll be right back."

All she wanted to do was run away.

"Stay here," Royal urged her. "You are safe here."

Grudgingly, she nodded. But mostly just because if she ran out of his office right then, anyone who saw her would realize what she'd been doing. Especially Simone. Simone could read her like a book. Violet knew she had to get her control back and she had to—jeez, where were her panties?

"Good. Thank you," he added grimly. His lips parted, as if Royal would say more, but then his jaw locked as he turned away. *He* hadn't lost any of his clothing, so he could just stalk right out. And he did. All aggressive and determined-like.

Meanwhile, she found her panties on the floor. Picked them up. And realized they'd been ripped in two.

* * *

ROYAL JERKED his office door shut behind him. He rushed forward and caught sight of his brother's head as the guy climbed down the stairs. "Beau!" A bellow.

Beau's head whipped toward him. Even from the distance, Royal saw Beau wince.

Royal crooked his finger at his brother. "Up here. Now." He knew Beau would be able to read his lips.

And even if he didn't, the lovely lady on the step below Beau had already elbowed him. His brother's fiancée, Avalon Trahan, appeared particularly disgruntled with

Beau. Not that the disgruntlement would last. With those two, it never did.

Mostly because Beau was wrapped around Avalon's little finger. The man would do basically anything for her.

As Beau and Avalon climbed back up the staircase, Royal's fingers clenched around the railing in front of him. Punishment had been a spur-of-the-moment investment for him. Beau tended to prefer more sophisticated venues— places where the best whiskey was always flowing. But Royal had known the city was ripe for something different. Something that would let the crowd roar and go wild.

Violet went wild for me.

The lights rolled over the partiers below.

Beau stepped off the stairs. His gaze shot toward Royal's closed office door, then back to Royal. "Uh, yeah." Beau scratched his jaw. "Didn't realize you were entertaining. Would have watched my mouth better."

And Royal remembered the words that his brother had fired off. *You didn't quit your extracurriculars.*

His teeth ground together. "I wasn't fucking *entertaining.*" Not like he was playing around with Violet.

Avalon inched closer. "We all need to talk." She looked down at the crowd. Then back at Royal. "Privately."

Shit. Beau and Avalon were the only two people in the world who knew about his unique *extracurricular* activity. Mostly because, until recently, Beau had been helping him with said activity.

Everyone needed a hobby, right? So maybe Royal's particular hobby involved killers. Hunting them.

Stopping them.

By any means necessary.

And maybe he'd allowed Avalon and Beau to think he'd given up that particular activity.

Because maybe I lied...

* * *

HER KNEES WEREN'T SHAKING any longer. And she'd put the remains of her torn underwear in her bag. Violet had smoothed her dress back in place. She'd finger combed her hair. Even applied a fresh coat of lipstick. She wore her heels again. Her heart rate had stopped galloping. At this point, she hoped that she appeared at least moderately normal.

Normal enough to get through the crowd and get back home.

Except Royal had asked her to stay.

She turned back to his desk. The desk they had wrecked. She'd *never* had sex on a desk before. And, technically, she still hadn't.

He went down on me. Right here. He'd been fully dressed, and I came against his mouth.

She should, ah, fix his desk. He'd shoved files to the side. Almost knocked his laptop to the floor. Her nervous hands fluttered as she grabbed a few manila files. She stacked them up, but...

Something fell out of one.

Her picture.

She stared at it as it rested on the floor. Then she bent and scooped it up. The picture trembled in her hand.

No, no, that's not me. Because the woman in the picture was dead. Her body covered in blood. Stab wounds were all over her chest. Her arms. Her neck.

A choked sob spilled from Violet's throat. She grabbed the file. Saw a stamp on the outside. Something about the police.

She yanked open the file. More pictures. More horror.

* * *

"It took me a bit of time to put things together," Beau snapped. "Because I was…distracted." His gaze darted to Avalon.

She rolled one shoulder. "We also were under the impression that you'd stopped. You know because you *said* you were going to stop."

"You two need to leave." And he needed to get back to Violet. "And you should stop worrying about me and my extracurriculars."

Beau leaned closer. "The woman will identify you."

Royal's chin lifted.

"You were hunting the killer, weren't you?" Beau's voice carried only to him. "But you found her instead. The dancer, Violet Murphy. You found her, and you saved her." He shook his head. "She saw your face. Dammit, do you know how much trouble this will bring raining down on your head?"

"What was I supposed to do?" Royal fired back, his voice just as low. "Leave her in the fucking trunk? She's scared of the dark."

Beau blinked. "Uh, what?"

Avalon pushed her hand against Beau's chest, an effort to get her fiancé to back up. He did. Just a bit. Avalon cleared her throat. "Beau just said that the woman saw your face. We've been arguing about this. I told him that you probably wore a mask."

No, he hadn't.

"There's no way she can *actually* identify you, right?"

Avalon continued with a nervous glance around the club. "I read the reports the police had."

Of course, she would have. She had so many friends at the PD. Avalon was a true crime writer. The cops and the DA were tight with her.

Meanwhile, those people tended to hate him and Beau. *So I have to resort to different tactics in order to get my intel.*

"She doesn't know your actual identity," Avalon continued in her ever-so-careful voice. "Please, tell me that she doesn't know—"

The door to Royal's office flew inward. Violet stood on the threshold. Her eyes were wide and stark and utterly horrified as she stared at him.

He remembered, too late...*the fucking files.*

Oh, shit. This would look bad. More like hellish to her.

She was opening her mouth, and he knew that she was about to scream. With the music blasting, most people probably wouldn't hear her.

But he couldn't take the chance on her drawing any unwanted attention.

He leapt for her. And even as she began to scream, his hand covered her mouth, and he shoved her back into his office.

Chapter Five

Fuck, fuck, fuck.

Her eyes were wide and terrified, and her hand rose up to claw at his. Fast—and carefully because he would be damned if he hurt her—Royal spun her around. He locked her back against his chest. One of his arms curled around her so that he could pin Violet's arms to her sides. His other hand hurriedly flew back to cover her mouth before she could scream. "Don't fight me."

Uh, yeah, she fought. Violet drove her high heel down on his foot. Shit.

"What are you *doing?*" Avalon's horrified voice as she rushed into the office after him.

Royal glanced toward his desk. He saw the crime scene photos spread out. He cursed beneath his breath. "I can explain," he said to Violet.

She trembled in his arms.

Beau hurried in right behind Avalon. He hauled the door shut. Locked it.

The click of the lock seemed oddly loud, and when Violet flinched, Royal knew she'd heard it. Immediately, he let her go. The room had been soundproofed. Their words wouldn't carry. Hell, even a gunshot wouldn't carry. Not with the material he'd used. "I can explain—"

She whirled and drove her fist right at his face. He caught it. Then realized he shouldn't have. She deserved to throw a punch. Probably a few of them.

"OhmyGod!" Avalon's cry. "*She's Violet Murphy.*"

Violet's gaze whipped toward Avalon.

Beau stepped forward as his stunned eyes raked Violet. "She's the one you were just—*fuck, man,* you are screwed."

Violet yanked her hand free of Royal's grip, and she immediately ran for the door. Only Beau blocked her path.

"It's not what you think," Beau said quickly. He held both of his hands in the air. Probably in a pose that he wrongly believed made him look non-threatening.

"He's a killer!" Violet cried.

Those words pierced right through Royal.

"He has pictures, he has—" A deep inhale as she gestured toward Royal. "I thought he saved me. He's the one who *took me!*"

"I'm not," Royal denied. He kept his voice flat with an effort. *He's a killer.* His hands had fisted at his sides. The better for him not to reach out and grab her again. "I did save you." One of the precious few times in his life that he'd done the right thing.

She darted around Beau. His brother made no move to stop her. Neither did Avalon. Violet's fingers were reaching for the lock.

"I was hunting the killer." Again, Royal's voice was flat.

Violet's shoulders stiffened. She spun toward him. One of her dress's delicate straps slid off her shoulder.

"I didn't kidnap you. I didn't ever plan to hurt you."

Except, in her eyes, he saw hurt. Pain. Betrayal. "I was after *him*."

Her terrified gaze darted around the room. From Royal to Beau to Avalon...then back to Royal.

"You weren't supposed to be there. But when I saw you and you asked for help, I couldn't leave you." His hands fisted even tighter. "I took you away, but that meant *he* got away, too. And he's still out there." He backed up. Focused his attention down on the photos that were scattered across his desk. "This is what he does. He takes something beautiful, and he wrecks it. He would have wrecked you." *No one can do that.* The idea that someone could take her. Use a knife on her...*No.*

Rage beat within him. The dark and hot rage that had haunted him when he was a punk kid who didn't belong any damn place. The one people had called trash because he'd been fucking thrown away on a New Orleans street. No one had even known his real name.

No one had cared about him.

He'd grown up. They still hadn't cared. But they had learned to fear him.

He'd almost come to enjoy the fear. People didn't mess with what they feared. Fear could lead to respect. Power. Except...

I didn't want Violet afraid of me.

But you didn't always get what you wanted in this world. Hadn't he learned that, so long ago? Back when he'd been a foolish kid, hoping that his parents would come find him. That there had been a mistake. That he should never have been thrown away.

Only I was.

"I think we need some serious de-escalation here." Avalon sounded all calm and poised. Like they were having freaking tea or something. Hardly surprising, though. Avalon spent too many days and nights interviewing killers. It took a whole lot to knock past her control.

Sympathy flashed on Avalon's face. "Violet, I am sure this scene is incredibly unsettling for you."

Violet shot her a look of utter disbelief.

Avalon winced. "Especially in light of, uh, what we interrupted earlier. You're undoubtedly feeling a rush of emotions. Fear. Betrayal. You don't know me. You certainly don't trust me. And given that you are probably suffering from PTSD—"

"Screw this," Violet threw out. "Screw it." She whirled back for the door. Flipped the lock and—

"I hunt down killers because the cops aren't catching them." Royal's voice wasn't so flat any longer. It was hard with the intensity that burned within him. "I was at the old winery that night because I was hunting the man who killed those other women. I didn't know he'd taken another victim, not until I heard you in the trunk. You weren't my prey that night. He was."

She looked back over her shoulder.

"Royal has done this before," Avalon added. "You might have even seen the stories in the news. You know about Everett Thomas? The Slasher?"

Violet's eyes widened. "He...he was found tied up for the cops. With a..." She licked her lips. "A bow tied around his neck."

"Someone has a bit of a sick sense of humor." Avalon rocked forward onto the balls of her feet. "Everett Thomas wasn't the first killer discovered that way."

Violet's eyes whipped back to Royal. Then to Avalon.

"The cops want to find the vigilante who has been beating them to the killers—and leaving those perps with red bows around their necks. The authorities aren't exactly looking to give him a big reward. Unless, of course, you count that reward as jail time." Avalon's brows climbed. "So, in light of that, you might understand why Royal wasn't rushing into a police station with you. His appearance would have raised all kinds of questions."

Royal was sure that Violet had plenty of questions. "I was not there to hurt you," he said again. She needed to know that.

She looked at him, then away. Too fast. As if she couldn't stand the sight of him.

Been there, done that before. His chin lifted.

Beau cleared his throat. "You protected him before. You didn't tell the cops anything about him. We know." He gestured toward Avalon. "We, ah, have some contacts who filled us in. You told the cops that you were in and out of it because of the blow to your head. That the escape and drive by the Good Samaritan were all a blur. Since Royal knew where to park his ride so that no security cameras would pick him up, the cops have nothing on him."

"That's why you parked so far away," she murmured. "You were avoiding cameras?"

He'd avoided them all through the city. No traffic cams would have picked him up.

"You trusted him then. You'd just met him." Beau watched her carefully. "Can you keep trusting him now? He isn't the bad guy."

Oh, but he was. And Beau knew that. Beau knew him better than anyone else in the world.

Beau wasn't his blood family. But what did blood matter? Their connection was deeper than blood. When Beau had escaped hell, he'd pulled Royal out of the fire with him. And over the years, Beau had tried to fight the darkness that they both knew lived and breathed inside of Royal.

But there was just no fighting some things.

"Can you trust him?" Beau wanted to know. "Or when you walk out of that door, are you heading straight for the police?"

Violet didn't respond. She also didn't look back at Royal again. Dammit.

Avalon inched closer to her. "My name is Avalon Trahan. I'm a true crime writer. Look me up when you leave. Or call the police station and ask to speak to the chief. The chief will vouch for me. The chief will say that I'm not just some random woman with crazy theories." A slow exhale. "I'm telling you that Royal isn't the man who took you. I'm also telling you that, if you go to the cops, he will be locked up."

"Why lock him up if he stopped predators?" Such a soft question.

"Because the stopping wasn't some easy takedown. Because the legal system isn't designed for what I did." And Royal had known that all along. He just hadn't let the "rules" get in his way. In fact, he'd made his own rules.

"I have to get out of here." Violet shook her head.

He wanted to grab her. Keep her. "You're in danger."

Her eyes snapped over to meet his.

"He's still out there," Royal reminded her. "He's not walking away from you." *Neither am I*.

Her hand flew out. Pointed to the desk. "Why the hell did you do that?"

That. Him going down on her like a starving man. Not really something he wanted to discuss with an audience, but, then again, he hadn't wanted to discuss any of the other shit with Avalon and Beau right there, either. "There are some things you just can't control." The way he felt about her was one of those things. "I want you."

She didn't say another word. She pivoted on her elegant heel. Wrenched open the door and left with a swirl of her red silk dress.

And every single part of him wanted to rush after her.

"Royal," Beau began.

Royal lifted his hand even as he turned away from his brother. "Not yet." He exhaled. *I still taste her.* And she'd just run away from him. Looked at him as if he were a monster and then fled. He inhaled. Exhaled. The bloody pictures were on the desk. Spread out. *It won't be her.* He pulled out his phone. Sent out a quick text to his buddy Kai.

V is on the move. Keep eyes on her at all times.

Three dots appeared as he waited for the response to show then...

On her.

He heard the door click shut softly. *Beau must have closed the door.* His shoulders stiffened, but he didn't look over his shoulder. Instead, Royal reached for the scattered photos. He tucked them all back into the folders.

"Royal..." Beau's seething voice. "If she goes to the cops, you are fucked."

"Tell me something I don't already know."

"You're just going to let her walk away?" Beau pushed. "She could be heading straight for the nearest uniform right now!"

She could be. She could be moments away from destroying his entire world.

"Aren't you going to stop her?" Beau seemed stunned.

He peered down at the desk. "No, I'm not." If she wanted to burn his world to the ground, he supposed he'd just get ready to enjoy the fire. Maybe he should even pick up some marshmallows.

Then a hard hand grabbed his shoulder and whirled him around. Beau glared at him. "You lied to me. You said that you'd stopped."

"I knew another killer was hunting. He started in the Atlanta area. That's where the first two bodies were found. Then he came here. Body three." *Violet would have been number four.* "Authorities are still piecing this shit together. People in power are keeping the truth from the media because they don't want to shout that a serial killer is at work."

But that is exactly who is searching for prey.

Royal stared into his brother's intense gaze. "He's fucking seeming to imitate the Slasher. His crimes are just as bad and as bloody."

Beau's eyes widened. Yeah, he had a personal tie to that prick.

"What was I supposed to do?" Royal demanded. "The cops weren't closing in. Someone had to do something. If I hadn't been there...*Violet would be dead.*" Guttural. "So you think I'm going to regret hunting? She's still breathing. She's still walking around. She'll be fucking dancing as the star of her show soon. She's living." A hard shake of his head. "I won't regret that. Not even if it means my ass gets tossed into a cell." A reckless smile curved his lips. "Hardly like it will be my first time."

Beau's nostrils flared. "And what you just did on the desk with her? You regret that?"

"Hell, no. I just regret that your bad timing interrupted me."

The door flew open.

Again.

The world seemed to be shoving into his office these days. Only...it wasn't the world.

It was Violet.

Maybe she is the world. A sudden, random thought that he immediately dismissed as he focused on her.

She'd pulled the loose dress strap back onto her shoulder. Her chest shook with her hard breaths, and her eyes were focused right on him. "You're hunting killers."

He winced. "Sweetheart, maybe shut the door and don't scream that out to everyone? I truly am trying to keep it on the down low."

Violet stepped forward. She kicked the door shut with one high-heeled foot. Then her hands went to her hips. "You're hunting killers."

"Guilty as charged."

She marched toward him. Beau backed up. Avalon didn't say a word.

Violet stopped right in front of Royal. She tipped back her head and stared up at him. "He got away when you saved me."

"Yes."

"And you think he's going to kill someone else...if he's not stopped."

His lips pressed together.

"Royal." Her voice vibrated with intensity.

"I think he's going to come after you, sweetheart. Not someone else. You."

Her eyes widened. "That's why you're trying to get close to me. Because you're still hunting him, and you are using me to do it."

"I'm still hunting him." *I don't want to use you.* But, yes, he was.

"Fine."

Uh, what was fine?

Violet jabbed her finger into his chest. "I'm hunting him with you."

Oh, the hell, no, she wasn't.

Her finger jabbed him again. "I'm hunting him with you," she repeated.

"We should probably go," Avalon murmured.

Royal didn't take his eyes off Violet. "The hell you are."

She leaned closer to him. "The hell I am." A nod. "Because if I don't, if you don't agree to partner with me, then I will be going to the cops. I will tell them that my memory has suddenly become one hundred precent crystal clear."

Royal blinked.

"We should definitely go." Avalon's voice was much firmer. "Great meeting you, Violet. Can't wait to see the show. I've heard you're an incredible dancer. Beau, *let's go*."

Royal cut a glance at his brother. Avalon was tugging on Beau's arm, but Beau was currently an immovable object.

"We aren't done," Beau informed him. "Not even close."

Right. A reckoning would come. Just not now. One crisis at a time.

Beau swung away and marched out with Avalon. And when that door closed again...

"Am I going to the cops?" Violet asked sweetly. "Or are we hunting?"

Royal clenched his teeth. "You don't want to fuck with me," he gritted out.

"Oh, but I do," she told him. "I *do*."

Chapter Six

You don't want to fuck with me.

Violet yanked back her poking finger.

I do. That—that wasn't what she'd meant. She didn't want to actually fuck him.

Liar, liar.

She wanted—

His hands curled around her shoulders. "You're out of your league."

A league that involved hunting killers? Yes, probably. Way out. A million times out. But she was also not going to just sit around and wait for the bad guy to come after her again. Being afraid every moment wasn't cutting it for her. "I recognized Avalon when I saw her."

His hold tightened.

"I read her books." Back when she'd been a true crime addict. Back before she'd become a victim, and everything had changed. "I know what she's done. I don't have to call the police chief or anyone else in order to get verification on her."

"You *aren't* working with me."

"Then I guess I will be making a trip to the police station so that I can reveal my miraculous memory turnaround." Blackmail? Is that what she was doing? Maybe. No, definitely. She backed away, expecting him to release her.

He didn't. He did haul her closer.

"You think this is a game?" His hazel eyes glittered down at her. "Women are *dead*. Go back to your brother's house. Go back to the guards I have on you—"

"You have *guards* on me?" Since when? Her mouth hung open in surprise.

"*Don't play with me.*"

"Don't you play with me!" Violet returned. "This is my life. *Mine*. He took *me*. He knocked me out. He tossed me in that trunk. And *I* am the one who was going to get up close and personal with his knife." *Don't think about the pictures. Don't.* "I want him caught. The cops don't seem to be doing much. They think he's just some stalker I picked up—"

"He *is* a stalker."

"A serial killer is far different from an ordinary stalker!"

"You'll get hurt with me."

A shiver skated over her body. "I think my best chance of not getting hurt *is* with you."

They faced off. Her chest rose and fell too quickly. His mouth was inches from her own. She was far too conscious of what they'd been doing—right there, on that very desk—not too long ago. Her body felt too attuned to him. But her mind? It was splintering apart.

Avalon had tossed out that line about PTSD. And, dammit, Violet knew the other woman had been right. Her nightmares. Her night sweats. Her panic—yes, she knew exactly what she had.

She also knew that the way to face her fear? It was to track down the bastard who'd taken her. "You think he's coming after me again."

A grunt.

Was that a yes? She took it as one. "So you're in my life now. We had our big dance earlier. Let's cement things. Be seen very, very publicly from here on out. If he's coming for me, then you stay close to me." It was what Royal had suggested earlier. Where was the problem? Now, they'd just be working together. "While he thinks he's closing in on me, you and I will close in on him."

"You don't want to play with me." A growled warning. He finally let her go. Stepped back.

And she felt colder. "I don't want to wind up like those women in your pictures. I want to stop him. I want to fight."

"You're fighting by blackmailing me?"

"That is such an ugly word."

"It's an ugly thing to do, sweetheart. Especially since I saved that sweet ass of yours."

"Why did you?" The question blurted from her. "I mean, don't get me wrong. Super grateful to be alive and breathing and not sliced into some horrible nightmare. Super. Grateful. But if you were there hunting him, why didn't you just leave me in the trunk? And get him first?"

"Because I couldn't be sure where he was on the property. I suspected he was there—"

"How?" How had he known where to go?

"I suspected he was there," Royal repeated. "But there was a whole lot of ground to cover. While I was hunting him, he could have circled back and taken you. Finished you. Leaving you on your own wasn't an option."

And now she was blackmailing her hero. What did that say about her?

"My rules," he suddenly snapped.

Her brows shot up.

"You do what I say, when I say it. No questions. No protests."

A lump rose in her throat. *What am I doing? What am I thinking?*

"And you swear—right here and now, you *swear*—that you will never reveal the truth about me to anyone. No matter what else I do, you'll take my secrets to your grave."

"That sounds super ominous," she whispered.

"I'm an ominous kind of guy." A half-smile teased his lips, and, yes, the faint smile somehow made him look ominous. "Do we have a deal? Or do you just want to run back to your safe life? I do have guards on you. They're watching you from the shadows. Protecting you. They'll keep doing that until I have the killer contained. I can end this for you. And you can have your life again and never have to look back."

"We have a deal." A fast retort from her. She shoved out her hand toward him. Weren't they supposed to shake or something? People shook on deals.

That half-smile of his vanished in a blink. Royal frowned at her hand.

She wiggled her fingers. "I'll keep your secrets. And you let me hunt with you."

His gaze was still on her hand.

"I need this." She did. More than she could say.

His fingers closed around her hand. Warmth shot through her, chasing away the growing chill that wanted to cling to her bones.

"Why aren't you afraid of me?" he growled.

She stared into his eyes and told him the absolute truth. "I am. You terrify me." But what she didn't tell him?

Despite her fear, she was drawn to him. Drawn to him more than she'd ever been to anyone else in her life. He was dark. He was dangerous.

And he called to something equally dark that she'd carefully buried deep inside herself.

* * *

HE PULLED her onto the dance floor. Bodies gyrated all around them. The lights rolled across the crowd. Concealing. Revealing. Concealing.

They wouldn't be out there long. Just enough to get the point across.

Royal kept Violet pinned closely to his body. He could feel every delicate inch of her against him. His hold was possessive. Consuming. His left hand dropped to her ass, and when she jerked, he pulled her against him even more.

She knew they had to put on a show.

Would she break before the show was over? Run away?

His left hand stayed curled on her ass. His right slid under her chin. Tipped back her head.

Her friends were still there. The men. The women. Her friends watched. Strangers watched. There were always eyes in Punishment.

The lights overhead rolled once more. Concealing. Revealing.

He took her mouth. Drove his tongue past her plump lips and tasted her like the fucking starving lover he was supposed to pretend that he was.

No pretending necessary. He'd discovered that when it came to Violet, he was quite ravenous. The taste he'd had of her upstairs had only whet his appetite. He wanted more. He wanted his mouth on her hot, wet core. Wanted his tongue licking her clit. Wanted her scent around him. And her cries of pleasure ringing in his ears.

He wanted her completely naked.

He wanted to lift her up against him. Wrap her legs around him and take her as the lights rolled over them.

The music pounded. He did lift her up. How could he not? And her legs curled around him. He'd already ripped her panties away. She wore no underwear now. It would be so easy to plunge right into her.

To take and take.

"Violet?"

His head lifted. At first, he just stared at her. Wet lips. Red from his mouth.

The lights rolled. Concealing. Revealing.

"Violet, we're leaving."

He slowly lowered Violet until her feet touched the floor.

"Violet!"

Violet jerked, and her head angled toward the blonde who'd called her name. "Simone."

Simone grabbed her arm and pulled Violet toward her. "We're leaving." Her suspicious gaze raked Royal.

He rolled back his shoulders. "Violet's coming home with me."

Simone's jaw dropped. "Violet doesn't go home with strangers!"

He smiled. The rolling lights caught his smile. "I'm not a stranger."

"Yeah, you're the rich asshole who paid ten grand to dance with her tonight. It was just to *dance*, dude. Violet isn't for sale." She tugged on Violet. "The group is leaving. Let's *go*."

"I'm all right." Violet's soft voice. "Thanks for checking on me. But I'm good."

Simone shook her head. "No, you're not—not if you're going home with some—"

"His name is Royal. And I'm safe with him. He's not a stranger."

Simone glanced between the two of them. "What is happening right now?"

Royal pulled Violet back toward him. "I'm glad that you were looking after her, but I have Violet now. You heard her. She's safe with me."

"Buddy, I don't *know* you—"

"It's his club," Violet blurted. "He owns it. This is Royal's place."

That didn't seem to reassure the other woman.

"He'll make certain I get home all right," Violet added.

"Absolutely," Royal murmured. Though it had been very good to learn that Violet didn't go home with strangers. *I don't want her going home with any bastard but me.*

When it came to Violet, his feelings weren't exactly rational. Not that he'd ever been an overly rational sort. Too close to the edge, too aware of a dark need inside, he'd spent most of his life pretending to be someone he wasn't.

Even the night he'd found her...

I pretended to be a savior. But I wasn't.

Violet hugged her friend. "I'll see you at rehearsal tomorrow."

Simone still didn't look reassured.

But the groundwork had been laid. When the other dancers left, Royal made sure to exit the building with Violet, too. He'd already ordered his car brought around. The convertible Benz was waiting, with one of his bouncers standing guard beside it.

Simone watched them approach the car. The jerk who'd tried to offer Violet the glowing shot glass earlier watched them.

Royal opened the passenger side door for Violet. She frowned at the car but didn't speak. He made sure she was buckled before slowly making his way to the driver's side. He tossed a wave to the people staring so intently at them.

Then a few moments later, he pulled the convertible away from the curb. "I don't think your friends like me."

"I don't think you care."

He didn't. Guilty as charged.

"This isn't the same car you used before."

Nope. It wasn't. The other car couldn't easily be traced to him. Something he'd learned from Beau over the years... cover your ass. Having a few dummy corporations set up and ensuring that lots of red tape secured your world? Oh, that could be priceless.

The convertible glided through the streets. He kept the top down, and the stars glittered overhead. They didn't speak again. Not until they pulled up on the short driveway that led to her rental house. The house was dark. Waiting.

The lights from his Benz lit the scene.

The engine growled.

"Thanks for the ride," she said. "And I hope that I, uh, put on a good enough show for you."

"You were perfect." He killed the engine. Unhooked his seat belt.

She'd already unhooked hers and was shoving open the door.

He shoved open his, too.

"You don't have to walk me up. I've got this."

He smiled. His new partner had so very much to learn.

When she walked away from the car, so did he. A quick

press of a button had the top lifting and settling back into place. The lights flashed when he set the alarm.

"Royal?"

"You wanted to be partners."

She paused in front of his car. "Yes."

"You wanted to be close to me." He moved, deliberately coming close to her.

"Yes." Soft.

"Then I will be close. If we're setting the scene, if I'm suddenly the hookup you can't resist, then I will be staying the night with you."

Her lips parted.

How could she look so innocent and so sexy at the same time? A freaking gift. Or a trick. Maybe both.

"I don't remember inviting you to stay the night."

"I invited myself." He looked away from her. Back at the dark house. "This is your first night here since the abduction. You really want to sleep all by yourself in this place?"

He wondered if she'd lie.

She didn't.

"No." Violet cleared her throat.

"I'll take the couch. I can do good behavior. Sometimes." His gaze cut back to her.

Only to find her focused on him. "I can't figure you out."

That was normal.

"But...yes, you can stay." She brushed by him.

His soft laughter followed her. And so did he. As he watched her unlock the front door, he had to confess, "I think this is the least excited any woman has ever been to spend the night with me."

Her head shot up, then whipped toward him.

"Most women are a bit more excited. Just saying."

"Really not interested in hearing about them."

Royal considered that statement. "Fair. I sure as shit wouldn't want to know about the men who've spent the night here with you."

"You're the first." She opened the door. The alarm beeped as she rushed over the threshold.

Taking his time, he followed her. He also made sure to shut and lock the door. He approved of the multitude of locks that had been installed. He should approve. After all, while Violet might think she'd been the one to hire the security crew, he'd actually been pulling strings. His people had shown up. They'd put in the system he'd ordered.

Probably not the time for him to mention that, after her attack, he'd purchased the rental from her previous landlord. Something to disclose on another day.

I needed to be able to keep watch on her. Someone had to look after her.

The alarm had stopped beeping. She stood by the control panel with her shoulders slightly hunched.

"You haven't been in town that long. Didn't find a man to date during that time, huh?" Why was he even asking the question?

"You're the first," she said again. "And that means exactly what it means."

It sure as shit could *not* mean what he thought it meant.

She turned toward him. "Do you have any idea how many hours I have to spend in rehearsals? How many tours I do? How very little free time I have?" Her lips curled down. She'd flipped on the overhead light, and the illumination revealed her perfectly. "And do you have any idea what it's like to be locked in a trunk and think that you're going to die—and you realize there are so many things that you never, ever got to do? Because you were too busy. Or too afraid to put yourself out there."

The drumming of his heartbeat seemed far too loud.

"Simone knows me well. I don't hook up with strangers. I always thought that was too dangerous. And half the men who are around me each day, well, let's just say that their interests often rest in other directions. I've had a hard time getting close...you are the first."

Fucking fuck. "You should go to bed," he rasped. *She is telling me that she hasn't had sex with anyone? I was the first one to put my mouth on her?*

I'll be the first to put my dick in her?

How the hell had this happened?

And how was he supposed to keep control? "Go to bed." A rougher order. "I'll...take the couch."

She pivoted away from him. Punched in a code. Set the alarm on STAY. "Does that change things?"

It changes everything.

She straightened her shoulders. Turned to him once more. "Want me less now?"

"That wouldn't ever be possible." He could never want her *less*. The longer he knew her, the more he wanted her.

She slid off her shoes. Held the straps with one hand. Became even smaller. More delicate. He closed in on her because he was helpless not to do so.

"Some men prefer women with more experience."

He wanted to fuck her right there. "Some women prefer a guy who doesn't have blood on his hands."

She looked at his hands. "I don't see blood."

"Then you're not looking closely enough." Her scent teased him. "It's late. You've already made your deal with the devil for the night. Go to bed. I'll keep watch."

"People will see your car in the morning. My neighbors will think we slept together."

"That's the point. Any reporters come around, wanting gossip on you, they'll find out you have a guy who likes to stay with you. You aren't alone."

Her breath shuddered out. "The other dancers will say it's too fast. That this isn't the way I operate."

"Let them say whatever the hell they want. *You'll* say I couldn't keep my hands off you." And it was hard. All he wanted to do was put his hands on her right then. "You'll tell the world that you liked them on you."

She stared at him.

How many times would he need to say the words? "Go to bed." *Before I lose the little bit of control I have remaining.*

Her head moved in a barely perceptible nod. She brushed past him. He inhaled, pulling in more of her scent. It was a one-story house. He already knew the layout perfectly. Two bedrooms waited down the hallway. Hers was on the right. The smaller room on the left? She'd made that into her workout room.

She started down the narrow hallway. Then paused. "I do."

"You do what?"

"Like your hands on me."

Sonofa—

"Good night, Royal."

And she walked away.

* * *

SHE WASN'T ALONE.

The Benz was in her driveway. Sitting there like it belonged. The house was dark. It was nearing three a.m.

She wasn't alone.

Anger built and twisted. Violet Murphy shouldn't be going back to her perfect life. She shouldn't be making headlines. Shouldn't be dancing as the star of the show.

She shouldn't have a life.

Not now.

She'd been taken. Everything would have been different. She'd been meant for other things.

Only now...

Violet isn't alone.

The watcher shuffled closer. Large, decorative stones edged the drive. Supposed to be pretty landscape work. Fuck that.

Fuck. That.

The stones could be perfect weapons.

* * *

WHAT IN THE holy hell was he supposed to do with a virgin? An actual virgin of all things?

Keep your hands off her. That was probably a good start. And, maybe, maybe that would have worked except...

His hands had already been on her. His mouth on her. And the idea that no one else had taught her just how very wicked and consuming pleasure could be—

The shriek of an alarm and a loud crunch had Royal lunging upright. He'd been stretching out on her piss-poor excuse of a couch, with his legs dangling off the edge, but at that sound, he leapt up and off the couch. He'd stripped off his shirt and ditched his shoes and socks. He'd kept on his pants and the boxers.

With adrenaline pumping through him, Royal rushed for the door just as Violet came running down the hallway. All of the lights were off, but he saw her shadowy form. He reached out before she could get to the front door, and he locked his arm around her midsection. He pulled her up against him. Felt the soft silk of her pajamas brush over his chest.

"Don't even think of running out there," he breathed against her ear. "Someone set off my car alarm."

She shivered against him.

"I'm checking things. You are staying *here*." He let her go. He also paused to retrieve his gun.

"*Where in the world did you get that?*" A startled whisper.

Probably not the time to mention he'd had the weapon on him the entire night. He was armed. The gun had been strapped to his ankle. When he'd lounged on her uncomfortable-ass couch, he'd tucked it close by. Now he gripped the weapon like the old friend that it was and advanced toward her window as—

Something hurtled at the window. Glass broke, splintering into a thousand pieces, and this time, her home alarm started blaring. A loud, piercing cry.

Sonofabitch.

Chapter Seven

Fear held her frozen.

"Stay here," Royal ordered her.

She wasn't sure she *could* move. The alarms—both her home alarm and his car alarm—kept blaring. Her window had shattered, and glass littered the floor.

"I'm going outside."

Going outside...with his gun. Showing no fear at all while she was biting her lower lip so hard that she worried she might draw blood at any moment. He'd shielded her right before that window had shattered. Covered her with his warmth and strength. But now he'd pulled away and he was just rushing right outside like it was nothing.

While I'm trembling like a victim. Because that was what the freak had made her. "Be careful," she ordered.

"Always."

Then he was gone. He'd slipped out the front door with his gun drawn. The alarms were still blaring, and she had to *move.* She whirled and rushed for the kitchen. Distantly, she was aware of the car alarm stopping.

Violet grabbed for the knife block on her countertop

and hauled out the butcher knife. Her sweaty palm closed around the handle even as a picture of a dead victim from Royal's file flashed through her mind. Violet's grip tightened on the knife.

The house alarm was driving her crazy. She rushed back through the dark and disengaged the alarm. The sudden silence sent unease racing through her. And she knew that she couldn't stay in that house any longer. What if this had been some divide and conquer technique? What if the attacker had circled around the back and he was coming for her while Royal was outside? Or, what if, heaven forbid, something had happened to Royal? What if he'd been lured outside and attacked? Killed?

Even as fear rose to choke Violet, her lights flashed on.

Violet blinked. Royal stood in the doorway. He'd come back inside, shut the front door behind him, and hit the light switch. Now he looked at her. Then the knife. One brow arched. "What are planning to do with that, sweetheart?"

Honestly? "Whatever needs doing."

He smiled at her. "That's what I like to hear." He tucked the gun in the waistband of his pants and closed the distance between them. "Awfully sharp. How about we just..." He reached for the handle of the knife. His fingers curled around hers.

Heated awareness pulsed through her.

Wrong time. So wrong.

But he felt right.

"Don't want you cutting yourself. Or me." He tugged the knife from her grip. "Also don't want the cops bursting in and finding you brandishing a knife. They'll be here soon, you know. The alarm will send them charging over. We need to get our story straight."

"Did you see someone outside?"

His jaw hardened. "I saw that some asshole had thrown a giant rock or brick or some shit like that through the windshield of my car."

She sucked in a breath.

"Then the same asshole threw another rock through your window. I can only surmise that the prick in question doesn't like me being here with you."

Someone had been watching the house. Watching me. Her racing heartbeat shook her chest. "Do you think it was the man who took me?"

"Do you have other enemies I should know about?"

"No."

"Then, sure, let's go with the idea that the sonofabitch came back tonight. In order to be *here* tonight, he would have needed to know that you moved out of your brother's place. That means he was watching you. Monitoring you."

Her stomach knotted.

"But then when he came here for you, you weren't alone."

I am so glad that Royal was with me.

"You won't be alone again. He just realized that I am going to be one very serious problem for him. In order to get to you, he'll have to go through me."

She could not look away from him.

"I'd had guards on you, but since I was staying here, I texted and gave them the night off. Dumbass move on my part. Just didn't expect the attack so soon." Rage drifted beneath his words. "Next time, be sure that I will have extra eyes outside."

Eyes that could catch the attacker.

"The cops will come," Royal spoke faster, and he kept holding the knife. A knife in one hand. A gun tucked at his waist. "They'll have plenty of questions. They'll want to know who the fuck I am and why I'm staying with you. We need to deliver the same story to them."

She inched closer to him.

"We met tonight. I paid for the dance with you at the fundraiser. We hit it off. Met up at my club. You invited me here. We were..." He stopped. His nostrils flared. "We were together when the alarm went off. *Tell them we were together every moment, understand?*"

She threw her body against his. Her hand curled behind his neck, and she pulled his head down toward her. Their mouths collided. Lips. Tongue. The kiss wasn't soft and teasing. It was demanding and savage and stark. The way that she felt.

And he kissed her back the same way. His arm wrapped around her. Did he still grip the knife? She didn't know. Didn't care. He was kissing her. She was kissing him. The killer had *come for her*. But Royal had been there.

The second time his presence had saved her.

The second time...

Sirens shrieked in the night.

Royal's head slowly lifted. "I need to drop the knife and ditch the gun."

His words didn't quite make sense at first.

"Or else they'll think I'm the bad guy." He kissed her again. "What the fuck am I going to do with you?" he whispered against her lips.

"Save me," she said. But, he already had.

"Always."

The knife hit the floor.

Chapter Eight

"MORE FREE PUBLICITY. YOU REALIZE, OF COURSE, that Micah and the other bigwigs are about to lose their shit." Simone dipped into a low stretch. "Ticket sales are apparently insane, and with you leading the news again this morning because of the vandalism at your place..." She slowly straightened her spine. "We are going to be sold out every single night."

Violet remained stretched out on the stage. "So glad that my personal tragedies can help the show."

Simone winced. "Okay, yeah, sorry, I sounded like a completely unsympathetic bitch, didn't I?" She hurried toward Violet. Did a split in front of her before she bent to grab the toes of her right foot. "But at least you weren't alone." Her head turned as she maintained the pose, and she grinned at Violet. "Have you been holding out on me? Since when are you dating mysterious club owners *and bringing them home with you?*"

The news hadn't just been splashing her image onto the screen. They'd captured footage of Royal leaving her house. Correction, of *her* and Royal leaving. His arm had been wrapped around her. His clothes had been wrinkled and very clearly the same ones that he must have worn the previous night.

Everyone in town who'd watched the footage would believe that she was sleeping with Royal. It was what the cops on scene had believed.

It was clearly what Simone believed.

And it was exactly what Royal wanted everyone to believe. Violet cleared her throat. "You're the one always telling me that I need to stop living like a nun."

Simone let go of her foot. She arched her back, rotated, and pinned her bright eyes on Violet. "There's living like a nun…" Her voice carried only to Violet. "And then there's jumping into the deep end before you know how to swim."

Or how to fuck.

Violet's chin lifted. She got exactly what Simone was telling her.

"That's a man who doesn't play around," Simone warned softly. "I think you need to be careful with him."

"I know what I'm doing with Royal." No, she did not. At all.

"I hope so." Simone's face softened. "I'm just worried about you."

"Thanks, I—"

"Practice time, people!" Micah clapped his hands. "I want a complete run-through of the production today. Special effects. All props. Impeccable timing. Lace up the shoes. Drink your water. And get your asses in motion."

Violet rose to her feet. Her head moved in a small circle as she tried to work the kinks out of her neck.

Micah stopped in front of her. Surveyed her. His lips tightened. "You look like shit."

Anger stirred inside of her. "Thanks, Micah. No, please,

don't worry about me. The incident at my house doesn't have me rattled at all, and I got plenty of sleep."

"You took home a man you just met, Violet. I'm sure you weren't getting much sleep even without the rock hurtling through your window." He tapped his chin. "Are you up to the rehearsal today? If not, Simone can step in."

"I'm good." She needed this. But...

I also want to be with Royal. Hunting down the bastard who took me. Surely, Royal wouldn't hunt without her? They were supposed to be a team.

Only they hadn't exactly discussed a thorough game plan.

"I don't need you to be good." Micah shook his head. "I need you to be perfection. Anything less won't cut it for me. Can you give me what I want?"

Such a demanding asshole. When she became an artistic director in charge of her own show, she would never be like him. And that was the plan. To step away from the spotlight and to be in charge of the performances. This show was going to be her last lead.

"Violet?" he pushed.

She flashed a hard smile his way. "Perfection. Coming right up."

"That's what I love about you."

Simone waited until Micah strolled away, then she closed in on Violet. "That man is such a dick."

Violet agreed.

"Totally makes me regret those three...no, four times I slept with him."

Violet looked at her friend and raised her brows.

"What?" Simone shrugged. "He's straight, gorgeous, and actually really good in bed. He's also a super bastard. That's the way nature works. Can't have it all." She pointed at Violet. "That's why I'm telling you now...your mystery club owner? He's gonna have some serious flaws. He doesn't get to be gorgeous and rich without having some major skeletons hiding in the closet. There will be red flags, mark my words."

Oh, he had a few red flags.

Like the fact that he seemed to enjoy hunting down killers.

* * *

"YOU'RE FUCKING the woman you saved?"

Royal had expected that to be the first question Beau asked. He'd gone straight to LeBlanc's, his brother's riverfront bar, because he knew a reckoning was at hand.

When Royal entered LeBlanc's, Beau had been standing behind the counter. A wall of the best whiskeys in the world waited behind him. When it came to his whiskey, Beau spared no expense.

"Caught the news story." Beau crossed his arms over his chest. "Me and everyone else. You were at her house last night."

"I was protecting her."

"Do tell."

He crossed to the counter. Flattened his hands on the top. "You really think you're in a position to lecture me about wanting to protect someone? Try that bit with someone else. I know how *long* and how closely you guarded Avalon."

Beau's eyes narrowed. "Completely different."

Was it? "You stalked the woman for years—"

Beau surged toward him. "I was watching her ass! The

arsonist who nearly killed Avalon wasn't caught. Someone had to keep her safe."

And, of course, the fact that Beau had been in love with his Avalon ever since a very long ago night when he'd saved her from a fire in New Orleans—a fire that had occurred when Beau was just a teen—well, Royal supposed that was irrelevant? Whatever. He forced a shrug. "The killer who kidnapped Violet wasn't caught. Someone has to keep her safe." He sent his brother a tight smile. "Guess you and I are more alike than you thought, huh?"

"You told me that you'd stopped hunting."

Yeah, well. "I lied."

Beau growled.

"And if I *hadn't* lied, if I had stopped, Violet would be dead right now. So how about you stop reading me the riot act, and you get on board with this hunt?" There was no need for the moral high road BS. Beau had once hunted with him. During their time in Savannah, they'd taken out two murderers in the area.

They hadn't killed those men.

They'd stopped them.

Two men. Sadistic predators who'd gotten off on torturing others. Murderers who'd needed to be stopped.

But those weren't the only hunts Royal had ever done. And even though Beau swore he was done with hunts...*I'll keep hunting without him.* Because Royal wasn't going to let the bastard who'd taken Violet just get away. Hell, no.

Royal rolled back his shoulders. "From where I'm standing, my last hunt counts as a win."

"Even though the killer got away?"

"*Momentarily* got away."

Beau grunted. "You're playing with fire."

"Nah. You're the one who does that. Not me. I'm just helping out a pretty dancer."

"You're fucking a pretty dancer."

He dropped his relaxed pose. "Watch what the hell you say about her." His hands slapped on the bar's countertop, and he leaned toward his brother. Got practically nose to nose. "She's an innocent in all this."

"An innocent who *knows* what you like to do for fun on the weekend. In case you missed it, your hobby isn't freaking typical. It's dangerous and scary as hell, and it's also the kind of thing that can get you tossed into a cage." Beau's eyes glittered. "I've been in enough of those over the years. I've tried to keep you out of them."

Beau had always been looking out for him. Ever since they were kids. Beau was the only family that Royal had in this world. The only person who actually gave a shit about him. So Royal took a breath and took a step back. "I'm in control."

"No, you're not. And I think that, with her, your control is going to get weaker and weaker."

Royal lifted his hands from the counter. "You're wrong."

"Am I? You were at her house last night. You gonna really try and sell me the story that you were keeping your hands off her?"

He actually had kept them off. Mostly. "I was on the couch. She was in the bedroom."

Beau's eyes narrowed.

"Someone tried to scare her last night. Someone who did not like the fact that I was in her home."

"You think it was the killer?"

"I think..." A slow exhale. "I think I need to call in a few favors. I've always had your back, right? Bodyguard work.

Some bending of the law. Whatever you needed." He would always give Beau whatever his brother needed. "This time, I need you to work some magic for me."

A furrow appeared between Beau's eyes. "I'm listening."

"You're tight with the Ice Breakers."

"I don't know if 'tight' is the word I'd use. But, yeah, I know some of them."

The Ice Breakers. A cold case solving crew that had been making headlines quite a bit in the last two years. From what Royal had been able to discover, the group had first started online. They'd all come from different backgrounds. Civilian life. Military. Former law enforcement. Billionaire Archer Radcliffe pretty much bankrolled the operation these days—mostly because his wife, one of the original Ice Breakers, had helped to clear him of a murder suspicion that had dogged the guy's steps for years.

One of the core Ice Breakers actually lived in town. A badass SOB who went by the name of Saint. Royal and Saint had crossed paths a few times. Mostly because Alice, Saint's wife, ran one hell of a speakeasy. Royal had picked up a few tricks and tips from Saint. But it wasn't Saint's help that he needed right now. Royal tilted his head to the right, ran a hand over the stubble that coated his jaw, and asked, "You ever hear about a woman called the doctor of the dead?"

Beau's face tightened. "People say she's almost psychic when it comes to finding dead bodies. She hunts with her dog, Banshee."

"I think I need her to do a hunt at the old winery where I found Violet."

Beau cursed.

"There were three dead vics that I linked to the perp, but I'm suspecting there are more." His instincts screamed there were. "And I think the doctor of the dead can help me find them."

"This is gonna go from bad to worse, isn't it?"

"Probably." He glanced at his watch. "See if you can work your magic and get her to town for me, will you?"

"And what will you be doing?"

"Ah, what I do best, of course." He flashed a tiger's smile. "Hunting the sonofabitch."

* * *

SWEAT SOAKED HER BODY. The rehearsal had been brutal so far. In a way that she absolutely needed. Her movements had needed to be timed down to the exact second. Her focus complete. Violet hadn't been able to waste energy thinking about the jerk who'd taken her. Or what could have happened at her house last night.

"Bring out the coffin!" Micah's voice rang out. "Looking great, people! Great! Violet, perfect death. You were delicate and tragic, and that was just what I needed."

"Praise from Micah." Simone—just as sweat soaked as Violet—slid toward her. "That's like winning the lottery."

Violet bobbed her head because Simone was absolutely right.

"Curtains will be down." Micah was holding court in the middle of the stage. "During the intermission, the coffin will be brought out by the crew. Violet, you'll get inside as soon as it is positioned. The curtain will rise, and the prince will come. He'll be desperate to awaken you."

The stage crew brought out the coffin. Made of glass—

and gold. Or at least, it looked like gold lining the edges of the coffin. It wasn't, of course.

"Beautiful." Micah hurried forward and ran his hands over the coffin once the stage hands put it in place. "Seriously, it's exactly what I wanted. The audience can see our poor heroine through the glass. Every inch of her. They'll grieve with the other dancers. Emotions will be high." He raised the lid of the coffin. "Violet, hurry, get inside!"

Right. Inside the coffin.

At least it's made of glass. Since she could see through it, she shouldn't feel claustrophobic. Her feet rushed across the stage, and she slipped inside. Violet stretched out her body. The coffin had been built so that it fit her body perfectly. Not a whole lot of wiggle room, but, it worked.

"Arms over your chest," Micah ordered.

She put her arms over her chest.

"Perfect."

She watched him lower the lid. Then she stared through the glass and looked up at him.

Micah smiled at her. "You're gorgeous in death."

A shiver slid over her body.

He tapped the lid. "Okay, eyes closed. We're going to lower the stage lights and send in the fog." He rose and turned to the crew. "I want the mournful music playing. This is our death march. The tone should reflect her sorrowful end..."

Her body had felt so warm just moments before. But now she seemed chilled. She hadn't closed her eyes. Not yet.

She kept her hands over her chest. The other dancers backed away. Violet knew they'd come out on their cue. When the curtain rose, though, she'd be the only one on the stage. The coffin would be the focus. Fog would swirl around her, like wisps of the evil queen's magic lingering in the air.

Violet breathed in and out as she tried to calm her racing heartbeat.

The lights overhead dimmed.

She jerked.

With all the darkness…

Back in the trunk. Closed in. Can't get out. She'd banged and banged her bound hands against the trunk's lid. She'd had bruises on her hands for days after her rescue. She'd pounded even when she'd been certain no one would save her.

Get a grip, Violet. You're not in the trunk. You're on a stage. This is a show. There is no danger.

But her racing heart didn't seem to get that message.

She heard the music start.

Violet squeezed her eyes closed.

Each rapid heartbeat seemed to echo in her ears.

You have this. You aren't going to break apart in front of everyone now. No big deal. You have this.

The music rose. She felt the vibrations on the stage and knew that the other dancers were coming closer. Her prince would be there soon to lift the glass top of the coffin. He'd press his lips to hers and bring her back to life.

Except…

He didn't.

She lifted her lashes just a little.

The top of the coffin hadn't lifted off.

Why hadn't the lid lifted? What was happening? She could see light. Not total darkness any longer, so that was a win. But what wasn't a win?

The lid still being shut.

"I can't get it."

The prince's voice. Only, she wasn't supposed to hear his voice. There was no speaking in the ballet. Her eyes flew wide open. She stared at Dante Baxter. *His* dark eyes were wide and worried as he frowned down at her. "I can't get it open, Violet!"

"You're not supposed to speak!" Micah's snarl. "This isn't freaking Broadway! It's the ballet! Shit. *Everyone, stop!* Dante can't open a damn lid."

She could hear his voice so clearly. Then she saw him. Micah bent over the coffin and pulled at the lid he'd closed moments before.

The lid didn't open.

She stared right at him, so she saw the surprise—and flash of worry—in his eyes. "It's...jammed."

Her head shook. Her hands rose and pressed to the glass.

"Crew! I need the stage crew!" Micah jerked on the handle—the lever? He sent Violet a wide smile. "Nothing to worry about. It's just jammed. We'll have you out in no time."

He'd *have her out?*

Her hands shoved hard against the glass above her.

Nothing happened. She just slapped the glass. The top section of the coffin didn't rise.

Most of the stage still seemed dark beyond the glow of light that surrounded Dante and Micah. Fog swirled around the coffin. But at least there was some light. There was—

Darkness.

The light died, and the whole stage plunged into darkness.

"What in the hell is happening?" Micah demanded. "Dancers—off the stage! I want everyone off but the freaking genius who built the coffin and who can now open the damn thing." Something tapped the top of the coffin.

Her heart raced faster. The darkness seemed so consuming. Panic flared inside of her. Too much darkness. Too much—

Light. A flash of light from Micah's phone shone onto her face.

"Power failure. Can you believe this crap? I have to get the dancers off the stage before someone breaks a leg, and I'm screwed." The light stayed on her. "You are safe here, Violet. Andy built the coffin, and he's coming. The lock just jammed."

Why was there a lock? Why had a lock been included at all?

"You're safe," Micah said again. "I have to get everyone else *off my stage.* But I'll be back. You just breathe and *don't* break the glass!"

She'd panicked and started pounding the glass. Her hands froze.

"We don't want to have to build another one. It's just a technical glitch. You know this sort of thing happens all the time." The light lingered on her. "I'll be right back."

He was leaving her? They were all leaving her?

The light pulled away as Micah's steps pounded to the right.

Darkness engulfed her. Panic built. *This was not happening.* They couldn't leave her there. She wasn't just going to stay in the trunk, helpless, until that bastard came back and finished her off. She couldn't die now. She wouldn't die. She'd get out of the damn trunk even if—

Not a trunk. You're not in a trunk. You're in a coffin.

And wasn't that even worse? Her right hand fisted, and she drove it at the glass above her.

Light.

Light hit her face. She squinted and expected to see—

"It's me, Violet." Royal's voice. And she could hear his fury. "I'm getting you the hell out of there, sweetheart. Roll to the side. Get as far to the left as you can."

She immediately rolled and hunched her body.

Thuds sounded behind her. The crack of glass and then...then a faint squeak as the coffin lid lifted. She rolled back.

"Easy." Royal's arms caught her. He hauled her up and into his arms. "Broke some glass when I shattered that damn lock." He pulled her tighter against him.

She was shaking.

"I've got you," he growled against her ear.

How was he there? Oh, screw it. Forget how. She was just grateful he was there.

"What the hell are you doing?" Micah's horrified voice. "The coffin! *What did you do to the coffin?*"

Held tightly in Royal's arms, Violet turned her head in the direction of Micah's voice. In that moment, the stage lights turned on again. Startlingly bright and too powerful. She blinked quickly. Over and over as her eyes tried to adjust to the sudden, almost blinding brightness.

"*What the hell were you doing?*" Royal snarled back. "You left her *trapped* in there." And, with his hold on Violet tightening, he took an aggressive step toward Micah.

She felt something whistle in the air. Or at least, it seemed like a whistle.

Some *thing* hurtled down right behind her and Royal and glass shattered. Not one little crack. *Shatter.*

With her in his arms, Royal bounded forward. Loud screams echoed throughout the theater and then...

"OhmyGod!" Simone's shocked voice. "If Violet had still been in the coffin, that light could have killed her!"

She strained and peeked over Royal's shoulder. One of the lights had fallen from overhead. Big, black, round. The light had hurtled into the side of the coffin. Broken glass littered the stage.

Everyone seemed to have frozen. Violet's horrified gaze was on the coffin. On all that glass. "Again," she breathed. She looked at Royal.

And found him staring down at her.

"You've just saved me *again*."

Chapter Nine

"Calm down, everyone—*calm down!*" Micah scurried toward the coffin. Glass crunched beneath his feet. "No one has been harmed." His hands waved in the air. "Calm. Down!"

Royal forced his gaze off Violet. He slowly turned his attention to his target.

The asshole frowning at the wreckage.

"Looks like one of the clamps came off one of the Fresnel lights that had been mounted above the stage." He grimaced. "Not ideal, certainly but..."

"Not ideal?" Royal echoed in disbelief. "You better be shitting me right now."

Micah's head swiveled toward him.

Royal realized he was still holding tightly to Violet. He also realized that he didn't want to let her go. But if he was going to rip apart the prick glaring at him, Royal did need his hands free so...

Carefully, he put Violet on her feet. His gaze swept over her. "You hurt, sweetheart?"

She shook her head. But there was fear in her glorious golden eyes. He hated that shit. "Stay behind me." He turned to face the artistic director who was begging for a beat down.

Happy to oblige you, asshole.

"You shouldn't be here," Micah snapped. "This is a closed rehearsal. Doesn't matter how much money you throw around to get a dance with Violet, you should not be here!"

Royal kept his hands loose at his sides. "If I hadn't been here, Violet would have still been trapped in that coffin when the light came hurtling down."

"It could have killed her!" Simone called out once more. She'd edged toward the stage. She peered up at them. She'd been near the orchestra pit, and the horror was clear to see on her face. Her gaze darted toward Violet. "My God, Violet..."

"Maybe some cuts," Micah dismissed. "Hardly a life-threatening situation. Just calm down, everyone. I get that you're a dramatic lot, but take a minute and breathe, would you?"

And Royal *lost it*. He bounded forward. Fisted his hand in Micah's shirt-front and yanked the dick toward him. "You think the prospect of Violet's face and body being *slashed* by glass is no big deal?"

Micah's eyes bulged. "I-I didn't say—"

Royal leaned in closer to him. Growling, he bit out, "If I slash your face, will it still be no big deal?"

All of the color drained from Micah's face. He swayed. "S-security!"

Knowing that only Micah could hear him, Royal softly promised, "Security won't be able to protect your ass from me. If Violet ever gets hurt and you just stand there saying it's nothing, believe me when I say that there will be no one on this earth who can save your sorry ass."

"Y-you wouldn't..."

"I would do anything." Still low. Still a promise straight from hell. "You do not know me. You have no idea what I am capable of." *But push a little more, and you will find out.*

Soft fingers tapped on Royal's shoulder. "Let him go, Royal." Violet's voice. "I-I really want to get out of here. We need to get a maintenance crew in. The mess has to be cleaned up. The theater reset."

She couldn't be serious.

"Please?" A careful entreaty from her. "Just let him go."

He knew a deadly promise would still be in his eyes, but Royal slowly released his prey. For the moment. "You're not calling a damn maintenance crew to clean up," he told Micah.

Micah's Adam's apple bobbed. "I-I'm not?"

"You're calling the cops," Royal snarled. "Because this looks like an attempt on Violet's life. So no one touches anything. No one moves *anything*, not until the cops and the crime scene team have gone over every single inch of this place." His gaze swept over the assembled dancers. The crew. They were all staring with wide eyes and...

Worry.

Fear.

"You...you aren't serious," Micah gasped out.

Royal glared at the idiot. "Do I look like I'm standing here making jokes, dumbass?"

Murmurs swept through the crowd. It was one thing to have a mishap with a piece of equipment. It was another to have just witnessed an attempted murder.

Suddenly, Micah was grabbing Royal's arm. "You think..." A swift glance toward Violet. "You think the man who took Violet just tried to kill her? In *my* theater?"

He didn't think this was the prick's MO. But he also didn't buy that two weeks after being taken, Violet suddenly had someone randomly throwing big ass rocks at her house and having a light fall and nearly kill her while she was trapped in a freaking coffin.

A few things needed to be made clear. Right the hell now. "The set will *never* be closed to me." Micah needed to understand that vital fact. "Where Violet goes, I go. Consider me her personal bodyguard."

Micah's hand dropped. His lips twisted as some of his cockiness returned. "A billionaire bodyguard? Is that even a thing?"

Royal stared back at him. Just stared.

And Micah lost his twisted smile. He backed up a step. More glass crunched.

"It's a thing right now," Royal assured him. "If I'm not with Violet, one of my team members will be. Obviously, you can't see to her safety. So I will." Her fingers still pressed to his shoulder. Was she trying to calm him down? Not going to happen. He was close to exploding. She'd been fucking trapped in a coffin. *A coffin.* The big light had hurtled right for her. *No way that was a coincidence.* "You will be providing me all-access to the theater and to Violet from here on out."

Micah bobbed his head in agreement. "I'm sure we can make arrangements for you."

"Good. And the next thing you'll be doing..." He looked at the crowd. "I want the name of every person here."

"Uh, you're not the cops..." Micah began as his shoulders stiffened.

"No, I'm something a whole lot scarier." He needed everyone to understand this. "Violet isn't going to be hurt. Anyone going after her will have to fucking claw through me first."

* * *

"They're my friends."

Royal and Violet were in her dressing room. The cops had come. They were currently still talking to the crew and performers. A crime scene team was collecting evidence. Hours had passed.

And Royal still hadn't calmed down.

He and Violet had recently gotten the all clear to leave, and he'd followed Violet back to her dressing room. No way was he letting her out of his sight.

She sat in front of a vanity mirror. Soft light spilled from the round bulbs that circled the mirror. He stalked up behind her as she stared into the mirror. Her gaze darted to his reflection. "My friends wouldn't hurt me," she said.

Was she trying to convince herself? Or him?

"They wouldn't," Violet insisted.

"Everyone out there isn't a friend, sweetheart." He put his hands on her shoulders. "You need to be careful who you trust."

A soft, almost broken laugh escaped her. "Those people out there didn't kidnap me. They didn't put me in his trunk. They didn't—"

"You were taken *from* the theater. You were just nearly killed *in* the theater." And there was something else that burned in him. Something that he needed to tell her. Something he'd held back, but they were supposed to be partners now and—dammit. This was going to hurt her. "I have the theater's security footage from the night of your abduction."

Her eyes were still on his in the mirror. "I want to see it."

Yeah, he'd figured she would.

Violet wet her lips. "And do I want to know how you got the footage?"

"I have my ways."

"Of course, you do." A shake of her head. "So, you're my bodyguard now, huh?"

"I've played the role before. I can do it again." Actually... "I'm pretty damn good at it."

"You saved me today."

He'd gone to the theater after talking with Beau because he'd had an overwhelming urge to see her. Was he developing his own obsession? Maybe.

She caught his hand. Brought it to her lips and pressed a kiss to his knuckles. "Thank you."

Okay, shit. *Probably.* Or even...*definitely.* He was definitely developing an obsession. He knew he had to tread carefully. He also had to tell her the truth. For some reason, the truth mattered with her. "I think someone else was in the video."

"What?" Her grip tightened on him.

He inhaled. Exhaled. "After you're taken...when the sedan drives off..." Because he'd kept watching. Hell, he'd watched and watched the video endlessly in the last two weeks, and each time he'd seen her attack, rage had filled him.

That same, dark rage filled him now.

"If you look closely in the footage," Royal told her grimly, "you will see the flash of lights."

In the mirror, her eyes narrowed. "I don't understand. What does that mean?"

"It's the flash of lights as in...someone is turning on a car."

Her lips parted.

"Someone could have been out back." *Someone had been out back.* "Parked in the theater's rear lot, just like you were, and that person could have *seen* you getting taken."

She shook her head. "No. No one reported that. No one said anything about seeing the abduction. You're wrong."

He'd like to be wrong. But Royal didn't think that he was. And, deep down, he wondered if she believed what she was saying. Or if she was afraid to face the truth.

"You are wrong," she argued. "Because if someone...if someone had seen him take me..." She leapt to her feet and spun toward him. "They would have helped me."

He stared at her. Such a lovely face. Silken skin.

Someone cutting her face? Micah being okay with her having a few fucking slashes? Oh, hell, no. He'd be paying a visit to Micah again soon. They needed to have a little one-on-one chat. Because when it came to suspects, Micah was at the top of Royal's list.

"If they didn't help...then...they'd be okay with me dying."

He stared at her. "You aren't dying." His hand lifted. The back of his fingers slid over her cheek. *Never going to get cut.* "You have me now."

"You're...dangerous."

"Yes." Why deny the truth? "But not to you. I'm not ever going to hurt you." The chair was between their bodies. In his way. With his free hand, he shoved the chair to the side. She inched toward him. Her body brushed against his. "Are you scared of me?" Royal asked her.

Seemed important to know.

"I think I am."

Fair enough. His hand dropped.

"But I want you far more than I fear you." Now she was the one to touch his face. Her fingers curled under his jaw. "Kiss me, Royal?"

His eyes were on her mouth. "Probably not a good idea."

"Why not?"

"Because I'm not in complete control right now."

"That doesn't sound like a problem."

It was. "If I start kissing you, I may not stop."

"Promises, promises," she murmured.

His hands closed around her waist. He lifted her up and sat her on the dressing room table. The soft lights were behind her, sending a glow spilling around her body, and damn if she didn't look like an angel.

Fitting, since he felt like the devil. But an angel wasn't supposed to wind up with the devil. That wasn't the way things worked in this world. "You shouldn't be with someone like me." Yet he didn't take his hands off her.

"Why not?"

"Oh, sweetheart, you don't know what I've done."

"Then tell me."

Maybe he should. But if he laid bare all of his deep, dark secrets, then she would fear him, more than she wanted him.

"Who are you, Royal Boudreaux?"

"Not even my real name," he heard himself say.

A faint line appeared between her brows.

"I was thrown away. A freaking two-year-old kid. Found wandering around Royal Street in New Orleans. No parents ever claimed me. The name I got came from the street I walked." An exhale.

Her eyes widened and then...a tear slipped down her cheek.

"What the hell?" Royal stared in horror at that tear drop. Then another fell.

"What are you doing?" he demanded. "Violet!"

She swiped at her cheek. "I'm sorry," she whispered. "That shouldn't have happened to you."

His chest burned. Ached. Burned.

Another teardrop fell.

"Stop it." He didn't like her tears. This time, he was the one to wipe the teardrop away. To catch it on his hand.

No one ever cried for me before.

Why was she crying for him?

"I like your name," she said, even as another tear leaked down her cheek. "I like you. I want you, Royal, and I—"

He took her mouth. He could taste the salt of her tears, and she should not be crying. Not Violet. She *should not be crying for me.*

His hand curled carefully under her jaw. Her mouth opened beneath his, and her tongue snaked out to meet his. She kissed him tenderly, as if he was somehow the fragile one, when the truth could not be further from that.

He pushed closer to her. Stood between her spread legs. And the hunger he felt for her burst free. He'd been riding a dangerous river of adrenaline ever since he'd seen her on that stage. Trapped in the coffin. Shoving her hands against the glass.

Get her. Save her.

Take her away.

He kissed her with growing hunger as his control

fractured. This wasn't the place for her first time. He knew that. Knew that he should exercise restraint and caution.

But restraint and caution had always been so very boring.

Letting lust reign. Letting need dominate? So. Much. Better.

She'd changed her attire after getting back to her dressing room. Put on soft, supple yoga pants that hugged her legs and delectable ass. A loose top that fell off one shoulder. Her hair was still twisted up into a bun, but loose tendrils had escaped to tease her cheeks.

A moan slid from her throat, and he greedily took the passionate sound. She hadn't turned away from him when he'd started revealing his past to her.

Thrown away. Left behind.

And she'd cried for him.

She knew about his hunts. About the twisted *extracurricular activity* as Avalon called it.

Hunting like a monster. Feeding the darkness inside.

And she wanted to be his partner. She wanted to hunt with him.

How the hell was he supposed to stop from absolutely consuming her?

Her hands slid over his back. She pulled him closer. "Royal..." A husky cry of his name.

He forced his head to lift. Violet blinked up at him. Eyes heavy with passion, not fear. She wanted him. No lie. He was ready to fight the world for her.

Or to just kill some deserving bastards. Whatever worked.

"You're coming home with me," Royal told her, all too aware that his voice had gone ragged.

She licked her lower lip.

Sonofa—

"Safer that way," he rasped. "I've got great security. You'll be protected at my place."

"Right. Protected."

Her voice dripped over him like the best sin.

He sucked in a breath and decided to give her a fair warning. "You'll also be fucked."

Chapter Ten

Her lips curled. "I was hoping you'd say that."

What. In. The. Hell? He shook his head. *What in the hell am I supposed to do with you, Violet Murphy?*

"Because I want to fuck you, Royal. And I don't care if it's right or wrong or anything and everything in between. I want you." Then she surprised the hell out of him—even more. Her hand slid between their bodies. Skated down his chest. Down his stomach. And her fingers pressed to the heavy erection that thrust against the front of his pants.

"*Violet.*"

"I want to go down on you. You tasted me. I want to taste you."

He had to close his eyes and *breathe*. Because the visual that just flooded his head was too incredible. Violet, on her knees before him.

Oh, hell, yes.

But the cops were in the building. Still talking to witnesses. Still checking the scene. Dancers rushed around the dark, back halls of the theater. Surely, he wouldn't be so bad as to fuck her mouth with everyone so close...

"I think you'll taste amazing."

His eyes opened.

Yes, he was that bad. But he wouldn't stop with just her mouth. *You pushed too far. I will fuck you now, Violet. And if anyone hears you scream my name, then they will just know that you belong to me.*

She blinked at him. "Is something wrong?"

Not at all. He backed up. Pulled her off the dressing table.

"Did I say something wrong?" Violet pushed.

They should be clear on one thing. Right now. "There is never anything *wrong* when it comes to you."

She smiled at him. A smile that lit her golden eyes and *almost* made sanity return, but, nope...her mouth—on his dick. Then his dick in her hot, tight core?

Yes.

She started to lower onto her knees before him. "I've only done this once or twice," she began.

"Fucking kill them."

Violet froze. "Royal?"

He unclenched his teeth with an extreme effort. "Don't talk about them." *Sure as shit not now.*

"I just meant that I'm not sure I'll do it right."

His eyes narrowed. "You'll do everything right. Didn't I just tell you?" And he bent. His lips brushed over hers. *"There is no wrong when it comes to you."* He straightened and stared down at her. *Want her. Need her.*

Her smile came again. Her knees hit the floor. Her fingers went to the front of his pants. She unhooked the belt. Undid the snap. Lowered the zipper.

His eager dick surged right toward her. No underwear. He hadn't bothered with boxers that day when he'd rushed home to change. Her fingers curled around him. Hesitant.

Soft. He thrust into her grip, and she tightened her hold. Squeezed him. Pumped. Moving uncertainly from the base of his cock to the tip. Then again. Again.

His hands slammed down onto the dressing table behind her. He couldn't touch her in that instance. He was afraid his hold would be too rough.

Her mouth opened over the tip of his cock.

He almost shattered the edge of the dressing table.

She retreated a bit. Her breath fluttered over his dick. Then she came back in. Her tongue licked over him, sampling him like he was a freaking popsicle and she was lost on a hot day, and a growl tore from him.

Want in her. Need in her. Want. Her.

Her mouth took him in deeper.

His grip tightened even more on that dressing table. And he—

Heard voices. Just beyond her door. Out in the hall. Coming closer.

Not again.

"Sweetheart..." He pulled her up. *Regretfully.* "People are close..."

A hard knock sounded at the door. And some SOB rattled the doorknob.

She stared up at him. Lips swollen. Gaze dazed. Absolutely fuckable.

"Locked the door this time," he muttered. Like he hadn't learned from his previous mistake.

Awareness flooded into her eyes even as heat flooded her cheeks.

He tucked his dick back in his pants. *Dammit.* "We'll finish that soon." His gaze swept over her. *Perfection.* He swung for the door. Marched forward angrily because that jerk was still rattling the doorknob.

Then...

"Violet!"

Micah's voice. Color Royal shocked.

"We have to talk," Micah continued loudly, his words followed by another demanding knock. "We have to talk *immediately!*"

Royal yanked open the door.

Micah's hand was poised to pound against the door once more. "Oh."

Royal tilted his head.

"I...thought you had left."

Then you thought wrong. "Told you already, I'll be with Violet from now on." *Until I'm sure she's safe, I'll be her shadow.*

"Don't you, ah, have businesses to run?"

"Quite a few of them, actually, thanks for your concern." *This prick has been investigating me.* The "billionaire bodyguard" line had told Royal that Micah had been looking into his life. Fair enough. *I'm looking into your world, too, asshole.* "But I know how to delegate, and I have people I trust who can manage things for me." He lifted a brow. "There a particular reason you are bothering me and Violet right now?"

"I, uh..." His gaze tried to dart around Royal so he could land on Violet. "I was worried."

"Were you?" Royal knew he sounded doubting.

"Violet has been through some very unsettling incidents."

Royal grunted. *Do tell, asshole.*

"I have a friend who is a shrink. Dr. Leo Barnes. I thought she might want to talk to him." His head craned more. "Violet, I've known Leo for ages. He can help you. I took the liberty of calling him a few moments ago, and he said that he'd be happy to talk with you today."

Royal heard the rustle of her steps. "I'm not talking to him."

"Why not?" Surprise flashed on Micah's face. "You need him! I noticed you were already shaking when you got into the coffin, and after what happened—look, I *need* you to be able to handle the show. I get that Simone is your understudy, but she isn't you. The tickets are selling because people want to see *you*. And I need to know that you won't leave me hanging when the show is ready to start."

Her soft steps padded closer. She touched Royal's arm, and he stepped to the side. But stayed close. "I am not going to leave you hanging." Her chin lifted. "I will be ready for the show."

"You should meet with Leo," Micah urged her. "He's good. Hell, half the dancers in the show see him already."

"Thanks for your concern." Violet inclined her head toward him. "But I have other plans for today."

"Here." Micah grabbed her hand. "This is his card. In case you change your mind." He dropped her hand a moment later, as if he'd just been scalded. His gaze skittered toward Royal. "FYI, big guy, one of the cops was asking for you. Thought you'd left but, ah, guess not? Detective... Curran Barlow, I think it was? He asked for you, specifically."

Good to know. "Come on, Violet."

"I need to talk more with Violet!" Micah protested.

Okay, this jackass was just getting on his nerves. "Then talk." He felt Violet put her hand in his. Automatically, his fingers curled around hers. A glance toward her showed Violet's cheeks were still flaming. Her lips so plump.

And when he turned back to Micah, he realized the guy understood that he'd interrupted at a very bad time.

And Micah looked pissed.

You won't have her, bastard. Get over it.

"I truly regret that you were frightened today," Micah said stiffly.

"Yes, I regret that, too," Violet returned, a little bite coming back to her voice. Royal really liked her bite.

"We're going to get the coffin repaired."

Royal tensed. They were going to put her back into that glass hell?

"Something happened to the lock—I don't know what. But we'll make sure all the kinks are worked out before showtime. You know there are always a few mishaps before the big show."

"Mishaps," Royal tasted the word. "Your leading lady often nearly gets killed?"

"No!" A fast denial. "This is very unusual. You can rest assured that additional safety precautions will be put in place, I promise."

Royal didn't trust the guy. Not at all.

"I'm afraid word leaked to the press. Probably because of the patrol cars that came rushing to the scene." Micah winced. "They're out front in force, so you probably want to slip out the back when you leave, Violet."

She nodded. "My car was out back anyway."

She wouldn't be driving off in her car. He'd be taking her from the scene. And Royal would make arrangements for someone else to pick up her ride.

Micah looked for all the world as if he had something else to say, but the guy retreated. Finally. Royal watched him scurry away and then said, "I don't really like him at all."

"I can see that." A pause. "You think he was involved, don't you?"

"I think I'll be finding out." Why not put his cards on the table? He tugged her closer. "And, yeah, he's at the top of my suspect list."

Time to get her the hell out of there. Especially if a hungry pack of reporters had already closed in. Violet grabbed her bag, tucked the business card she'd been given inside, and they headed into the hallway. They maneuvered through the tight quarters and past some dancers, and Royal spotted Curran.

Detective Curran Barlow. A very new promotion.

Curran caught his eye and dipped his head in acknowledgement. He approached Royal slowly. His holster was attached to his right hip. With one quick glance, Curran took in Royal and Violet and the fact that Royal was still holding Violet's hand.

Like he'd be letting her go anytime soon.

"Boudreaux," Curran announced loudly. "Heard you were the big hero today."

"Hardly," Royal dismissed.

"Yes, he was," Violet declared, voice adamant. "Royal got me out of the coffin just in time."

"So glad he could save the day." Curran raked her with a speculative glance. "I know you spoke with some of the other officers here, but I haven't gotten to interview you. It's Violet Murphy, correct?"

"Yes."

"I know you were at the station two weeks ago. I saw you, but you didn't see me." Curran stood just an inch or two shorter than Royal. Curran's dark eyes were sharp. Assessing. "I'm the new detective on the block. They're not exactly shoving high-profile cases like yours my way. They leave that to the seasoned guys. So when you were at the station reporting your abduction, I didn't get to speak with you."

Curran was a better detective than anyone else on that force, new guy or not. He *should* have been the one on Violet's case.

"Then the Feds came in, of course. Since we were dealing with a kidnapping. Then it just turned into a pissing match between the local cops and the Bureau." Curran's tone was annoyed. "Waste of time." A shake of his head. "I got called in today because it seemed to just be a situation involving some faulty equipment. Supervisors thought I'd be in and out."

"Yet you're still here," Royal noted. Very much not in and out.

"I don't think the situation is as simple as others may have believed." Curran leaned closer. He pointed upward. "You could access the lights from the catwalk. I went up there. Wanted to take a look at things myself. Checked all the other lights. *Very* secure. Those babies wouldn't come down, not unless you *wanted* them to fall."

Royal understood exactly what Curran was saying. *Someone wanted the light to fall. Someone wanted Violet to be hurt.*

"Haven't found any conclusive evidence yet," Curran added. "But I've got some good crime scene techs checking every inch of the place. When I know more, you'll know more." He rubbed a hand along his jaw. "Heard there was an incident at your place last night, Violet."

She nodded. "Someone broke the front windshield of Royal's car and threw a big rock through my window."

"You got any enemies?" Curran asked.

Her chin notched up. "Just the jerk who abducted me."

Curran stared hard at Royal. "I'll repeat the question for you, Royal. Got any enemies? Someone who might be looking to send you a message by targeting your girlfriend?"

Royal didn't even blink.

But Violet surged in front of him. "Royal didn't even *know* me when I was abducted. What happened to me is in no way linked to him. And as far as what happened at my place, it was *my* place. I think his car was hit just because he happened to be there with me. Then I was the one targeted today, not him. Royal saved me. Let me be very clear, none of this is on him."

"Protective," Curran noted softly.

"Yes," Violet fired right back. "He is protective, and I appreciate—"

"I meant you were protective of him. An admirable trait. One I am sure Royal enjoys very much." Curran pursed his lips. "Did you see anyone suspicious around the coffin before you were sealed inside?"

"The *only* person around the coffin when I was put inside was Micah. He closed the lid."

"Hmm."

"But some of the stagehands brought it out. I'm sorry—I wasn't paying attention then. I can't tell you who they were." She threw a glance over her shoulder at Royal. Then she looked back at the detective. "To be completely honest, plenty of people in the theater would have been able to get to the coffin. It was just stored in the prop area. So if someone did something to make the lock stick, it could have been...anyone." Fear breathed in the last word.

Curran's hard expression softened. "We'll figure this out."

She swallowed. "Showtime is coming up fast. We're in final rehearsal stages. I would hate to think something else could happen. I-I don't want another dancer hurt because someone is targeting me."

"And I don't want *you* hurt," Royal told her. She was his focus. Her safety was key for him. He shared another long look with Curran, and he knew the detective understood his message.

Report to me. Find the bastard. I want him stopped.

Royal inclined his head. "I'm taking Violet back to my place. If you have other questions, you know where to reach us."

Curran moved to the side, clearing the path so they could exit. But just as Royal and Violet passed him...

"One quick follow-up." Curran cocked his head.

Hell.

"Just why were you here today, Royal? Don't get me wrong, I'm certainly happy you were able to help Violet, but what brought you to the rehearsal?"

Royal slanted a glance at the detective. "She did. I—"

"I invited Royal to the rehearsal," Violet said quickly. "Last night, when we were together, I asked him to stop by. He was here because of me."

Curran's eyes gleamed. "Protective," he repeated. No missing the hint of admiration. "Hold tightly to her."

"I intend to."

* * *

GET AWAY. *Get away. Get away.*

All Violet wanted to do was break and run out of the theater. She didn't want to talk to the cops. Didn't want to chat with the dancers who milled around and told her just how *horrifying* the coffin scene had been to witness.

She wanted to run. She wanted to flee.

Instead, she had to walk slowly through the back corridors of the theater. She had to answer more questions. She had to pretend like she was not close to absolutely breaking apart on the inside.

I couldn't get out.

Trapped.

Again.

Royal opened the theater's back door. She hurried out. It was still daytime, and the sunlight spilled onto her. Violet blinked quickly and—

"Violet!" A shout of her name that had her head jerking to the right.

"Violet, was there another attack on you?"

Then her head whipped to the left.

A swarm of people—reporters?—waited just beyond the rear stage door. Some were filming with phones. Some had bigger cameras. They all closed in.

She shuddered and backed up and ran straight into Royal's powerful chest.

His arms immediately closed around her. "It's all right," he whispered into her ear. "I've got you." And he did. His body curled protectively around hers, and he rushed forward with her. He was big and strong, and he shielded her completely.

The questions flew. The phones and cameras kept filming, but Royal didn't stop. He got her to his car. Tucked her into the passenger seat of the Benz—a Benz with an already repaired windshield—and then, in seconds, he was in the driver's seat beside her. The crowd jumped back as he reversed, and then Royal got them the hell out of there.

Her hands fisted in her lap. Micah had told her that the reporters had gotten wind of the story, but that...*that* had been a whole lot more than just a small contingency of local journalists.

"So much for them just being out front," Royal groused.

She forced her hands to unclench. "I don't get why there were so many of them."

"Because your story was leaked, sweetheart. Someone tipped off the press, and if I had to guess, it's that prick artistic director. He's trying to sell more tickets by using *you*. You're freaking PR gold to him. The dancer who was the tragic victim."

She stiffened. *I'm not just a victim.*

"You got away, and now he's selling tickets like mad. And I hate to tell you, but national outlets were already picking up the abduction story. Now with this attack..." A long exhale. "You will need to stay with me. Not just for tonight. The reporters are going to be hounding your steps. They want a story, and you're the perfect, juicy lead."

"Because I'm so...tragic." A brittle note entered her voice.

He slowed at the stop sign. Turned his head toward her. "Because you're beautiful. Because you're breakable. Because people look into those big, golden eyes, and they want to help you. They want to fucking destroy anyone who hurts you. Rip the bastards apart and bury the remains so deep in the ground that *no one* will ever find them."

Um, okay. She fiddled with her seatbelt. "I'm not sure that's what most people would want to do for me."

"Guess it's just what I want to do for you." A pause. "You just lied to a detective for me."

She had. "You shouldn't be a suspect. Lying seemed like the easiest way to get you cleared."

"You sure about that?" His hands gripped the steering wheel easily as he turned and drove down the road on the left. "Maybe I came to the theater just to see my handiwork up close and personal. Maybe I wanted to rush in and save you because I want you to keep thinking I'm a hero. Perfect timing, don't you agree?"

"That's not funny." Anger stirred in her. Adding to her already brewing batch of emotions. "Why are you trying to make me doubt you?"

"I don't know." Low. Muted. "Maybe because you're the first one—other than my brother Beau—who has believed in me so much." He cut her a glance. "Not real sure what to do with you. You know my deepest secrets. You could get me locked away at any time. Guess I'm trying to find out what your tipping point is. When will you turn on me?"

She sucked in a breath. "I'm not going to turn on you."

He stared at the road again. "He's not my blood brother. Not like with your family."

Oh, shit. My family. Her brother Dawson would see the news. She fumbled with her phone.

"Beau's past is a lot like my own. He's the one constant I always had. He's done his best to make sure I don't go completely off the deep end and get lost in the dark."

She stopped fumbling with the phone and focused on him. "You honestly think that could happen?" Then before he could answer, Violet shook her head. "I don't. You have far too much control for something like that to occur."

A red light stopped them. His head turned slowly toward her. He flashed a smile that sent a shiver chasing down her spine. "Don't be too sure."

But she was. For some reason, she felt completely sure of him. And... "I feel safe with you. When I was in that coffin and I looked up and you were there, I knew I'd be okay."

His smile slowly slipped away. He stared into her eyes as if trying to figure out some big mystery. No need for that.

"I'm what you see," she told him. "No secrets from me. I'll tell you what I think and what I feel."

"And what do you think and feel about me?"

So many things. "I feel all tangled up," she answered him truthfully. "And I think you're the bad guy and the good guy all wrapped up in one package."

"Wrapped up in a bow," he murmured.

She thought of the killers he'd stopped. *Left with bows around their necks.*

Violet swallowed. "Part of me does fear you, but a bigger part of me feels connected to you. Feels safe with you. *Wants* you. And I trust you. I know you'd have my back if things went to hell around us. I mean, you saved me when I was a complete stranger. Now you *know* me. And you're still saving me."

A horn sounded behind them.

"Maybe you're saving *me*," he said.

She frowned. No, she hadn't saved him. Not once. But if he needed her, she'd sure try her best.

He turned and faced the repaired windshield. No sign of the damage remained. Perfect glass.

Would it be so easy to repair the glass coffin?

Royal drove forward.

Violet sent off a quick text to her brother. *Okay, so you'll see a scary news story, but I promise, I am okay.*

Three dots appeared. Then Dawson replied...

What. The. Hell?

Right. Her brother. Typical.

Another text fired from him: *I've already seen one scary news story. I don't want to see more. Violet, what is happening? Do you need me? Are you safe?*

She bit her lip, then typed her response. *Safe. Going to a friend's house for the night. Do not worry about me.*

Her phone rang three seconds later. Her finger swiped over the screen right before she put it to her ear.

"What news story?" her brother barked. "*And what friend?*"

Chapter Eleven

She was in his home. Secured behind his doors. Protected by the best security system that money could buy. And he was trying hard not to *pounce*.

"Make yourself at home," Royal instructed. Did he sound hungry? Freaking lusty? She'd been padding near the floor to ceiling windows that overlooked his pool. Her back was to him, and his eyes were drinking her in.

Slow down.

He'd gone too far in the dressing room. Check. Understood. But the woman had wanted his dick in her mouth, and how was he supposed to resist that? And right then, all he wanted was to strip her and fuck her where she stood.

But a gentleman wouldn't do that. Not after the nightmare of her day. Hell, a gentleman wouldn't have put his dick in her mouth after the attack, either. *But there you are.*

He wasn't a gentleman. Wasn't a real hero. He was just the selfish bastard who wanted to lay claim to everything that she was.

"It's a beautiful place," Violet said. She kept looking at the pool.

"There's a wine cellar downstairs." Maybe she wanted a drink—or three—after her day. "And there are two guest rooms upstairs. You can pick whichever one you want. Kitchen is to the left." He motioned needlessly because she wasn't looking his way. "You're probably starving." *Like I am starving for you.* "I can fix you dinner, if you'd like."

"You cook?"

"Oh, I'm a fucking fantastic cook."

Apparently surprised, she peered over her shoulder at him.

Royal shrugged. "Not bragging." Maybe he was. Sue him. He had one or two skills that didn't involve killing. "Even have plans to open a restaurant soon."

"Here? In Savannah?" Now she turned to fully face him.

But he hesitated. Before meeting her, he'd been planning to leave Savannah for a while. Beau had gotten settled with Avalon, and Royal had thought that it might be best to disappear for a bit. He'd done that, over the years, gone in and out of Beau's life. "Not exactly sure of the location yet."

She nodded. "What type of restaurant?"

"Creole." He laughed. "You can take the punk kid out of Louisiana, but you can't take the Big Easy out of the man."

Violet took a hesitant step closer to him.

"I can make some jambalaya that will have you thinking you're tasting heaven."

Her gaze searched his. "You grew up in New Orleans."

"Guilty."

"You miss it?" Her head tilted, and her hair slid over her shoulder. "I've actually never been there. Thought I'd do a performance at the Saenger in New Orleans last year, but I got beat out of the role."

"I'll have to show you the city one day." The words just slipped from his mouth. And, dammit, he hadn't meant to say them. Saying them implied there would be a future. That there was more than just now for the two of them.

Don't you want more than just now with her?

She took another step toward him. "I'd like to see the city with you."

He forced a laugh even as he eliminated the last bit of distance between them. Now they practically stood toe to toe. "Not like I grew up in the swanky mansions that fill the Garden District. That was more Avalon's style."

"You knew her when she was younger?"

Now *that* was a very complicated story. And it wasn't his story to tell. It was Beau's. "I knew about breaking into houses like hers and boosting rides in her neighborhood." A shrug. He caught the flash of surprise in her eyes. "Sweetheart, I ran with a gang that would give you nightmares. Beau and I fought our way out."

"How?"

His hand lifted and cupped her jaw. "Simple. We took over the gang. Then we ripped it apart. When we were done, nothing was left."

"You can be a scary man, Royal Boudreaux." But instead of appearing scared, her head turned, and her lips skimmed over his palm. "Show me."

His heartbeat accelerated.

"You're in this *swanky* house right now. I just saw your gorgeous pool. I have no doubt that you have some state-of-the-art kitchen that will give me serious envy, and, apparently, you have a killer wine cellar downstairs." A pause. "But I'm not interested in those things right now."

"What are you interested in?"

"You knew where a serial killer would be lurking. You have caught two other killers. And I watch enough true crime shows to know that you must have some sort of research area or crime room somewhere in this massive home of yours."

"This isn't *Criminal Minds*."

"I love that show. Or at least, I used to. Until I started being one of the victims and not the people chasing the monsters."

He stared at her, and he made his hand drop.

"You would keep that room hidden," Violet mused. "Can't have casual company just strolling inside on accident. How embarrassing would that be? *Oh, pay no attention to my murder board.*"

His eyes narrowed on her.

"And not like the room is going to be located in Punishment, though, I do get the name. On the nose, isn't it? You like to punish those who deserve it. You had files there, the ones I saw. The ones that gave me new nightmares. But there's more. There has to be." Her gaze darted around. "So, are you going to Scooby Doo it and show me some secret room?"

"Scooby Doo it?"

"Most people really liked Fred. Personally, I always thought he could use a bit more of a dark side."

He could only shake his head. "I take it you're Daphne in this version of the show?"

"No, I really liked Velma. The quiet brains behind the

operation." Her lips pressed together. "I always wished I could be as smart as she was. And even when Velma got rattled, she still solved the case." A pause. "I also wanted a dog just like Scooby. Never got one." She squared her shoulders. "Are you going to show me?"

"My secret lair?"

"So you *do* have one."

Didn't every good villain have a secret lair? "You could go upstairs. Get some rest."

"It's the middle of the day."

Nah. "Closer to evening."

A ghost of a smile teased her lips. "I'm betting it's downstairs. Does it connect to your wine cellar? Because suddenly, I find that I'm incredibly thirsty."

"Then how about a drink?" He turned on his heel and headed for the black door on the right. He swung open the door. A spiral, black metal staircase stretched down below. Without hesitating—because he knew Violet would follow—Royal descended the stairs. When he reached the landing, he immediately turned to the left. He opened the door that waited. Entered the temperature and humidity-controlled wine cellar. The lights turned on automatically. Two hundred and four bottles of wine were stocked in the cellar. All individually selected. The wooden shelves gleamed.

He heard her footsteps behind him. "What's your poison?" Royal asked her.

"Something sweet."

Yeah, I could go for something sweet right now. You.

Without another word, he made the selection. In moments, he'd poured the wine into two glasses and was offering her the dark red drink.

She took the glass from him. Their fingers brushed.

He lifted his wine glass. "To new partnerships."

She lifted hers. "To stopping killers."

Their glasses clinked. "I do like the way you think," he said. Then, watching her, he took a sip of his wine.

Violet gulped hers. Truly, she drained the glass in about three swallows.

Soft laughter escaped him. "You always drink your wine that fast?"

"False courage. I could use some." She put her glass down. "Show me?"

Very well. He set down his glass, too. Then... "Your Scooby Doo loving heart will adore this." He pushed down on one of the champagne bottles nestled on a tall shelf to the right.

Another door opened.

"I adore it," Violet breathed.

He took her hand and led her inside.

* * *

"How much longer are the cops going to be here?" Simone demanded. She sat at her dressing room table, but her back was to the big, lighted mirror. Her entire focus was on the man who'd just entered her room.

The bastard. The all-around asshole.

The handsome sonofabitch who was way too good in bed.

Micah grimaced and shut the door. "They have to finish their investigation." He braced his legs apart. "They grilled me. Can you believe that shit? And I'm pretty sure that Violet's new boyfriend threatened me." He marched forward and rubbed a hand over the back of his neck. "But, damn, sales are about to go through the roof." He flashed her a wide smile. "You can't pay for publicity like this! We are going to have to extend the run of the ballet. People will be flocking here every night. They'll all be waiting with bated breath to see if Snow White dies in her glass coffin."

Chill bumps rose on her arms. "You said she didn't nearly die. When—when her boyfriend said she could have died, you said that she could have just gotten some cuts."

"Yeah, and did you *see* that asshole's reaction to those words?" Micah's expression tightened. "I swear, for a second, I almost thought he'd pull out a knife and slice *me*." He rolled back his shoulders. "The man pays for one dance with her, and suddenly he's acting like he owns her. And Violet was the fucking Ice Queen before he strolled into her life. Now she's into screwing strangers?" A disgusted shake of his head. "Guess money does buy anything. Or anyone."

"I saw a reporter taking pictures of the coffin." She ignored what he'd said, for now. "I thought the theater was supposed to be off-limits while the cops were investigating."

He winked at her. "There's off-limits, and then there's *off-limits*."

"You let him in."

"If you don't have a dramatic shot to show the public, did the dangerous scene even happen? It's like the old saying...if a tree falls in a forest, and no one is there to hear it, did it even make a fucking sound?"

Her hands twisted in her lap.

"There was a big sound today. *Shatter*. That glass shattered so hard it even scared me. And in order to fully understand the scene, people needed pictures. To see is to believe."

She licked her lips. "Did you have something to do with the light falling on Violet?"

"She's my star!"

Simone flinched at that angry outburst.

"Like I would risk her." He closed in. Stared down at her. "Though, of course, if something did happen to her, I have an amazing understudy ready in the wings, don't I?"

"You didn't lock her in the coffin." A statement.

He bent and brushed his lips over hers. "Of course, I didn't lock her in the coffin. What kind of monster do you think I am?"

The kind that would do anything to make sure his show was a resounding success.

"I worry, though," Micah continued as his voice turned musing, "that our poor, traumatized lead may break before showtime. I tried to get her to go and pay a visit to Leo. You remember Leo, don't you, love?"

The psychiatrist. Leo Barnes. Yeah, Micah had introduced her to him at the fundraiser. Simone nodded.

"I was *attempting* to help her, but she refused." A sigh. "Some people are their own worst enemies."

"She should talk to someone," Simone heard herself say. The words were the truth. After the abduction, Violet had been so different. *Brittle.* And Simone had thought Violet might just be in danger of breaking, too.

"If she falls apart before the show, well, you are ready, are you not?" Another soft kiss. "All you need is the wig. That wig transforms you into our Snow White."

Was that one of the reasons that Violet had gotten the role over Simone? Because Violet *looked* like Snow White, no wig necessary? Hell, Simone would have dyed her blond hair in an instant. Or worn the stupid wig that was in the top drawer of her dressing table. She would have gladly worn it twenty-four, seven.

Or did Violet get the role because Micah wanted to fuck her? The dark question rolled through her.

Simone knew she was just as good of a dancer as her friend. *Is this just about Violet being an unattainable fuck?* Simone pulled in a deep breath.

Dammit, she is my friend. I hate feeling this way about my friend. But she'd been jealous when Violet got the role she'd wanted so badly.

"When the cops leave, I'll be cutting out," Micah said, completely oblivious to her sudden tension. "Want to meet me at my place?"

No, she didn't. They were a mistake. He'd been stringing her along. Making promises he wouldn't keep. And he'd started to scare her a bit because...*I'm not sure I trust him.*

But...

He kissed her again. "This show is going to change everything," he promised her. "National news teams have picked up Violet's story. Her getting abducted was the best thing that could have happened to us."

God, that was cold. "She could have died."

"But she didn't." Such a glib response. "And now she has her billionaire bodyguard. What a freaking prick." He straightened. "Lucky girl, though, am I right? Two escapes from death. And a new boyfriend with money to burn."

Simone swallowed. "Some people have all the luck." And some didn't. Some had to fight and bleed for every bit of success they achieved.

He headed for the door.

She stood and hurried to follow him out. "Micah?"

He opened the door but glanced back at her.

"You didn't hurt Violet?"

A frown pulled at his brows. "I didn't hurt Violet. What do I look like? Some crazed killer? I want publicity, not blood."

Right. Some of the tension slid from her shoulders.

Micah caught her arm and pulled her closer. And he kissed her. Even though he knew better. They didn't ever kiss when someone could see them. *The door was open. Someone could be watching.*

He let go. When he walked away, Micah was whistling.

Frantic, she looked to the left. No one was there. Her head whipped to the right. No one was—

The cop. Correction—detective. Tall, dark, silent, and too watchful. His intense gaze was on her. No expression was on his face, but she knew he was making all kinds of conclusions. Wasn't that what detectives did? Crap. He'd seen the kiss. Had he heard her question Micah?

Detective Curran Barlow ambled toward her. Part of her wanted to turn and flee. Instead, she locked her body down and refused to budge. *Never show fear.* That had always been her motto. She didn't show fear when she faced total prick casting directors. She didn't show fear when she had grueling instructors who wanted her to dance for hours and hours until her feet were bleeding, and she could only limp home.

Never show fear.

Hell, Violet had been the one to first whisper those words to her. At Simone's initial audition at the conservatory, she'd been shaking like a leaf. Then Violet had sidled up to her and whispered those words. *Never show fear.* And Violet had smiled at her. The first hint of kindness she'd had in ages.

I am such a shitty friend.

"You're sleeping with the artistic director," the detective said.

Her chin notched up. "Don't really see how that's your business."

He didn't argue. Didn't agree, either. But he did ask, "You think he might have hurt your friend?"

The cop *had* heard her question. "I think it was an accident." Simone chose her words very, very carefully. "I don't think anyone here wants Violet hurt."

"No enemies?"

"Violet is nice to everyone she meets." Which was true. "She's never said an unkind word about anybody on set. She freaking brings in bagels for the crew. She mentors new dancers. She will stay for hours and hours when a certain very demanding artistic director thinks she is not getting a routine exactly right." She pasted a smile on her face. "Violet has no enemies."

"But you still just asked your boyfriend if he'd hurt her."

She tried to remember her exact words. "No, I didn't ask." Her heart slammed into her chest. "I made a statement. I *said* he didn't hurt Violet."

"Sure sounded like I *heard* a question in your voice."

"Then I am sure you *heard* his response. He very clearly indicated that he had *not* hurt her. She's the star of his show. Why would Micah try and hurt his star?" Her heart raced in her chest, but her voice remained cool. *I am not just a dancer. I've always been a fabulous actress.*

His stare raked her. "Why, indeed?" He turned away. Took two steps.

She began to relax—

The detective glanced back. "You're her understudy, aren't you? I mean, you have other roles that you play, but if Violet were to be unable to perform, you'd step into the spotlight."

And her heart drummed even harder. "Yes."

"You're sleeping with the artistic director. Maybe your boyfriend wants her out of the way so that you can shine.

That could very well be the reason *why*." He sent her a little salute. "If you think of anything you might want to suddenly share with me because, oh, say, you realize you can't trust your boyfriend—"

"He's not," she cut in to say. Micah wasn't her boyfriend. Their relationship—no, it wasn't a relationship. They just hooked up. He kept their hook-ups secret. Except...

I told Violet about him.

And now the cop knew. Crazy how secrets could spread.

"Well, if you realize you can't trust your *not* boyfriend, reach out to me. I'd love to hear anything else you might have to say about this case."

Her stomach twisted. "I don't know anything else."

"Not about the coffin? About the light falling?" he pushed.

She shook her head. "Nothing."

"Not a single detail? Not even about Violet's abduction?"

Do not change expression. "How would I know anything about that?"

"Guess you wouldn't." A shrug of one broad shoulder. "Never hurts to check, though, right?"

She didn't like the detective or his questions. So what if he looked a bit too much like Shemar Moore, that hot actor from the *Criminal Minds* show that Violet used to watch all the time? *She was always trying to get me to watch that show with her. We'd curl up on Violet's ratty couch and watch after a grueling day. She'd said watching killers get captured relaxed her. Even if they were just fictional ones.*

After Violet's abduction, Simone was willing to bet that

her friend didn't still love to watch a show about sadistic killers. *Because Violet has changed. That night changed her.*

The detective was watching Simone too closely. Time to get away from him before she slipped up. "I need to collect my things. Get home. I'm exhausted."

"Sure. Be safe out there. You never know who is waiting in the dark." He strolled away.

She slammed her door closed. Locked it. Her fingers were trembling. Every part of her trembled.

Simone rushed back to her dressing table. She yanked open the top drawer and hauled out her little bottle of pills. She popped two and swallowed them down without water. Her shaking fingers tossed the bottle back into her drawer, and her gaze lit on the wig.

A wig that turned her into Violet.

Into Snow White.

She pulled out the wig. Stared at her reflection in the mirror. Lately, she hadn't liked herself very much. Mostly...

When I look at Violet, I don't like myself. Guilt could do that to you. It could tie you up and have you squirming. It could make you hate yourself.

Simone pulled the dark wig into place. Tucked her blond locks beneath it. She stared into the mirror. *You need red lipstick. Violet wears red lipstick for the show.*

She picked up a tube of lipstick and spread it over her lips. Her reflection stared back at her.

A tear slid down her cheek.

If she let her gaze unfocus...*maybe I can be her.* "I'm sorry," Simone whispered. The guilt was eating her alive. And she wanted to say those words to Violet so badly.

Was Violet still at the theater? Or had she already left with the new boyfriend—Royal?

When Micah had burst into her dressing room, he

hadn't told Simone that Violet had left. Maybe she *was* still there. Maybe they could talk.

Maybe...

She shot to her feet. Ran for the door. She flipped the lock and wrenched the door open. There was no sign of the detective, and she was damn glad he wasn't lurking around. Her feet thudded over the old wood flooring in the hallway. She snaked around a corner, took a left, and saw Violet's room ahead. She hurried straight for the door. Her hand curled around the knob, and she threw the door open. Simone rushed inside with a confession ready on her lips.

The room was dark. Empty.

She's already gone.

Dark and so still.

She stood there a moment, with her hands at her sides. Her shoulders slumped. Violet had been her friend. For so long.

And what had *she* been?

I saw her that night. A horrible, terrible truth. *I saw him take her, and I didn't do anything.*

Tears splashed down her cheeks.

The door creaked behind her. "Violet?" A gruff, male voice.

"She's not—" Simone began. But she didn't get to finish. She'd been about to say...*She's not here.* Only she never got the chance to utter those words. Because someone grabbed her from behind. Someone big and powerful. One hand slapped over her mouth even as an arm locked around her midriff. She was yanked up against a strong body, and she thrashed and clawed, and terror blazed inside of her.

She felt the wig slide off her head. It slithered to the floor.

His grip slackened. His fingers fell away from her mouth.

Oh, God. He thinks I'm Violet. "Not...her!" Simone gasped out. She sprang to the left as she tried to flee.

His fingers curled around the back of her neck, and he just slammmed her—and her head—into the nearest wall.

She crumpled.

Chapter Twelve

For some reason, she didn't expect all the computers. Or rather, she didn't expect quite so many of them. Five screens. Hard drive boxes blinked near them.

A massive, black desk waited in the middle of the room. There were maps on the left wall. One with a red circle in the middle, and when she leaned in closer to get a better look at that circle...

"The winery," Royal told her. "After narrowing down locations, it seemed like a prime spot for the killer to use. Based on his other kills, I knew that he liked isolated spots. He preferred areas that weren't currently inhabited. Not like he wanted his work interrupted."

His work. She flinched.

"After Fiona Law's body was discovered on the outskirts of Savannah, I knew he was hunting here. He'd been in Atlanta before that. I've linked two victims who were found there to him. Though, you already saw them, didn't you? In the files at Punishment."

She spun away from the map. Her gaze fell on the desk.

Familiar files were perched on top of the gleaming, black surface.

The wine she'd gulped had her feeling a little dizzy. Or maybe that was just the memory of those bloody pictures. "How did you know..." Her voice was low, so she cleared her throat and tried again, "How did you know a serial killer was hunting?"

"At first, I didn't. Just thought some sick bastard who got off on hurting women had left a body in an old botanical garden on the outskirts of Atlanta. The garden—hell, once upon a time, it was something to see. But the owner died, the place withered, and everyone seemed to forget about it."

Everyone but the killer.

"An...acquaintance of mine knew the woman who was found there. Marcella White. He wasn't exactly thrilled that she'd been tossed away like garbage. He thought Marcella deserved a hell of a lot better."

Her gaze lifted to collide with his when she heard the rage in his voice.

"So he reached out to me. He didn't have a lot of cash. He couldn't hire a PI to help him, and the cops seemed to have hit a dead end on the investigation."

"Did this friend know about your, ah, hobby?" And how in the world had Royal ever started this hobby? How—and when? How long had he been hunting the predators who hid in the night?

"No, he didn't know about my hobby. He just knew that I was a dangerous sonofabitch who'd never liked it when someone hurt a lady." His lips twisted. "Tyrone—Ty—and I knew each other from back in the day. Hadn't seen him since we'd left New Orleans, so for him to reach out to me, I knew it was important to him." He opened one of the files. Rifled through the photos. "He loved her, and it gutted him that some bastard took her away. Ty was always good to me, so I told him that I'd make sure the SOB got what he deserved."

Punishment.

"Another woman from Atlanta turned up dead four months later. Like Marcella, she was living in Atlanta, but the authorities didn't connect the cases right away because this victim..." He pulled out a photo. Turned it toward Violet. "Bailey Brown. She was found in an orchard about forty-five minutes from Atlanta."

Violet forced herself to look at the photo.

"Then he came here. I was hunting him, and the bastard just came straight to my town. What are the odds of that?"

She had no idea.

"He took Fiona Law." Another horrifying photo was slid toward her. "He took her approximately four months after Bailey was discovered dead. Fiona was later found in an abandoned corn field."

Her gaze had locked on the photo. All the women...*so much like me.*

"He'd been waiting four months between victims. I thought there was time. But he took you sooner than the four-month period he usually followed." He grabbed the photos and shoved them back into the file. He moved from behind the desk and toward the maps. "I plotted out places where I thought he would go. Abandoned sites that might work. Like I said before, he liked isolated spots. Abandoned property or property that had been for sale so long it might as well be abandoned. I figured out a couple of possible locations, and I set up cameras so I'd be alerted to movement out there."

She backed up a step in surprise. "You had cameras at

the winery?" She didn't remember seeing cameras, but so much of that terrible night was a blur.

He turned toward her. "The feed went to my phone. I saw the sedan pull up. That boring as hell, unobtrusive sedan—at night, in a dead winery. I knew it had to be him. Who the hell else would it be—at that time, at that place?"

Damn. "You're really quite good at hunting, aren't you?"

A dangerous smile curved his lips. The smile a tiger probably sent his prey right before those teeth ripped into the prey's neck. "Not my first ballgame, sweetheart."

No, she supposed it wasn't. Violet swallowed.

"I hauled ass out there as fast as I could. I wanted to catch him, but instead, I found you."

And the killer had gotten away. *But I got to keep living. Because of Royal.*

"This is the part where you can walk away." His smile had vanished. "You can turn around. You can realize that you don't want to really be tracking down a killer with me. That it's more than you anticipated."

The drumming of her heartbeat filled Violet's ears. It was more than she'd anticipated. No doubt about it.

"You can be assured that I will protect you." His head inclined toward her. "I will make sure that you have guards. You need those guards, Violet. You see, I happen to believe that he stalked you before he took you."

Goose bumps rose onto her arms. "Why do you believe that?" *Please do share with the class.*

"Because that's what he did with the other victims. You can't just snatch someone without watching the person first. Ty picked Marcella up from work every single night... except on Tuesdays. Because on Tuesdays, Ty worked as a volunteer at the local fire station. Guess which night Marcella was taken?"

"Tuesday." Not a guess.

Royal nodded. "He knew her routine. He knew when to take her. Knew when she'd be vulnerable. Same thing with Bailey. He took her when her roommate went out of town on a cruise with her fiancé. When Bailey was alone for five days."

Violet wet her lips. "What about Fiona?"

"Got her in the morning when she was doing her daily jog. There was one stretch where she cut through a park. She went in the park—a street sweeper saw her. But she never came out. He knew exactly when to take her."

Her goose bumps got worse. "And you think he knew exactly when to take me."

"As you got closer and closer to the show date, your rehearsals got longer, didn't they?"

A nod.

"On the night of your abduction, you were the last to leave the theater."

"I-I needed to be perfect." Micah had been particularly vicious that day. So she'd stayed, and she'd worked until her body had been near collapse. *Is that why I couldn't run from him fast enough? Why I couldn't fight harder? Because I was already so weak?* She could remember her knees trembling...

"You *are* fucking perfect." A snarl.

She jerked.

He rolled back his shoulders. "Sorry."

"Royal?"

He cleared his throat. Sawed a hand over the carefully trimmed beard on his jaw. "As I was saying, this is the part where you can change your mind. Where you don't actually have to go into the night and hunt with me as I stop a sadistic killer. No need for you to get your hands all bloody. I can do the dirty work for you."

Her chin notched up. "You think I'll be too scared, don't you?"

"Are you scared?"

"Yes."

He waited.

"But I *want* to do this." More than that, she needed to do it.

"He's still watching you. You get that, don't you? The first night you left your brother's house, the first night he thought you were unprotected, he followed you home. He threw the big landscape rock through your window because he was pissed as hell. He thought you'd be alone. Only I was in his way." He advanced toward her. "FYI, I intend to keep being in the bastard's way."

She bumped into the desk.

His hands reached out and curled around the desk behind her. "I'll need you to be bait, Violet. You really going to be okay with that? With me dangling you in front of him like some sweet treat that he can't resist?"

Her chest ached, but she said, "If it stops him, if *we* stop him, I can be okay with just about anything." What she *couldn't* be okay with? The monster just remaining free. With living the rest of her life in fear because she was afraid he'd come for her again.

Royal's gaze searched hers. What did he see when he looked into her eyes? Fear? Probably. When she looked into his eyes, she saw...

Darkness. Strength. Desire.

The hazel swirled. Brown. Gold. Green.

His right hand rose and curled under her chin. "I bet

you've never hurt anyone in your whole freaking life, have you, Violet?"

"I've tried not to."

"If it came down to a choice—your life or the prick who took you, what would you do?"

She didn't look away from his eyes. "I'd hurt him."

One eyebrow arched.

"I would kill him if it meant I escaped and he didn't," she whispered.

"Such bloodthirsty words," he murmured. "Careful, Violet, or I will think—"

"And if he turned on you...if something happened and you stopped being the hunter and became the prey, I would hurt him before I ever let him do anything to you."

His eyelids flickered. Then he let go of her chin and reached for her hand. His head tilted as he looked down at her hand. Automatically, she glanced down, too. His hand was so much bigger than her own. Stronger. Rougher.

"You're so fragile. Far too breakable."

"I am stronger than I look." She was. She trained for at least eight hours most days. Sure, she wasn't exactly the weight-lifting champion of the world. A dancer's strength was different. But different held its own power. "I'm not going to break."

"It would be a shame if you did." His fingers stroked along the inside of her palm. "I would be quite angry if something or someone caused you to break."

A shiver darted over her.

"Because I've discovered that I quite like you." He let her go. Retreated behind the desk.

She exhaled on the breath that she'd been holding. *I quite like you.* She didn't confess that she quite liked him, too. *Liked.* Ha. What a lie. Her feelings were far more twisted and complex than a mere *like*. Her hand—the hand that could still feel his touch—gestured vaguely. "Wh-what's the deal with all the computers? Is this the part where you tell me that you're a closet hacker?"

"Yes." No humor. Just a statement.

Violet blinked.

His mouth quirked into a half-smile. For a moment, real amusement seemed to dance in his eyes. "What? Didn't think some seedy club owner could know tech?"

"You're not seedy." She crept toward the desk.

"Sure, I am. Seedy. Dangerous. Manipulative. So many interesting adjectives apply to me." A roll of his shoulders. "I told you before that, in a different life, I ran with a gang in New Orleans."

Violet nodded.

"It was with them that I first realized I had a talent with tech. Don't get me wrong, I was always an asshole gamer." That mocking half-smile lingered on his lips. "But I went to a whole other level when I got access to equipment I needed." Slowly, the smile faded. "Teachers used to tell me I had so much potential. They wanted me to enter competitions, they put me in all the AP classes. But they didn't know what life was like when I left their school. They didn't get that a different life controlled me. Beau—hell, he wanted me to cut out, too. He wanted me to go to college. He fought like hell for our freedom. He'd bought into the stories the teachers told. I remember that when I turned eighteen, he did this bullshit talk with me about how I was special. That I could do different things." His gaze darted to the monitors. "I don't think this is what he—or all those teachers—meant when they talked about me living up to my potential."

Violet found herself taking another creeping step toward him. "Did you go to college?"

"For a while. I didn't fit in there. Didn't care about the football games and the frat parties. And I could already do one hell of a lot more with a computer than the professors could teach me." A shrug. "So I went back to living life my way."

Her gaze darted around the room. "Based on the house and the club and the expensive cars you seem to favor, living life your way has worked out for you." Her stare returned to him. "How do you use the computers to help you hunt?"

"I tear into the lives of anyone I suspect when I'm looking for my prey." A roll of one shoulder. "Because I'm an asshole, I routinely tear into the lives of the people who enter my world." His gaze had come to lock on her. "Take you, for instance, Violet Murphy. I know everything about you now."

She laughed.

He didn't. But he did begin checking off items, as if going through a mental list. "Bra size. Shoe size. Bank account. Credit history. I know when you went on your last date. I know your favorite food."

"That's..." Violet stopped.

"Scary?"

"Well, yes, it is," she admitted honestly. "You could have just asked me those things. I mean, ah, not my bra size. But..." She trailed away. "Why would you want to know all of that?"

"Because I'm trying to figure out why he took you. You look like his prey, yes, but I think there is more to it than just a surface attraction. I was trying to figure out that more."

By learning everything about me. She swallowed. "There is nothing special about me."

"Oh, I think there is. It's not every woman who decides she wants to hunt killers. Most victims of crimes let the police do that job. They don't want to get their hands dirty." He opened the top desk drawer. Pulled something out. Curled his hand around it and skirted around the desk as he walked back toward her.

She didn't retreat. She'd been heading toward him. Why retreat now?

"I keep expecting you to run." A little furrow appeared between his brows, as if he couldn't quite understand her. "I tell you my secrets. I scare you. But you still stay."

Yes, she did. "I'm not going anywhere." Her head tilted back so she could stare up at him.

"You should be pissed at me for tearing into your life."

Maybe. "I would have freely told you anything you wanted to know. No tearing necessary."

His jaw hardened. Then his hand lifted. There was a faint snick. And she realized the item he'd taken from the desk drawer had been a knife.

The blade had slid out. Gleaming. Sharp. Deadly.

And he was pointing the knife right at her.

"Scared?" A rasp.

"You aren't going to hurt me."

"I hurt a lot of people." Grim. "But, no, never you. I'd cut off my own fucking hand first." Then he reached for her hand. Royal curled her fingers around the knife's handle. "I saw the mace and the taser in your bag. But I want you keeping this on you at all times."

She started to nod.

"No, sweetheart, I mean it. *All* times. It's small enough

that you can even have it on you when you're on the stage. I need to know that you have a weapon with you at every moment."

The weight of the knife was light in her grip. She hit the small button on the side, and the blade vanished. He was right. The weapon was small enough that she could keep it with her. It would be easy enough to hide.

She pushed the button again. The blade sprang out.

"You've never used a knife on anyone, have you?" he asked.

Definitely not. But something about his voice...She peered up at him. "You have."

Royal shrugged.

He has. Violet pulled in a deep breath. "I'll willingly tell you every secret that I have. In return, I want to hear yours." Not like she could hack her way into his life. Not exactly her skill set.

"No, you don't want to hear them." He rubbed the back of his neck. "You must be tired. Adrenaline crash will hit soon. You can take your pick of the two guest rooms. My bedroom is the first room when you get off the stairs. I'll—"

"Have you ever killed someone, Royal?"

His hand froze. His eyes glittered.

And she took that as a yes. Her hold tightened on the knife.

"You don't want to play this game with me," he growled.

"I wasn't playing a game."

"Twenty questions."

No, she hadn't been—

"You'll find out things you don't like. Wouldn't it be better for you to just go on thinking I'm the guy who saved you? I like it when you think of me that way. Better for you not to see all my dark places."

The weapon felt cool in her grip. "We all have dark places inside ourselves. Some of us just do a better job of hiding them than others." But maybe there had been enough secrets revealed for one day. And maybe it was the wine she'd greedily gulped or the whole near-death experience, but her knees didn't seem quite steady. Her body kept wanting to tremble, and perhaps she should walk away.

While she could.

Besides, it wasn't like he was desperately grabbing for her and saying that he just couldn't live without her for another moment.

Are we going to talk about what happened in the dressing room? She still couldn't quite believe she'd done that. With him. But need had pierced through her. Her emotions and longings had raged out of control. And...

And we didn't finish what we started.

But he was making no move to turn things physical. So she walked away. Her steps were silent as she headed for the door.

"I'm not going to be able to let go."

So low and rumbling that she almost didn't understand his words.

"I'm *trying* to stay away. Trying to warn you that I am not what you need."

Oh, was that what he was doing? What a waste of energy. "I can be the judge of what I need." She threw a glance over her shoulder. "And of what I want."

His lips parted.

"You don't have to protect me from myself," she added.

"I'm not. I'm just trying to protect you from *me*." Stark. "Until you, I never would have said I was possessive. Not fucking territorial in the least. But when I look at you, I want to own you, Violet. The fact that you haven't been with another man makes me feel damn near savage. I want to take you and claim you and never, ever let go." An inhale. "I did the right thing when we first met. You thought I was a hero."

"Uh, you were." Just as he'd been her hero on the stage.

"Heroes don't want to do the things I want to do with you."

All of the moisture dried from her mouth. "What do you want to do?" A husky question.

He took a step toward her. Seemed to catch himself. Royal's powerful hands fisted at his sides. "Run while you can, sweetheart."

But what if I don't want to run? "If I run, will you chase me?"

The gold took over his eyes. Burned. "I'm not someone you play with, Violet. I've warned you about that."

"Does it look like I'm playing?" She sucked in a breath. Slowly let it out. "Did it look like I was playing when I was on my knees in front of you when we were in my dressing room?"

He bounded forward. *Lunged.* Royal reached out for her, only to fist his hands once more right before he could touch her. Then his fisted hands shoved back down to his sides. "You're scared, and you want me because you think I'm the thing that saved you from the dark. Sweetheart, I am the dark."

Her heart slammed into her chest.

"Get upstairs. Go to the guest room. Put space between us," he ordered starkly. "Or I will fuck you so completely that you will never be free of me."

* * *

SHE FELT THE PAIN FIRST. Simone's head throbbed in a heaving, stomach-churning rhythm, and her eyes cracked open. But she could only see darkness.

Something wet slid down her cheek, and she raised her hands to wipe it away, only to realize that her hands were bound together—locked at the wrists.

And her feet were bound.

A grinding filled her ears, and she...*rolled* a bit. Understanding and horror flooded through her when her bound hands slammed into something hard and metal above her. *Grinding*...like tires rolling on a rough road.

Darkness.

Trapped.

Oh, God.

She was in a trunk. In the trunk of a car, just like Violet had been. Her hands flew up, and she touched her mouth— no, the tape over her lips. Her bound hands caught a loose edge of the tape that covered her mouth, and she ripped it away. Simone screamed at the pain because it felt like her skin and part of her upper lip ripped away, too.

Muffled sobs broke from her.

I saw Violet get tossed into the trunk of that sedan. I didn't try to stop him. I was scared. Terrified, at first. Stunned into immobility. But then...

Then he'd driven away.

I grabbed my phone. I intended to call the cops. Even thought about following the sedan.

But she hadn't.

Because...

I also thought about what would happen if that sedan kept going and Violet never came back.

And now...

Now her bound hands slammed upward and into the metal edge of the trunk. Now she was the one trapped. And she was the one begging, *"Help me! Somebody, please, help me!"*

Chapter Thirteen

HER HANDS SLAMMED INTO THE TOP OF THE TRUNK. The duct tape pulled at her skin. The metal cut the edge of her fingers. She'd been rolling around in the trunk forever. But then they'd stopped. The car wasn't moving any longer. "Help me!" The scream tore from her. "Someone, please help—"

"*Violet!*" Hard hands closed around her shoulders. She was shaken once, lightly. "Violet, wake up. It's just a bad dream. *Sweetheart, wake up!*"

Her eyes flew open. The bedside lamp was on, spilling light onto her and onto Royal as he leaned over her body. He sat on the edge of the bed, and worry covered his hard features.

Her breath heaved in and out.

He didn't let her go.

"You were screaming," he said, and his voice was off. Ragged at the edges. "I thought someone might have gotten past me. Gotten *to* you." His hold tightened, but then he released her. "Just a bad dream." He rose.

Her hand flew out to curl around his wrist. "I was in the trunk again. I was screaming, and you weren't there."

"I'm right here."

He was. Standing beside the bed. Wearing battered jeans that hung low on his hips. Showing off his muscular abs. His powerful chest. Looking dangerous and sexy and strong. And she was still shaking.

"I have the same dream every few nights." Her brother had come into her room the first night, absolutely terrified because of her dreams. He'd had a baseball bat in his hands because he'd been sure an intruder was there. "Sometimes, I wonder if I'll have the same nightmare forever."

Maybe she should talk to the psychiatrist Micah had mentioned. Dr. Barnes. But she'd never been comfortable baring her soul to anyone. She didn't talk freely with most people. Didn't share her inner thoughts.

Except with Royal. Maybe because he'd already seen her at her breaking point? With him, she could talk. With him, she could let down all the walls that she usually kept around herself.

"Violet." Her name slipped from him like a soft, savage growl. One that oddly comforted her. "You have to remember that nightmares can't hurt you."

"No, they can't. But psychotic serial killers can." She was still holding his wrist. She should let go. "Sorry." Violet cleared her throat. "I'll be fine now. Really." *Not at all.* She was lying to him just like she did to so many others. "Sorry if I woke you up." Her hand fell back to the bed.

"Two things," he rasped. "First, don't ever apologize to me because you're scared. When you get scared, you call for me. I will be there immediately."

She found herself tugging up the covers. Clothes had been brought over for her—or, rather, they'd been waiting at the top of the stairs in a suitcase for her. Everything perfectly in her size. But then again, the man had said that he even knew what bra size she wore, so she could hardly feel too much shock that he'd gotten garments that fit her.

She'd put on a soft, silken black gown. One that dipped a little low in the front and skimmed the tops of her thighs. Suddenly too aware of the gown's dipping neckline, Violet pulled the covers up to her chest.

Royal sat back down on the bed. He caged her between his hands as they pressed into the mattress.

"Second thing," he rumbled. "You didn't wake me up. I was in the bedroom right next door. Thinking about you. Remembering how close to heaven I got when you put that sweet mouth of yours on me."

Her mouth dropped open.

"I should walk away right now," Royal continued in his deep, dark voice. "You're good. Too damn good for someone like me. And I shouldn't take advantage of you after you've had a nightmare. Fuck. I should not be here." But he was leaning toward her.

She was inching her head toward him.

"Tell me to leave," he ordered. "Tell me."

He gave lots of orders. Something she'd noticed about him. Maybe it was time for her to give a few orders of her own. "Kiss me," she told him.

He sucked in a breath. "Violet."

"Kiss me," she demanded once more.

And he did.

His mouth took hers. Her lips were open, waiting, and so ready for him. His tongue thrust inside, and desire blazed through her. Royal kissed with skill. Drugging passion. With a consuming possession that she could not ignore.

Every cell in her body *felt* his kiss. She yearned and needed and wanted more.

When Royal kissed her, when Royal touched her, when Royal gave that delicious growl in his throat that told her he *wanted* her, Violet wasn't afraid. She forgot her hell and focused on the heaven she felt with him.

Passion.

Pleasure.

A desire that made her want to do every wicked thing with him that she could imagine...and all the wicked things she knew he would do so very perfectly.

But he pulled back. He nipped her lower lip, a sensual bite, then slid back a bit.

She let go of the covers. Her hand pressed to his chest. The heat of his body sank into her.

"I can stay with you." His voice was deeper. Rougher. "Sleep on the floor. Keep my hands *off* you. If you have another bad dream, I'll be right beside you."

She shook her head. "That doesn't sound like what the bad guy would say." Her hand began to slide down his chest.

He tensed beneath her touch.

"You keep trying to play the bad guy," she added as her hand dipped a bit more. "Like you're trying to warn me away from you."

"I'm not playing."

"Neither am I." She knew what she wanted, and there was not going to be any more running. "I believe you mentioned something about fucking me so completely that I'll never be free of you? Weren't those your words?"

He growled. That savage sound that made her sex clench.

"But I had a thought..." She was nervous but wouldn't

let that stop her. Her fingers fumbled and undid the snap of his jeans. Pulled down the zipper. *No underwear.* His hard cock shoved toward her. "What if I fuck *you* so completely that you're never free of me?" Bold words. Especially since she was barely more than an amateur in this department, but she wanted to try. She wanted to learn.

She wanted her first time to be with Royal because he felt *right* in every way. Even when he said he was wrong.

"I *tried*," he gritted.

Her gaze lifted.

His stare seemed to eat her alive.

"You had the chance to get away, but now I'll have you."

That certainly sounded promising.

Royal—

He took her mouth again. Harder. Deeper. If possible, even more possessively. And he ripped the covers out of the way. Cool air hit her skin, and Violet gasped into his mouth. Then his hands were on her breasts. Stroking her through the silk, and his mouth tore from hers...but only so he could follow his hands. His lips closed over one nipple—through the silk. He licked and sucked and her whole body jolted.

And his hands kept moving on her body.

Down, down they went. He grabbed the hem of her gown and shoved it up. Then he was touching her through the panties she wore. Stroking and sliding with his fingers even as his mouth still sucked her nipple.

She arched up against him. Her body throbbed and ached, and she wanted the gown and the panties gone. Violet wanted to feel every inch of him against her.

His mouth lifted from her breast. "No condoms...in here..."

Uh, no, she didn't have any. She—

Was in his arms. He'd scooped her off the bed and was

carrying her through the bedroom. Her arms wound around his neck, and since he was right there, she decided to lean closer and press a kiss to the hard edge of his jaw. Then down, she skimmed her lips over him. Violet pressed her mouth against his throat.

"*I want in you,*" Royal snarled.

That was exactly where she would like for him to be.

And then he lowered her.

Put her carefully on another bed—his bed. A big, king-size bed with dark sheets. No lamp light in that room. The only illumination spilled from the open doorway. He stood by the bed, towering over her, and shadows clung to him. His hands slid under the gown. He caught the panties and pulled them off her. Then he pushed her legs apart. Bent. And feasted.

Her hips surged up against him. Her hands fisted around the sheets. She opened her mouth wide and cried out his name, but he was merciless. And she loved it. Loved every lap and thrust of his tongue. Loved the way he licked her clit again and again, and, even while he worked her with his mouth, his hands rose to pluck her nipples.

She screamed when the orgasm hit her.

And he kept right on licking her.

Violet collapsed against the mattress. Her heart thundered hard in her chest. Over and over and over.

The gown had hiked up to her stomach. Her tight nipples thrust against the silk. And her sex was completely bare to him.

His head rose. Her breath sawed in and out as the pounding drumbeat of her heart seemed to echo in Violet's ears.

He straightened. Took a step back.

She tensed.

But he just opened the bedside drawer and pulled out a condom. A couple of them. Okay. Violet licked her lower lip. "Ah..." *What to say now?*

Royal ditched his jeans. His cock shoved toward her. She decided not to worry about talking. She twisted and rolled and leaned forward so that she could curl her lips around his cock.

"*Violet.*" Guttural.

In a flash, she was on her back. In the middle of the bed. Spread-eagle beneath him. He towered over her. "I'm coming in *you.*" He ripped open one of the condom packets and rolled the condom on in an easy, fast move.

A breath later, she felt the head of his cock pushing at the entrance to her body.

She looked down, then her stare whipped up. So many shadows and so much darkness. Violet couldn't see his face clearly, but she felt the intensity of his stare. And something else she felt? The thick, broad tip of his cock as it thrust into her.

She was slick and swollen from her release. He wedged inside, and her inner muscles strained around him. Her breath came in fast, shallow pants.

"Thought you weren't afraid of me," he rasped.

"I'm not."

"You're tense. Just give me a minute, I'll get you—"

She didn't want a minute. She wanted *him.* Her hips surged against him, and a quick cry of pain broke from her, but the pain vanished in an instant because he filled her. Oh, he filled her. So completely. Every thick inch of him— and there were lots of inches.

Her eyes squeezed shut.

His fingers slid between their bodies. He rubbed her

clit. Slow at first, then faster, harder. The way she'd learned that she very much liked.

But he didn't thrust. Didn't withdraw. The thick, hard length of his dick stayed rammed all the way inside of her.

She felt her inner muscles soften around him. Then she deliberately squeezed him.

"*Baby…*"

Her eyes opened.

"Ready for me now?"

She nodded.

He withdrew. Pulled back. Drove deep. Her breath heaved out. Her legs locked around his hips. When he began thrusting fast, pistoning his hips against her even as his fingers worked their magic on her core, she knew another orgasm was imminent.

"So fucking *tight*." He withdrew. Plunged into her again. "Tight and hot and *mine*." He slammed into her.

The headboard thudded into the wall.

Her orgasm detonated through her.

"Hell, yes. *Hell, yes.* Squeeze me, sweetheart. So good. Insane. *Fucking heaven.*" Then she felt him erupt into her. His big body shuddered. His mouth took hers.

And as the pleasure rolled through every cell of her body, she realized he was right.

Fucking heaven, indeed.

* * *

I WANT HER AGAIN.

Royal stared at his reflection in the bathroom mirror. He'd just ditched the condom. Seen the faint traces of blood on the damn thing.

I was her first.

Selfish bastard that he was, he'd like to be her only. He'd like to claim her forever and never let any other man get close enough to so much as touch her sweet body.

He'd tried to warn her. But she'd given herself to him anyway.

He wanted her again already. Hell, already? More like endlessly. But he was trying not to be a completely selfish prick. His fingers gripped the edge of the marble counter as he sucked in a breath. Then she appeared behind him. Soft steps that he hadn't heard when no one ever snuck up on him. Usually, he was far too aware. Hyper alert.

But there she was. Naked. Tapping his shoulder. He spun around, locked his hands on her waist, and in a flash, he'd turned again and had her up on the marble before him. And he was between her legs.

Her eyes widened. "Uh, hi."

Fuck me. She is going to break something inside of me. "Hi?"

She swallowed. "You were in here a while. Thought I should check on you."

She was checking...on him. "I took your virginity."

"I believe I gave it to you. Not like it was doing anything overly useful. Just kinda hanging around."

He blinked. "Uh, come again?" Strangled words.

"I'd like to do just that," she said, voice all serious.

His eyes narrowed on her. "*Violet.*"

"I got worried you might be in here, feeling all guilty and remorseful about something I wanted more than my next breath."

Her honesty cut through him better than any knife.

"And I want you again," she added, softer. "Are you going to tell me that's wrong?"

He reached behind her. Turned on the warm water and

grabbed for a cloth that had been on the edge of the sink. He let the warm water soak the cloth, and then he brought it between her legs.

She gasped at the contact.

"Easy, sweetheart. I hurt you. I'm trying to make it better." He stroked her gently, cleaning and soothing. *I took her. She's mine. I will always protect what's mine.*

Violet caught his wrist. "You didn't hurt me. You haven't. You won't."

He stared into her eyes. The gold seemed even brighter to him. What had she asked just a moment before? If wanting him was wrong? "Nothing is wrong when it comes to you."

Her lips curled in the faintest of smiles. So beautiful that she made his chest ache.

Can't let go. Won't let go.

He dropped the cloth behind her. Pulled her toward him. Carried her back to the bed. When he put her down, she bounced lightly on the mattress. Royal remained standing, at least long enough to grab another condom. *I want her again. I think I'll always want her.*

"Is it always like that?" She moved to her knees as she watched him. Her breasts thrust toward him, beautiful nipples tight.

Want to taste them again.

"Like what?" He rolled on the condom.

Her tongue darted out to skim over her lower lip. "So good."

His back teeth clenched. "No." He climbed onto the bed. She scooted back. *Oh, hell, no.* He curled his hands around her hips and lifted her up and over him.

A gasp slid from her, and her hands clamped over his shoulders. He was sitting up, and she straddled him. His dick pushed at the entrance of her body, but he didn't go in, not yet. *Be careful this time. Gentle.*

He'd put a stranglehold on his desire. He would not pound into her like a crazed madman. He would not take and take and take.

He'd give her the control this time. Give her the pleasure.

Pleasure. "Not like that with everyone," he bit out. No damn way he wanted to think of Violet fucking someone else.

She sent him that smile again. The one that lit her eyes and made him want to put the whole world at her feet. But instead of doing that, his dick pushed into her.

She'd turned on the bedside lamp when he'd gone into the bathroom. He liked the light. Normally, he craved the dark. But he wanted to see her. Every single inch.

"You control me," he told her.

She shook her head. "I don't think anyone can do that."

His hold tightened on her. *Oh, sweetheart. You have no clue. I'd do just about anything for you.* A sobering realization.

Violet leaned forward and pressed her lips to his neck. She nipped him with her teeth.

It took all of his strength to hold back and not thrust deep into her. *Deep. Take. Claim.*

Her hips wiggled against him. He didn't let her press down, though. Not this time. She'd taken him in fast before. *This time,* it would be slow. Inch by inch.

"Royal." A sensual demand. "Are you teasing me?"

Never. "I'm not hurting you. You take me. Bit by bit."

Her head lifted. She stared into his eyes with her lush lips slightly parted. Her knees pushed into the mattress as she searched his gaze. Her hips dipped down.

One inch.

He could feel sweat gathering on his brow.

She slid down a little more.

More.

Her breath came out on a heave.

The fingers of his right hand slid between them. He stroked her just where he knew she needed his touch the most. Her head tipped back. She lowered onto him even more.

Half-way down his cock.

Her hips thrashed against him. One of his hands still held her hip, preventing her from driving all the way down. The other stroked her clit in a merciless rhythm.

"Royal!" Her breath choked out. Her eyes squeezed shut. "Royal, I'm coming!"

She was. Already. Fucking fantastic. He felt the vibrations along his dick and he—

She took him all. Jerked down hard against his hold and slammed their bodies together completely. The contractions of her inner muscles rippled along his dick as she cried out his name. A litany that went on over and over again.

He held himself perfectly still inside of her. He wanted Violet to pull every single drop of pleasure from her orgasm.

For her. For her. Her.

Her nails bit into his shoulders. She'd closed her eyes when she came, and now, they slowly opened. The gold gleamed. Gorgeous.

Mine.

He kissed her. Drove his tongue into her mouth and tasted the sweetness that waited. A sweetness that belonged to him.

"Royal..." Soft. Confused. "You didn't..."

"I will." Absolute certainty. "And you will again." He

spun them. Had her beneath him on the bed. And the time for holding back was gone. He withdrew. Thrust. Sank into her again and again and soon she was bucking and arching beneath him. Her short nails raked down his back. Her legs curled around him.

In and out.

Again and again.

Sinking into heaven time and time again.

The devil wasn't supposed to touch heaven.

His fingers skimmed over her. Breasts. Hips. Legs.

The devil wasn't supposed to taste heaven.

His mouth claimed hers once more. He'd never, ever get enough of her.

He plunged into her again.

The devil wasn't supposed to take heaven...

But he was. He took her and when she came again, he was right with her. He detonated on a release that was hotter than any fire from hell could ever be.

* * *

THE TRUNK OPENED. The screeching of the hinges seemed horribly loud to Simone's ears. She had no idea how long she'd been in the dark. She just knew that she had one chance. Just one.

"I'm not Violet!" she screamed even as gloved hands reached for her.

The hands froze.

Her fingers knotted in the stupid wig she'd found in the back of the trunk. It had fallen off in the dressing room. She remembered that, and her attacker must have tossed it in after he'd dumped her body in the back of the car. She shoved the wig forward like an offering. "That's why you took me, isn't it? Because you thought I was her?" Her throat hurt. Her mouth felt far too dry.

I was in Violet's dressing room.

I had on the wig that looked like her hair.

I'm the same size she is.

And he'd attacked Simone from behind. He hadn't seen her face when he'd grabbed her.

The gloved hands snatched the wig.

She didn't look up. She didn't want to see his face. If she saw his face, didn't that mean he wouldn't let her go? "It's a mistake," she whispered. "You just made a mistake." *You don't want me. You want her.*

Silence.

No, not total silence. She could hear the distant call of insects.

He wasn't moving. She was barely breathing.

The thick tape he'd used to bind her tugged at Simone's wrists. "You can just let me go." A plea. "I don't know who you are. I-I won't say anything."

He dropped the wig. It slithered into the trunk with her.

She could feel each hard thud of her heart. *Boom. Boom. Boom.*

Then she saw the knife. A sharp flash of the blade illuminated beneath the moonlight.

"*No!*" A sharp, desperate cry. "I-I can get you Violet! I can call her! Get her to meet me!" The feverish words tumbled out, one right after the other even as her gaze remained locked on the knife. *I don't want to die. I can't die. Not. Yet. No!* "We can trade! Me for her. I'll get you her, and you let me walk away!" *Please, please, please.* "I'm not the one you want. She is. I can get her for you. I can get—" Her words broke off as the knife came at her again.

The tip of the blade pressed to her cheek.

She froze.

And felt a rivulet of blood slide down her face. "I can get her," she whispered. "I can call her. I can get her for you. *Please.*"

Something shoved into her bound hands. It took Simone a dazed moment to realize it was a phone.

The tip of the knife pressed harder into her cheek.

"Then do it," he ordered.

Her breath shuddered out. *My phone.* She was staring at her phone screen. The image on the screen was one she'd taken backstage. A cluster of the dancers all around her. Even Violet was there, smiling her shy smile.

Violet's life for mine.

"Do it," he rasped.

She called Violet. The phone rang. Once. Twice.

Violet, pick up. Pick. Up.

Chapter Fourteen

SHE COULD HEAR A PHONE. THE DISTANT PEAL OF sound penetrated the heavy sleep that had pulled Violet under. Dazed, she cracked open her eyes and reached out her hand.

The bedside table was empty beside her.

She jolted upright. Not the guest room. Royal's room. Only Royal wasn't there.

Darkness filled the room. Still night. They'd had a second round of sex. She'd had...three, four orgasms? Violet wasn't exactly sure. But she'd gone to sleep in his arms.

And he was gone now.

The peal came again. Demanding.

She knew that ringtone. Didn't she? Still a little confused, Violet climbed from the bed. Her gown was on the floor, and she put it on automatically as she followed the sound. Her gaze darted to the bathroom.

Dark.

Where was Royal?

The phone stopped ringing.

But she kept walking. The rings had been coming from the guest room. From her phone.

* * *

Voicemail. *No, no, no, no!* He'd put the phone on speaker, so Simone's abductor knew that Violet hadn't picked up. As soon as the voicemail started, his finger pressed down to end the call.

One hand on her phone.

One hand still gripping the knife.

But then he dropped his hold on the phone, and the knife lowered so that the blade pressed to her throat. Tears spilled down her cheeks. "I-I can get her," Simone stammered. "Give me another chance. I can get Violet for—"

The phone rang. A loud jangle of sound. The ringtone she'd assigned to Violet long ago. The cry of the phone shocked Simone, and she jerked. The blade sliced over her neck. A gasp broke from her at the pain, but then she was grabbing for the phone and ignoring the knife. Or trying to ignore the knife. "It's Violet!" The screen had lit up. Violet's picture smiled back at her. "I'll get her! *I'll get her!*"

"Say exactly what I tell you." A low order. "Or I will cut you from ear to ear."

* * *

Three thirteen a.m. A call that late was never a good sign. Violet gripped the phone tightly in her hand as she called Simone back.

One ring.

Two.

Three—

"Violet?" Simone's voice.

Violet's breath shuddered out in relief. "I was so scared something had happened to you!" Another long exhale. "I was worried—"

"Violet, I need you to come meet me."

Violet blinked. "Now?"

"Yes, right now. *Now.* I'm in trouble, and I'm scared, and I-I need you."

Violet spun toward the doorway. Still no sign of Royal. "What's happening?"

"Micah...got rough. Crazy. I'm...I'm afraid, Violet. Come get me. Please. Please, come get me."

She put the phone on the bed and turned on the speaker so that she could ditch the gown and throw on real clothes and underwear. "Give me the address. Royal and I will be right there."

"*No!*"

Violet stilled with the jeans half-way up her legs. "No?"

"The cops came back," Simone said quickly. "That detective. He told me things about Royal. Royal is *dangerous*, Violet."

She jerked up the jeans. Hauled on a bra and her top and toed into her flats.

"You can't trust him," Simone continued with her voice breaking. "You...you aren't with him right now, are you?"

"I'm at his house."

"*Get out of there!*" A fierce demand. "Get in your car and come meet me. *We're both in danger*. Ah!"

Violet swiped up the phone. "Are you okay?"

"N-no..." A gasp. "Micah dropped me off...middle of nowhere. My phone battery is dying, and I don't know how long the call will last. I need you, Violet."

"My car isn't here." Was it still at the theater? Or had Royal gotten the vehicle taken to her house? Her temples throbbed. "I have to tell him. I need his car—"

"*Just take the keys!*" A screech. "Violet, Violet, I'm desperate. If you don't get here...I-I'm dead." A quick gasp. "I just need you."

Violet grabbed her bag. She shoved her new knife inside it and then spun for the door. She rushed forward and nearly slammed straight into Royal. He filled the doorway, broad shoulders stretching to nearly rub the wood on either side of him. Surprised, she staggered to a stop. The phone was still on speaker. Still clutched in her hand. Violet knew he'd heard everything.

So why was he blocking her path? They needed to *go*.

Violet began, "Royal is—"

"You can't tell him!" Simone cried out, her words cutting through Violet's sentence.

Because Violet had intended to say...*Royal is right here. He can hear you.*

"The detective...I *told* you that he said Royal is dangerous. A criminal. A killer. The cop thinks...this is going to terrify you, but he thinks Royal might be the man who abducted you!"

She stared into Royal's eyes. He didn't so much as blink.

"Royal has ties to some other women who were abducted and murdered. He knew a victim in Atlanta. One of his gang banger friends dated her, and Royal had some crazy jealousy thing going on because he wanted her for himself."

Royal slowly shook his head.

"You're his type, Violet!" Simone rushed to say. "He wants you because you look like her, and he is obsessed with the woman. The detective thinks...he thinks Royal killed her in some jealous rage. The Atlanta PD and the local cops are working together. They are going to bring him down."

Violet didn't look away from Royal. For just a moment, she could have almost sworn that she heard someone whispering in the background of the call. Talking behind Simone?

"He doesn't want you," Simone told her fiercely. "He wants the lover he killed, but he can't get her back, so he is going through this insane routine over and over again. *He* is insane. Get away from him, Violet! Steal his damn car if you have to do it, but get away from him! Come to me. We'll be safe together. I'll be safe when you get here!"

It was hard to pull in a deep breath. Royal showed no sign of getting out of her way.

He raised a hand to his lips.

Shh.

Her breath heaved out.

"I-I am near an old gas station. I'm going to ping you my location from my phone before it d-dies. There's just freaking miles of farmland out here. Micah just *left me here.* He was driving and saying wild things, and I had to get away from him."

Miles of farmland. "You should call the cops. Now."

"I can't! Micah will fire me if I do, and I need this job! Violet, I am begging you—*begging!*" And the tears were in her voice. "Come get me. We'll be safe together. You get away from Royal and I get away from this...this mess."

She lifted her chin and stared straight into Royal's swirling eyes. "I'm coming."

"Thank you." A long exhale. "And...hurry? *Please.*"

The call ended.

A moment later, the phone pinged with Simone's location.

"I'm going to need you to move, Royal." She thought the words came out surprisingly normal. Very level.

He didn't move.

Her chin lifted. "Royal..."

"Your friend is a liar, Violet. And I think she wants you dead."

* * *

"Done." Euphoria filled Simone, making her a little dizzy. Or maybe that was the insane amount of fear and adrenaline flooding through her body that made her dizzy. Either way... "Done," she repeated. "I said everything you wanted. I gave her the location just like you asked. Violet will come here. You'll get her, so...let me go?" *Please, let me go.*

He removed the knife from her throat. She sucked in some deep, gulping breaths. While the blade had been pressed against her jugular, she'd been afraid to breathe too deeply. Every word she'd spoken had made her acutely aware of the knife. When she'd begged Violet, Simone had felt the blade dig into her skin.

And she'd felt the blood trickle down her neck.

"You'll trade her life for yours." His voice was still a soft rasp. That was all it had been the whole time. He'd been talking in that low rasp while she'd been on the phone. He'd told her what to say. And she'd followed his orders because she wanted to live.

Simone still didn't look at him. *I won't. If I don't see his face, then I'm safe.* Simone nodded.

"I want to hear the words. Tell me that you'll trade your life for hers."

But she didn't want to say them. Saying them...saying

them made her feel like she was killing Violet. *Except I'm not. I'm not the one with the knife. He is.*

"Say the words."

He'd taken the phone away.

And the knife came toward her again.

"I'll trade my life for hers!" Simone cried out before he could bring that blade any closer. "I'll do it! You can take her, and I swear, I won't tell anyone about tonight!" How could she? The world would hate her. They'd say she killed her friend.

But I'm not killing her. I'm not even going to touch Violet. He's the one with the knife.

And who wouldn't do the same thing? If given a chance to live, she was sure even precious fucking Violet would turn on a friend. *Yes, yes, Violet would sacrifice me. It's just about survival. Nothing personal.*

Nothing.

Personal.

"I haven't seen your face," she whispered. "I don't know you."

"You can't see my face, bitch. I've got on a mask."

She was too scared to look. What if he was lying? What if that was a trick?

And then...on the heels of that thought...

What if he's been lying to me this whole time? What if he isn't going to let me go, even when he gets Violet? A sob caught in her throat.

He backed up.

The trunk slammed down. Total darkness consumed her again.

"*No!*" Simone screamed. She slammed her bound hands into the metal roof of the trunk.

"Don't worry," his grating voice told her. "Once I see Violet, you'll be free."

Her breath shuddered out.

Don't be a lie. Don't be a lie. Don't be a...

* * *

"You're lying," Violet said. Her chin was up. Her hair a gorgeous tangle around her shoulders. She'd dressed. She stood facing him with her back perfectly straight and with fear and determination both blazing in her wide eyes.

In that instance, Royal almost wished that he could be lying. He didn't want to break her heart.

But breaking her heart was a whole lot better than letting Violet die. You could keep living with a broken heart. You couldn't keep living if, say, some psychotic asshole shoved a *knife* into your chest and carved out said heart.

"I need you to get out of my way, Royal. Simone needs me."

"Simone watched you get thrown into the back of the sedan on the night of your abduction, and she didn't do a thing to get help for you."

Her eyes widened even more. Did her skin turn paler?

I'm breaking her heart.

"You don't know that," Violet whispered. She inched closer to him. "I don't have time to waste. She's alone, and she's scared."

Fine. They could talk on the way. "I'm coming with you."

She blinked.

Hell. Had Violet truly thought he'd let her leave on her own? "She's *lying*," he snapped. Dangerous tension pooled through him. "I didn't hurt Marcella. I'm not some sick stalker who is hunting and killing the same woman over and over again." *Why is Simone trying to frame me?* But the hard twist in his gut told him the reason why. "I didn't fuck you because you looked like Marcella."

"Why did you fuck me?"

His hand rose and his fingers skimmed across the silk of her cheek. "Because I've never wanted anyone more." His hand slid down, and his thumb brushed over her lower lip. "You're mine, Violet."

"Get out of my way, Royal."

A bite filled those words. Determined bite. He could admire that.

He could also think her determination was a pain in his ass.

His hand fell, but he did not get out of her way. "There's no way that you are gonna leave this house without me."

"She's *scared*."

"She's setting up a trap for you. I was just downstairs, accessing street cam footage from the night of your abduction. I've been searching through that footage for hours." *More like days* because there had been so much footage to review. "I've been trying to figure out who might have been in that parking lot and seen you get taken. It was *her*. I found a street cam about four blocks over. Got a pic of her behind the wheel of her red Mustang. She was the only person from the theater that I could find near the site after your abduction. Everyone else left before that time period. I've looked at every bit of footage I could locate. It goes back to her." Violet had to understand this. "Your best friend left you to die."

The lower lip he'd just stroked...trembled.

His jaw hardened. "The detective didn't tell her jack

shit about me." Another lie. One designed to destroy any trust that Violet might have in Royal. *A lie designed to take you away. To put you far from my protection.*

"How do you know that?" Violet asked. Her hair slid over her shoulder. "How do you know she didn't talk to him?"

Easy. "Because Detective Curran Barlow is on my payroll, sweetheart. The man reports to me, so he wouldn't sell my ass out." No, something else was happening. Something far more sinister. "She's luring you out in the middle of the night."

"*Simone was terrified.*"

On that, they could agree. "It's a trap." Every instinct told him that truth. "I think he has her."

She retreated a step.

"A three a.m. phone call?" Royal shook his head. "A desperate plea to meet in the middle of nowhere? To go without me? Come on, we both know this is a setup. You go alone, and you're dead. Hell, she's probably dead, too." *She may already be dead. He could have killed Simone the minute the phone call ended.*

There was no stunned shock in Violet's gaze.

His own eyes narrowed. "But...you suspected that already, didn't you?"

"I didn't believe her when she said you were a threat to me."

His heart raced a little faster in his chest, but his pose didn't alter.

"I didn't believe her when she said that you were insane. I know you didn't abduct me. But what she didn't know—Simone didn't know that you'd saved me. I kept that secret. I didn't tell it to the cops. Not to my brothers. Not even to my best friend. It was our secret."

Our secret.

"You wanted to use me as bait." Violet squared her delicate shoulders. "This is our chance. We have to make it *look* like I'm going alone. Like I ditched you. But you'll be there, won't you? My backup."

Your shadow, baby. Watching every single step you take.

"It could be Micah," she said. Violet bit her lip. "He could have taken Simone. Forced her to make the call. They've been involved, but they try to hide their affair from most people."

"He's been screwing her, but the bastard wants to fuck you."

She didn't deny the words. She did raise her chin. "I have to go. *Now.*"

Yeah, *they* did. "I'm driving."

"If he's there, he can't see you!"

"He won't see me." Royal was certain. "Trust me. Can you do that, Violet?"

Her hand lifted. Extended toward him. He looked down at her delicate palm.

"You're my partner," she told him. "Of course, I trust you."

He took her hand, and then hauled her forward. His mouth took hers. Deep. Hard. Desperate. "Do everything I say," he growled. "No hesitation. No questions."

Her gaze held his.

"He'll think you're alone when you arrive. *He won't see me.*" Because Royal had a plan.

She licked her lips.

"He won't kill you from a distance. He'll want to get up close. When he gets close, you shove your knife into him, you got it?"

Violet nodded. "The knife is already in my purse."

That was the kind of dirty talk he liked to hear. "I'll show you where to cut him. The best spots to drive that blade ever so deep in order to bring him to his knees."

Violet paled, but she didn't back down.

"Going to be able to do that, Violet?" he pushed. "You really gonna be able to shove a knife between someone's ribs? Or to drive it into a man's stomach and twist the blade?"

"I'll do what's necessary. Especially if it means saving Simone and stopping a killer." A pause. "How many times do I have to tell you? I'm not backing down."

"Good." Gruff.

"Nothing about this feels good," she murmured. "But she needs me. And he *can't get away*."

"The knife will be step one." An exhale from Royal. "And then we'll take care of everything else." *Because the sonofabitch will not be getting away from me. Not this time.*

Violet would never need to fear his attack again.

Royal wasn't going to leave this perp subdued. This wouldn't be like the last two hunts that he'd done with Beau. For those instances, he'd left the killers waiting for the cops.

Not this time.

No bow would be wrapped around this killer's neck while he waited—bound—for the police to arrive.

This hunt was different. Personal.

You will be dead before the sun rises because you never, ever should have touched Violet.

Dead.

Chapter Fifteen

SHE PULLED THE CAR TO A STOP NEAR THE SMALL, rundown gas station. The lights from the big Lincoln she'd been driving lit up the old pumps. Pumps that had run dry long ago. Windows with broken glass—crisscrossed like spider webs—reflected her lights back from the front of the station. Violet leaned forward as she peered through the windshield. Farmland stretched for miles on either side of the station. Withered crops that had been abandoned probably as long ago as the gas station.

From where she sat, there was no sign of Simone.

Shivering, she reached for her phone. She kept the car running. She dialed Simone's number. It rang and rang and...

Voicemail.

"Hi, you've reached Simone. I'm out dancing my life away. Leave a message, and I'll hit you up later."

Her breath rushed out. "Simone, I'm here. Where are you?" Violet hung up. Clenching her back teeth, she turned off the car. The lights immediately died away. Violet opened the door. She looped her purse over her head, wearing it across her body. Her mace and her taser were in that bag. Slowly, she exited the vehicle, and as she did, she made sure to keep a grip on her phone—and to slide the knife out of her pocket and curl it in her right hand.

"Simone!" Violet called out.

No response.

Dammit.

The moon and stars shone down on her. She didn't see anyone around. Not for miles and miles.

But I'm not alone. Royal is here.

Her finger swiped over her phone's screen once more. She called Simone and—

Violet stiffened. She could *hear* a phone ringing. Simone's phone. The ringtone her friend had assigned for Violet ages ago. Turning slowly, Violet looked again at the old station. Part of the building had one of those big, sliding doors on the side. Like you'd see at a repair shop. A garage door that lifted up so you could drive your vehicle inside for maintenance work.

Back in the day, maybe the place had been a full-service shop. Get gas. Get a quick tune-up.

The phone kept ringing.

Violet shuffled forward. She used the light from her phone to illuminate that big, sliding door. Through the dark, dirty glass, she could just make out a car inside.

A sedan.

Her shuffling steps stopped.

The ringing stopped.

"Hi, you've reached Simone. I'm out dancing my life away..."

Violet lunged forward. She slammed her hands into the glass of that sliding door or garage door or whatever the hell it was. "Simone!" She didn't see her friend beyond the glass. Just that damn car. *The sedan. The car he took me in.*

She slammed her hands into it, harder. "*Simone!*" A desperate scream.

And then...

Then the glass started to lift. The door started to rise. A grinding filled her ears even as Violet stumbled back a step. The gas station had appeared abandoned. But someone was raising the old garage door. And someone had parked the sedan.

Someone had taken Simone.

Higher, higher it went and then...

It stopped.

About two feet off the ground—maybe even just one foot—such a tight fit, the garage door stopped rising.

"You bastard!" Violet screamed. She knew what he wanted. For her to crawl under and go inside. He was opening the door just enough for her to fit through the gap.

He wants to make sure I go in alone.

Simone's phone had pealed from inside that garage. Probably from the trunk of the sedan. Maybe her friend was trapped in the trunk, just as Violet had been trapped.

And maybe Simone *had* watched the freak take Violet from the theater on that terrible night. Maybe she had just stood there and watched...

But I'm not going to do that.

"I'm coming, Simone!" Violet yelled. She dropped to her stomach. She crawled beneath the door. She held her breath and prayed the ancient thing wouldn't come crashing down on her. And she prayed that she and Simone would get out alive. "I'm coming!"

***

HE UNDERSTOOD EXACTLY why Violet hated being stuck in a trunk. Who the hell *wouldn't* hate being enclosed in the dark back of a vehicle? Being trapped in the trunk was damn well like being buried alive.

But as he heard Violet's steps retreat and then the banging of her hands on what sounded like some kind of door or window, Royal pulled the small, glowing lever in the back of the trunk. He'd made sure she'd taken this ride deliberately. One, because the trunk was big enough to hold his burly ass. And two, because the Lincoln had the perfect, easy-to-see trunk release lever. One that was *inside* the cavernous interior of the trunk. Some people didn't know that every car built after 2002 had to include a release lever *inside* the trunk.

That's why the SOB used that freaking ancient sedan. He wanted a ride that didn't have a release lever inside. No way for his victims to get out. So he'd deliberately used the old sedan to trap them.

After Royal tugged on the small lever, the trunk lid slowly rose, but he grabbed the edge, making sure it didn't pop open all the way. Then he slithered out, touching down soundlessly and lowering the lid back in place.

If the prick had been watching the Lincoln arrive, he would only have seen Violet. No one else in the car with her. About two miles from the destination, Royal and Violet had stopped so he could slide into the trunk. No way did he want to risk being seen and blowing things to hell and back. After he'd gotten in the trunk, Violet had driven the rest of the way to their destination. Royal had instructed Violet to park the car in such a way that the trunk would be hidden so he could make his escape.

And she had. She'd parked the rear of the vehicle right against an overgrown patch of bushes. Plenty of shadow and hiding space for Royal. He crouched in the darkness, and his gaze swept around the decrepit gas station.

"*Simone!*" Violet's desperate voice.

He stiffened. His gaze instantly zeroed in on her. Violet was crawling under an ancient, barely lifted garage door. Dammit, not good. If she got inside there, she'd be separated from him.

He rushed forward, still sticking to the darkness and cloaking his body. *Violet.*

But then Violet's legs disappeared. She'd made it into the garage.

And the garage door lowered with a groan and screech of metal on metal.

Sonofabitch. So much for Royal's well-laid plans. Time for the option B. *Go in with guns blazing.* Good thing he'd come packing.

* * *

VIOLET CLAMBERED to her feet just as the door shuddered down behind her. Her breath heaved in and out. She still clutched her phone. And her knife. The knife was hidden in the palm of her right hand while her left hand held tightly to the phone. "Is someone here?" Violet called out. Someone had to be there. The jerk who'd opened and closed the old door.

Did she hear the faintest rustle of a footstep?

Her light swung back to the trunk of the car. Not closed. The lid of the trunk was open, maybe just an inch. Her breath heaved in and out as Violet advanced toward the trunk. "Simone?"

No answer.

It's a trap. I know it's a trap. He opened the door for me. I crawled inside. And now he wants me to go toward the trunk. Maybe he was waiting to shove her inside. Or maybe he was waiting to shove a knife into her back when she moved forward.

So...

She didn't move. For an instant, Violet just froze. *Think. Figure this out.*

"I know you took Simone!" Her voice was clear. Calm. "Just like you took me. And Marcella White. Bailey Brown. Fiona Law." Deliberately, she said their names. "I know what you've been doing. Watching us all. Taking us when you think no one else is around to see. You hide in the shadows—just like you're hiding now—and you steal us away from our lives. You bring us to the middle of nowhere, and then you take our lives away completely."

Another faint rustle. From the right. She turned that way. Maybe it was him. Maybe it was a rat. Her chin lifted.

I'm not alone. Royal has my back.

"You're not taking my life away," Violet told him. "You're not taking Simone's life away. You're—"

His soft laughter stopped her. The laughter was low and mocking and it came from the darkness just a few feet away.

She stiffened even more. Her spine was so straight it almost hurt.

"Simone is your friend." His voice came to her. Low. Rasping. Disguised?

"Y-yes."

"Yet she traded your life for hers."

Violet's heart shoved into her chest.

"She's gone. And you're here with me. Now we'll finish what we started when I had you at the winery."

Gone?

Violet shook her head.

"Aw, so sweet. You think a friend wouldn't do that? She did. She left you all alone."

It was him. The bastard who'd taken her. He was right there. He thought he'd been the one making the trap. But they'd pulled *him* out into the open. "I'm not alone." Soft. Husky. Had he heard those words from her?

Didn't matter. She lifted up her phone and flashed the light right at him. Time to see the monster who hid in the dark.

Tall. With shining glasses over his eyes—glasses that reflected the light back at her. *Night vision? Is that what those glasses were?* And some kind of black fabric covered the bottom of his face. A black, half-mask. His clothes were big and bulky. His hands were loose at his sides. One of his hands held a big, long knife.

One hell of a lot bigger than mine.

Wait, was something on that knife?

Something wet?

As her light hit him, he let out a heavy grunt, and his head jerked away from her. He tapped the side of the goggles, and then his masked face turned back toward her.

Did he turn the goggles off? Lower the intensity?

Violet backed up a step. "Simone?"

"Told you." That same rasp. "She's gone."

The sedan was behind Violet. He was right there. And Royal...

Royal, where are you? He could come rushing in at any moment. Any. Moment. The sooner the better.

But...*The garage door lowered back into place.*

"There's no one to save you this time," he murmured. "You are going to be mine."

The hell she would. "No, sorry. I have other plans."

He laughed.

Then he lunged for her. And as he lunged for her, glass shattered on the garage door. Broken shards hit the floor even as thunder seemed to echo around the station. Stunned, surprised, her attacker whirled toward the sound. Violet skirted around the car, heading for the driver's side and away from the masked man. She killed the light. Darkness closed around her.

Another explosion of glass.

Shatter. The shattering of the glass was just like it had been on stage. The glass breaking and shattering. Automatically, her head whipped toward the garage door. She knew who was breaking in to get to her side. *Royal.*

Before he'd gotten into the trunk, he'd promised to have her back. Always. She knew he would keep that vow because she trusted him. One hundred percent.

"Get the fuck out of there, Violet!" Royal shouted. Then he fired his gun again. He also kicked at the glass of the garage door, breaking it more as he punched his way inside to her.

"No!" A bellow that broke from the masked man. "You bitch!"

He rushed toward her. He had his big knife raised up. He was going to slice it down on her.

But another bullet fired. The attacker hit the floor, slamming his body down hard just before the bullet sank into the side of the sedan. She heard the distinct ping of it hitting metal. She also heard the knife clatter when it fell from the masked man's fingers.

Violet's breath panted out. And she attacked. She hit the small button on her knife. The blade sprang forward. Not as big as his blade, but it would get the job done.

He was rising and coming for her. But she didn't stop.

Her sweaty fingers had curled tightly around the handle of the knife, and she plunged it hard into his side. And she twisted it.

He howled. A cry of shock and pain even as he heaved her back.

But she didn't go back far. Violet dropped her phone and grabbed the taser from her purse. She left the knife in the bastard's side, and she drove her taser at him.

His body bucked and shuddered, and he let her go. He fell again, and she jumped over him. She ran for the shadows on the right where he'd been moments before. She was going to get the garage door open for Royal. *If he was in this corner, the chains to lift the door must be here. I can pull them and get Royal inside.*

Except Royal was already there. He grabbed her arms.

He'd broken through the glass to reach me.

"Baby." His grip was almost bruising. "Get the fuck out of here. I'll go after him."

Go after him?

She peered over her shoulder even as she heard the thud of footsteps. Her attacker was fleeing. Rushing toward the back of the station. The taser hadn't kept him down for long.

"I'll end him," Royal swore. "Leave. I'll finish this. You don't need to see what I do."

He let her go. Bounded after those fleeing footsteps.

Violet knew she should get to the Lincoln. She should get inside. Lock the doors.

Only she didn't do that. Her feet stumbled as she went back to the side of the sedan. She picked up her discarded phone. Turned on the light once more.

Her fingers shook. Her whole body shook. But she went

back to the trunk. It was open that scary inch. She reached out and pushed it higher. Her light shone inside.

A sob broke from her.

Simone.

Her friend was in the trunk. A dark wig covered her hair. Her hands were bound with gray duct tape. Her ankles secured with the same thick tape. Tape that had been used to subdue Violet, too, just weeks ago.

Same trunk. Same tape.

But...

Simone's eyes were closed. And her clothes and body were covered in red. Blood.

"Simone?" Violet whispered.

So much blood. Too much.

Her left hand went for Simone's throat. She searched desperately for a pulse. The scent of blood clogged her nostrils. How many times had Simone been stabbed? How much pain had she endured?

A flutter moved beneath Violet's fingers. The smallest beat of a pulse. Her imagination? Reality?

Be real. Be. Real. Violet dialed nine-one-one.

Chapter Sixteen

Fury pounded through Royal's veins. The sonofabitch had been too close to Violet. *With a fucking knife.* Royal had fired his gun, and he thought he'd hit the bastard. But the wily prick had dropped to the floor.

The SOB could have killed Violet.

The thought had fury flaring even hotter within Royal. *I did this. I brought her here. So cocky and arrogant. So sure I could take him out.*

But the arrogance had died when the jerk had charged at Violet. Terror had clawed through him, and all Royal had wanted to do was get to her.

Cuts and slices littered his arms. Blood dripped down his hands because he'd clawed his way through the glass. He would have clawed his way through hell if it meant getting to her.

Violet was behind him. *I left her. Left. Her.*

And a huge part of him just wanted to whirl around and rush back to her. But the attacker had fled. He could not get away again. If he got away again, he'd come for Violet once more.

She couldn't be in danger again. The nightmare had to stop for her. Royal didn't want Violet afraid for the rest of her life. Always looking over her shoulder.

The thudding footsteps had gone to the right, and he swerved to the right, too. Royal saw that the bottom part of the wall had been torn apart just enough that a person could slide through to exit. Nostrils flaring, he twisted and contorted and got his ass through that opening. When he broke into the night, he stilled a moment as he tried to figure out where the attacker had gone. If the jerk had circled the building in order to go back for Violet...

But, no. *Footsteps.* Straight ahead. Coming from an old, dead farm field. Royal raced forward. A quick turn and he shoved his way through the dry-as-dust corn stalks that were in his way. Overgrown. Twisting. Pale in the moonlight. The dry stalks were everywhere, but those steps... they were—

Got you.

He surged through the corn stalks and tackled his prey. The man let out a sharp cry as he hit the ground.

Royal spun him over, he brought up his gun, and he put it right in the middle of the prick's face.

"No!" Micah Wright cried out. "Don't shoot!"

"You're dead," Royal told him. And he squeezed the—

A hard voice thundered, *"Freeze!"*

Royal stiffened. He didn't drop his weapon. Hell, no, he didn't.

That hard, *familiar* voice continued, "Royal, put down the gun. Do not shoot him. That's an order—from your friend and from a police detective."

Because the voice shouting orders? It belonged to Detective Curran Barlow.

Slowly, Royal turned his head toward Curran. The detective had just shoved through the twisting corn stalks.

"I know what you've been doing," Curran gritted. "It ends, *now*."

"You shouldn't be out here," Royal told him.

"Neither should you."

Micah squirmed beneath Royal. Royal was on top of the bastard, with one hand slammed against his chest and the other holding the gun dead center on Micah's face.

"H-help me," Micah gasped.

"That's what I'm doing," Curran snapped.

The moonlight showed that the detective had his gun up—and aimed at Royal.

"I'm not as dirty as you think," Curran said. "I don't just turn a blind eye to murder."

Micah whimpered. "I-I'm...hurt...st-stabbed..."

Royal's teeth ground together. "She stabbed you, asshole. When you tried to hurt *her*." His head whipped back to Micah. He glared down at the bastard. "You thought you'd take Violet from me? The only thing you'll be doing is going to hell."

"Don't!" Curran roared. "Don't make me shoot you, Royal! I'll do it! Dammit! I'll shoot you in the back if that's what you make me do!"

"He's crazy!" Micah screeched. "I'm here...Simone c-called me...was...just attacked...Someone...knife..." His words ended in a wail. "I'm bleeding! Get...*help!*"

"Violet is the one who stabbed you," Royal threw right back. "Because you attacked her. You killed all those other women. You are going straight to hell."

Grass and corn stalks crunched as Curran advanced. "If what you're saying is true, Royal, then a judge and jury can decide his fate. You don't get to do it. Put down the gun."

Royal smiled at Micah. "There's no need for the judge and jury."

"*Royal!*" Curran roared his name. "Don't make me do this! Put down the gun. Put it down or I will—"

"*Royal!*"

His whole body jerked.

"Royal, help me!" Violet screamed.

He lunged up and off Micah. But then Micah immediately scuttled away. The prick made it to his feet. *No, no.*

Royal grabbed him. Spun him around.

"*Don't shoot!*" Curran shouted.

Micah swung at Royal. Missed with his punch. Royal headbutted Micah. He drove his head hard into Micah's face. Micah howled.

Royal shoved the gun into his waistband. Then his fists went straight for Micah. But before he could hit—

Curran hauled Royal back.

A whimpering Micah fell to the ground.

"What the hell are you doing?" Curran let him go, but he put his body between Royal and Micah.

"Subduing the suspect." His breath heaved. "Put cuffs on him. Put a bullet in his head. Do what you have to do. *But do not let him go.* He's a killer."

"*Royal!*" Violet's desperate voice. The corn stalks crunched. She burst through them.

A light hit her. Curran had hauled out a flashlight, and the beam shone straight onto Violet—perfectly illuminating her figure and the blood that soaked her.

For a moment, Royal could not breathe.

She was hurt. I left her. Thought she was secure. She's covered in blood.

"Help me!" Violet cried again. "I-I can't get her out of

the trunk. I can't stop the blood. *Simone is dying.*" She grabbed Royal's hand. "I called nine-one-one. But, please, help me!"

Always.

He rushed with her back to the old service station. Back through the small entrance in the rear. Back to the garage and to the body that was waiting in the trunk.

His breath hissed out.

Violet had propped her phone inside the trunk. The light illuminated Simone.

"I couldn't leave her in the dark. That's why I left the light with her. She can't be alone in the dark." Violet pressed her bloody fingers to Simone's chest. "I called nine-one-one," she said again. "Help is coming, but she needs us now!"

He didn't think any help would save her. The woman looked dead. So much blood. "Violet," he began.

"She's alive!" Violet shouted. "I felt her pulse! *Help us!*"

His hand went to Simone's throat. He didn't feel a pulse, but he leaned closer. He—

"M-Micah..." Simone whispered.

Shit. She *was* alive.

He pushed his hands against some of her biggest wounds.

* * *

ROYAL DIDN'T KNOW how the press found out about the attack, but they rushed to the scene. Hell, maybe they'd just been listening to the police scanners. Wasn't that how they usually knew when drama and death went down? The reporters flew up right behind the ambulances and the cop cars that came spilling to the old service station.

He knew cameras were rolling. Knew plenty of pictures were being taken.

Simone hadn't spoken again, not after that one word. He was pretty sure she hadn't breathed after that one word, either. At least, not on her own.

Curran had cuffed and secured Micah, and then the detective had come to help them. They'd performed CPR. They'd tried to stop the terrible bleeding. But blood had literally soaked the trunk beneath Simone.

Too many slashes.

When the EMTs arrived, they immediately took over CPR and rushed Simone away on a gurney. They loaded her into the back of their ambulance, and the sirens screamed when the vehicle raced away.

The reporters kept filming.

Royal had blood on his hands. On his body. His clothes. So did Violet. She stood beside him and she shivered and her gaze followed the ambulance as it left.

"She's not going to make it," Violet murmured. "Is she?"

He wanted to touch her, but he didn't want to put more blood on her. He didn't respond, but Royal knew that was answer enough.

"Royal." Curran cleared his throat. "You have to go to the station with us."

Royal had known this moment would come. He smiled at his friend. "And here I thought we had an agreement." A shake of his head. "But you were playing me all along." He could almost admire that trick.

Curran stared back at him. "You can't commit murder. Doesn't matter if the people you're after are the scum of the earth, you aren't their final executioner."

He would have been, that night. If Curran hadn't

stopped him from pulling the trigger on Micah. "You saw what he did."

None of them would ever be able to forget Simone's blood-soaked body.

"You really think he should get to live for the next fifty years?" Royal asked. "After what he did to her?"

Curran didn't answer. The scene was now lit up like the freaking Fourth of July. The cops had brought in so many lights. Uniforms rushed in every direction, and a female EMT made her way steadily to Violet.

"Miss?" The EMT reached for Violet. "I want to check you out."

"I'm not hurt." Violet turned away from the EMT. Moved toward Royal. "We'll both go to the station," she informed Curran.

Curran dipped his head. "Right. I have questions for you, too, Violet, but Royal..." A wince. "I don't want to use the cuffs in front of the crowd."

Royal laughed. "Why the hell not?" And he extended his wrists toward Curran. "You have a job to do." *You have your job. I have mine.*

Curran swore. "Just get in the cruiser, would you?"

Royal didn't move. Not yet. His gaze swept over Violet's profile. "Violet..."

"*You're arresting him?*" she demanded. "For what? Saving me? Trying to save Simone?" And she edged so close to Royal that her arm brushed against his. "You can't do that! You can't put him in a cage when he hasn't done anything wrong."

Oh, Royal had done plenty over the years that counted as wrong.

And, apparently, Curran knew all his dirty secrets.

Again, he was impressed. He'd always thought the guy showed talent and promise. Nice to be proven right.

"This isn't the time," Curran breathed. "I need to get Royal out of here. You can come to the station, too. But he's gonna need a lawyer."

"*He attacked me!*" Micah suddenly screamed.

Yeah, that prick was still there. Being loaded into the back of another ambulance. One hand was cuffed to the rail of the gurney. Micah's free hand flew up and pointed at Royal. "Arrest him!" A screech. "He killed Simone! He attacked me! Put a gun to my head!"

That's what happens when you're a murderous prick. "Should have let me kill him," Royal muttered to the detective who'd turned on him. "That mistake will come back to bite you in the ass." He still kept his wrists extended toward Curran.

Swearing, Curran took the cuffs and locked them around Royal's wrists. "I'm sorry," he whispered.

"You will be," Royal assured him.

"No!" Violet's voice broke through the night. And all eyes seemed to surge toward them.

Curran began leading Royal to a nearby patrol car. Micah had been sealed inside his ambulance.

"No!" Violet blasted again, the denial even louder and even stronger this time. "Royal saved me!"

The reporters pushed closer.

She grabbed Royal's arm. Held tightly. She stared straight up at him. "I'm not letting you get locked up."

He smiled at her. "You're safe." She was safe. Beautiful. Determined. Strong. Alive. *What would I have done if she'd been the dead body in the trunk?*

Violet shot onto her toes. Her hands curled behind his head, and she dragged his mouth down to hers. She kissed him. Hard and deep and wildly. Right in front of the reporters and the cops.

"Move," Curran snapped.

She slowly let Royal go.

Then she spun to face the crowd. "Royal Boudreaux saved my life tonight! He's a hero, and the cops are locking him up."

"Freaking fabulous," Curran groused. He pushed Royal forward.

Royal advanced, but his eyes slid back to Violet.

Fragile, breakable Violet. With blood on her body and her clothes. Looking like a weak victim, but speaking so clearly. "Royal has been protecting me. Guarding me." She peered into the biggest camera. "He's been my bodyguard since my abduction. He's a hero. Not a criminal. *Hero*. If it wasn't for him, I'd be dead."

The cruiser's rear door was open. Curran guided Royal inside.

Royal kept watching Violet. "She can't be left alone."

"I have a feeling she won't be."

Violet turned her head toward Royal. "His only crime is stopping the man who came at me with a knife. So why is Royal being sent away?"

"You have a few more crimes than that one, but still, nice touch. She is painting one stellar picture of you. Royal, hero extraordinaire. The press will eat that shit up." Curran slammed the door. He slapped the top of the car. The driver was already in place. The young cop started the engine and drove the vehicle forward. Royal kept his eyes on the person who mattered.

Violet.

The reporters closed in on her.

Chapter Seventeen

"SHE MADE YOU INTO A FREAKING HERO."

Royal rolled back his shoulders. His neck ached. The chair was stiff as hell. And the weak coffee in front of him had gone ice cold.

He'd been at the station for most of the night. Cooperating. Or, at least, giving the appearance of cooperating. He needed to see just what the cops had on him. That way, he could launch his own attack. So he'd been talking a bit—and letting the cops talk more.

"Violet. She made you a hero." Curran hauled out a chair across from Royal. He sat down at the narrow table. Ran a weary hand over his face. "Your picture—blood-covered, brutal you and fragile Violet—that picture is all over the Internet, FYI. All over every TV news show in the *nation*. The world is calling you a hero. I'm getting pressure from my boss to cut your ass loose when just yesterday, I was being told to lock you up at all costs."

Royal tilted his head. "Funny how things can change." He smiled at the detective. "Take you, for example. Who would have thought that you'd be leading the charge against me so passionately? And to think, I considered you a friend." He put a hand to his heart. "It hurts. Right here."

Curran's gaze cut to the right. To the one-way mirror that hung against the wall. Then he looked back at Royal. But Royal got the message.

We're being watched.

Like he hadn't already figured out that shit. What was this? His first time in interrogation? Hardly. He knew exactly how to play this game. Royal let his hand drop and released a dramatic sigh.

"We found the camera," Curran revealed.

Royal didn't change expression. "Uh, good for you?" He cleared his throat. "What camera?"

"The one out at the winery. Did you forget to move it?"

He hadn't forgotten. But when he'd gone back, it had already been removed. "Sorry. I'm having trouble following along."

Curran's hands flattened on the table top. "Then let me draw you a map."

"Whatever gets you going."

Curran's eyes narrowed. "A surveillance camera was found at the winery. The winery where the perp took Violet. It was *your* camera."

"Why would you think that?" He let his own eyes widen. "Were there prints on it that led you to me?"

"You know there were no prints recovered on it."

Because he wouldn't make such an amateur mistake. "Then did you somehow trace the camera's purchase to me? I'm just—sorry, I'm not following along. The map needs to be more detailed."

"Bullshit. You follow everything. You and that crazy tech mind of yours. Look, we both know it was *your* camera."

"A statement, not a question." The camera could not be traced back to him. "I think you're supposed to ask questions. Not that I want to tell you how to do your job."

Curran's lips twisted. "You're damn good when it comes to tech."

"Thanks for noticing. I try."

"But we've got someone better."

He didn't change expression. "Do tell."

"A lady from Quantico. She came to town with the Feds. See, you aren't the only one who thought a serial killer was hunting here. The Feds had been watching and evaluating. She got the camera from the winery. She did some tech mojo, and she was able to trace the signal back to you and your phone."

He didn't buy that for even a second. *No one can trace jack back to me.* "Why are you lying to me? I'm not going to make some grand confession." He laughed. "I'm not the serial killer the Feds are after."

Curran stared stonily back at him.

Let's see what all the cops know. Royal shifted a bit in his uncomfortable chair. "The killer that the Feds want to catch? He has claimed four victims so far. Four women who all look the same." An exhale. "Marcella—"

"Marcella White. Bailey Brown. Fiona Law." A pause from Curran. "And Violet Murphy. Only Violet wasn't murdered like the others. You saved her."

So the cops *were* tying all the pieces together. Finally. "I didn't kill those women."

"I never thought you did. Feds might have suspected you. But...you're not into hurting women. You don't go after the vulnerable."

"Tell me more about what I do—or what you think I do." *Tell me everything.*

"I think you're the man who has been *hunting* the killer."

Ah, well, on that, Curran would be right. Good for him. And if the Feds had put those puzzle pieces together, too? Bravo.

"And you were hunting him the night Violet was taken. Only instead of finding the killer, you found her." Curran leaned forward. "What I don't get is why you didn't just leave her in the trunk and finish him off then and there."

He held the detective's stare.

"Simone Wilmont is dead." Curran slumped back in his seat. "Hell, we both knew she was dead even when they loaded her into the ambulance."

Beneath the table, Royal's hands clenched into fists. *Where is Violet? How is she?* Her friend's death would hit her hard. Violet had tried so desperately to help Simone.

I need to get to Violet. Enough of this bullshit with him *cooperating.* He had places to be. And a Violet to hold.

"I want to know how you and Violet wound up at the crime scene. How did you get to that old service station?"

He could share this part and get things rolling. Besides, he was sure the cops had already asked Violet plenty of the same questions. Violet—being Violet—she'd tell the truth. So he'd stick to the truth as much as possible, too. "Simone called Violet. She was scared. Desperate. She asked Violet to come and get her." A pause. "She said Micah had left her in the middle of nowhere."

Curran's jaw hardened. "Micah says he got a call from Simone, too. That her car had broken down. That she needed him. She asked him to come and find her. Only when he got there, he said some guy ran at him in the dark, stabbed him, and then the next thing he knew, you had a gun in his face."

"Some people are good at lying."

Curran nodded. "Yes." His stare bored into Royal. "They are."

Oh, was that supposed to be a hit? Whatever. This whole scene was a pain in his ass. He'd sat patiently for hours. He'd chatted politely with too many cops, but his patience was slicing away. "Violet stabbed him. I saw her do it. I'm sure she has already told you that when her attacker charged at her, she used a knife on him. A knife I'd given her for protection."

"You *saw* her stab Micah?"

"I just said that, didn't I?" He'd said it before, too.

"Where were you when she stabbed him?"

His nostrils flared. "I was punching my way through the glass in the garage door in order to get to her." A moment that would replay in his mind on a hell-loop pretty much forever, thanks so much.

"Is that when you were also firing your weapon?"

The weapon that had been seized by the cops. "Yes. He had a knife, and he was trying to use it on Violet. I wasn't going to let that happen. I happen to take deep offense to the idea of anyone cutting her skin." Great offense. The kind of offense that would result in someone getting killed. *Micah should be dead, but Curran stopped me.*

Royal could forgive a lot of things. Curran's conscience getting the better of him and the guy arresting Royal? Sure, he could even let that go. Bygones. But Curran letting that prick Micah *live?*

No forgiveness on that one.

"Let's cut the bullshit," Curran suddenly announced.

Royal quirked one brow. "Oh, have we not already done that? My bad."

Curran glowered. "You went to that shitty old gas

station with Violet because you knew that the killer you were after had taken Simone there."

He exhaled. "I hear so many statements. Not so many questions. I get that you're new to the detective gig, my friend, but you have to ask questions during interrogations. That is the way this works."

"I *know* that Simone and Micah were an item. I also know she was Violet's understudy, and I suspect that Simone wanted the lead role with every breath in her body." Curran cleared his throat. "Simone was having an affair with Micah. I know it because I saw them together at the theater."

Royal waited.

"But word from some of the other cast members is that Micah wanted to fuck your dancer."

She is mine. But Royal just shrugged. "We don't always get what we want in this world."

"You weren't going to let him have her."

"I wasn't going to let him *kill* Violet, if that's what you mean. Look, she stabbed him. Violet has no doubt told the cops that she stabbed her attacker. And Micah has a stab wound—"

"One that he says someone else gave him." Curran stared straight at Royal. "Not Violet. A man who charged at him from the darkness."

Royal grunted. "Convenient, don't you think? Violet stabs her attacker, and, oh, look, someone else just happens to stab Micah in basically the same spot? That's not coincidental. That's impossible." Curran should see right through the lie.

"You almost killed him," Curran whispered.

Too bad you interrupted the job.

"Violet says she tased her attacker," Curran added. A long exhale. "Did you see that happen?"

He frowned, trying to remember. No, no, dammit, he couldn't recall her doing that.

"Huh." Curran scraped a hand over his jaw. "Pieces don't add up." Low. Very low. His stare cut to the one-way mirror, then back to Royal.

"Is she watching?" Royal asked, truly curious. "The Fed you think is better at tech work than me? Is she in there? Are a whole team of Feds in there just salivating because they think you're taking me down?"

"*They* thought you were the serial who'd hurt those women. That's why they originally wanted me tailing you."

Royal laughed.

"This shit isn't a joke. The camera at the winery? They have a theory that it was set up because the perp wanted a replay of his crimes. They think you were at the winery the night of Violet's abduction. And then, bam, you were there when Simone was killed at the service station. You had Simone's blood all over you."

Ah, yes, his bloody clothes. They'd been removed. Bagged and tagged as evidence. Now he wore some borrowed jail clothes. The kind of crap that they gave prisoners to wear in holding. Orange and garish. Royal looked down at the shirt in distaste. "Not really my color."

"Blood isn't your color?"

"No, this hideous orange." His head tilted back so he could eye the detective. "You have five more minutes, then I'm calling my lawyer. I've cooperated, but my patience is at an end."

"Fine." A muscle flexed along Curran's jaw. "Did you abduct Violet?"

"No."

"Did you *save* Violet that night at the winery?"

"Do I look like a fucking savior?" His heart slammed into his chest. *Has Violet revealed my secret? Did she tell them what I did that night?*

"Then let's switch things up. Are you the man responsible for subduing and restraining Everett Thomas and Owen Bell?"

Royal stretched out his legs beneath the table. "Refresh my memory. Who are they?"

"You know damn well who they are. Killers. Sadistic, twisted killers who had been murdering women. Cops and Feds couldn't find them. But someone else did. Someone trapped them. Secured them. Put freaking bows around their necks and left them for the cops to pick up." A long exhale. "Everett Thomas was called the Slasher because of what he did to his vics. And as for Bell? That freak was using horse tranquilizer to knock out his victims and make them helpless while he attacked. Two straight-up, real-life nightmares. Killers who were all but gift-wrapped for the cops."

"Oh, right." Royal smiled. "I do remember those stories. And you think I'm the one who stopped them?" He let his smile stretch. "I am flattered. Truly."

"After some prompting and serious badgering from me, the Feds revealed there have been other killers who were... stopped." Again, he glanced toward the one-way mirror. "Like a real bad piece of work named Will Kelly. He was found in Lafayette, Louisiana."

"Huh. Will Kelly, you say? What were his crimes?"

"He abducted and murdered girls. *Girls*. Not women. Kids."

Royal forced his back teeth to unclench. "I'm guessing

he was found subdued and with a bow tied around his neck?"

"Subdued? Sure, you could say that. He was found with a bullet to the brain." His eyes glittered. "Seem familiar to you? Because when I found you and Micah, you had your gun aimed at his brain."

"Technically, I had my gun aimed in the middle of his face. Details matter."

"This shit isn't a joke. The Feds are trying to tie you to *murder*."

"Seems to me like that prick Will might have deserved what he got. You shouldn't hurt kids. They're too breakable. Fragile."

"And you don't like it when fragile things are hurt, do you? Kids...and say...a certain ballerina. One that somehow worked her way beneath your skin. See, this is what I think happened."

"Oh, yes, please, tell me what you think happened."

"I think you've got a whole lot of rage and darkness inside of you, Royal. I think that darkness cut loose with Will."

Still with the statements, not questions.

"But I think maybe...maybe you had some help on the other two hunts. Everett and Owen. Maybe someone stopped you from going too far. You subdued them. Didn't kill them. Is that what happened? You have someone put you on a leash and yank you back from the edge?" His narrowed stare watched Royal like a hawk.

Royal looked at his wrist and the watch that wasn't there. "I think those five minutes are up."

"But last night, when the attacker tried to take Violet away—your new, *fragile* thing—you lost it, didn't you? And you were going to pull the trigger and blow out Micah's brains."

Royal cocked his head and returned his focus to the detective. "Did you miss the woman who'd been savaged in the trunk? I counted at least ten deep stab wounds on her. And I saw the defensive cuts where she tried to lift her *bound* hands and stop her attacker."

"I didn't miss her." Grim. "She's burned in my mind."

In Royal's, too. "Some people won't ever stop. Something is twisted and wrong inside of them. They do bad things and they never, ever stop."

Curran nodded. "You got something twisted and wrong inside of you? See, the more they look at you, that's what the Feds—and their profile on you—is saying. Is that why you're hunting these killers? You doing your own *bad* thing?"

He'd always felt twisted. "I was there last night to protect Violet. I wasn't hunting anyone."

Curran's eyes widened. "I think that's your first lie." Soft. "You used her to hunt, didn't you? And the fact that she almost died in front of you—how the hell does that make you feel?"

Like he was splitting apart on the inside. Like his control would disintegrate at any moment. Like he needed to see her—touch her—or he would lose his mind.

"She's out there telling the world that you're a hero, but that couldn't be further from the truth, could it?" Curran pushed.

Oh, so *now* the man started asking actual questions. "I never claimed to be a hero."

"So you're the villain of the story."

"No." Not that, either. "That would be the man who abducted and murdered Marcella White, Bailey Brown, Fiona Law, and now, Simone Wilmont." A pause. "The same man who also abducted Violet Murphy just over two weeks ago. The same man who tried to kill her last night." His words came out flat and hard. "The *same* man you should now have in custody. How convenient is that? Almost like he was tied up for you with a red bow around his neck."

"Royal—"

"Hope you don't let him out. If he gets out, who knows what could happen?"

"Are you threatening to kill him? Telling a cop that you are going to kill someone?"

Royal shook his head. *There's a difference between a promise and a threat, my friend. You should know me well enough to understand that fact.* "I'm telling you something that I am sure your new FBI buddies have already said. And if they haven't said it, they should. Killers like this one—they don't stop. They can't stop. Compulsions drive them. If you let him go, he will attack again. He's come after Violet twice now. He'll try for a third time."

He should be dead.

"Micah willingly gave us his phone," Curran revealed. "The call from Simone's number was there, just as the call from her was listed on Violet's phone."

That didn't prove jack. "Maybe Micah was standing right the hell next to her when she made the calls. Maybe Micah had a knife at her throat and he ordered her to call his phone so he could try and set up this BS story. Then he got her to call Violet. Or, considering they were fucking and Simone wanted Violet out of the way, maybe they planned the scene together." Another option that had to be considered. "A trick to get Violet out in the middle of nowhere. See, Violet was told to come alone. I insisted on going with her."

"The better for you to hunt and use her as your bait."

His shoulders tensed. "*Maybe* the plan wasn't for Simone to die, but Micah decided she was expendable. After all, she wasn't really his type, was she? Wrong hair color. He likes dark hair. Hair like Violet's. Like Marcella White's. Bailey Brown's. Fiona Law's."

"There was a bloody wig in that trunk. Same shade as Violet's hair."

Royal's lashes flickered.

And—

The door flew open. "Gentlemen!" A woman crossed the threshold. About five-foot-eight, with shoulder-length, black hair. She wore a blue business suit. Better quality and style than most FBI suits, Royal would give her that much credit, but he still recognized a Fed when he saw one.

"The hacker, I presume?" Royal murmured.

Her blue gaze flickered to him. "I have a question for you."

"Seems to be that kind of day."

"I'm Agent Teresa Duncan, and I want to know why..." She moved to the side. Another woman appeared. Golden skin. Long, dark hair that had been braided and now fell loosely over her shoulder. The woman's intense gaze immediately landed on Royal. "I want to know *why*," the federal agent continued, "the famous doctor of the dead has just shown up at the Savannah police station and requested to see *you*."

Well, well, well. What a perfectly timed development. Fate could occasionally smile on him.

Royal rose and inclined his head to the doctor. "Dr. Rossi."

"In the flesh." Her gaze assessed him. "Didn't expect to encounter you in prison orange."

"A temporary situation," he assured her.

Holy hell. Beau had actually done it. Pulled off one major favor for Royal. *I will be repaying him for years to come.* Because Royal was standing and staring at the real-life doctor of the dead. Dr. Antonia "Tony" Rossi. A woman who could find the dead better than anyone else in the US. Her exploits were legend, and, based on the way Agent Teresa Duncan eyed her, the Fed understood just what a big deal it was to have Tony make an appearance in town and ask to see Royal.

What perfect timing. He truly was gonna owe Beau forever.

"Got some bodies you want me to find?" Tony asked, voice tinged with the faintest note of curiosity. "And it's Rossi-Warner now."

Right. Because she'd married the rich billionaire who'd fought a killer with her not too long ago. Royal was kind of surprised the man wasn't trailing behind—

A tall figure in a damn expensive black suit appeared behind Tony.

And there he is. Aiden Warner.

"What in the hell is going on here?" Curran demanded. The legs of his chair screeched as he shoved it back. He sidled around the table. "Someone want to explain this shit to me?"

Royal motioned to his hideous orange gab. "Sorry for the attire. The cops and the Feds seem to mistakenly think I'm some sort of criminal."

Tony's eyes narrowed. "And you're not?"

"I'm not the criminal you're after today." *I need to speed this scene along. Get out. Get to Violet.* "No, I'm like you."

Tony took a determined step toward him. "How so?" The curiosity in her voice had deepened.

"Just consider me a junior cold case solver. An Ice Breaker in training, if you will." He motioned toward an ever-so-watchful Curran. "As the detective can tell you, we have a serial killer at work in Georgia."

"Serial killers are often at work. A sad and terrifying truth." Tony's stare assessed him again.

"I think Savannah is this killer's home base."

"Are you making a confession right now?" Agent Duncan asked.

He shook his head. "Feds are wasting my time. I do have places to be. And I think you have bodies to find," he told Tony. So he'd cut to the chase with her. "The winery. It's important. Violet Murphy was abducted two weeks ago—"

"I saw her story on the news," Tony cut in to say. "And *your* story. She said you're a hero." A shake of her head. "Heroes don't usually get locked up."

"Just being questioned. Not tossed into a cage." A smooth reply. And back to the winery and its sprawling vineyard... "Violet was taken to the old Freemont Winery outside of town. I don't believe she was the first victim taken there."

"Cops and crime techs searched that area," Curran muttered.

"They didn't search well enough. Obviously." He smiled at Tony. Royal certainly hoped she lived up to all the hype he'd heard about her. "That's why we needed the big guns."

Behind Tony, her husband shifted his position ever so slightly. A small ripple of menace.

"If you review the reports on the victims—reports that I'm sure the resourceful Agent Duncan has somewhere close by—you'll find that a very diligent crime scene tech discovered grape leaves near Marcella White's body. Same thing happened with Fiona Law. That discovery made me curious."

"How did you get access to the reports made by the crime scene techs?" Aiden Warner asked.

Royal waved away the question. "When I learned that interesting detail—"

"How?" Aiden asked again.

"Through the usual channels." *I hacked my way to the details.* "The grape leaves stuck out to me. Something unusual. I had some acquaintances do some research for me. Those grape leaves? Turns out, they were from—"

"The Freemont Winery," Tony finished.

Indeed. "Four victims so far. I'm no expert, but it seems strange that someone would just start so strong and so perfectly with his kills. Again, no expert, but don't serials usually work up to the attacks? Perfect them? Going by that logic, wouldn't it be possible that our killer had started longer ago than we realize? That there could be other—"

Curran grabbed Royal's shoulder. "You think the guy has more vics? And he hid them at the winery?"

"I think someone who is good at finding the dead should give the place a much more thorough look than it's had before, and since the doctor of the dead has come all this way, it would be a crying shame not to use her specific talents."

Tony put her hands on her hips. "Who owns the property?"

"Funny thing, that," Royal returned without any pause because he'd already been digging down this particular path. "It belongs to Jonathan Freemont. He's spent the last seven years in a memory care facility. The place withered over the years because he had no immediate family who wanted to help with the place. Though, interestingly, *some* of the vines are still producing. Even though no one is supposed to be taking care of them. That would be where those precious leaves came from. Vines that should have been completely dead."

"You have captured my attention," Tony informed him as she raised her eyebrows. "Maybe it's the orange outfit, but I just can't look away."

He rolled one shoulder. "I have that effect on people. I seem to have caught the attention of the Feds, too. Agent Duncan thinks I'm the serial killer."

Tony tilted her head to the right. "Again, according to the stories I'm seeing, I thought you were supposed to be the hero."

"Hero, killer. It's so hard for people to ever figure things out completely."

Tony's gaze shifted to Curran. "Can you get me approval to search that property?"

"I—"

"We can get approval," Agent Duncan interrupted to say. "It's still a crime scene because of Violet Murphy's abduction." She hurried closer to Tony. "I've heard about you. You've worked with several colleagues that I have at the Bureau." A brief pause and then, "I would very much like to see you in action."

"There may be nothing to see," Tony returned without missing a beat.

Royal thought that—unfortunately—there would be plenty to see. "Shame the Feds and the local PD all missed following up on such an important clue. So glad I could assist in the investigation." Now, enough of this interrogation BS. He slanted a glance at Curran. "I believe that last allotted five minutes have come and very much gone. Shall I call my lawyer? Or is this gonna be the part where you just let me walk out...because we both know you have jack and shit to hold me on?"

Curran and Teresa Duncan shared a long look. Then she inclined her head.

Ah, so the Feds were very much in charge and pulling the strings. An important point.

"I'll escort you out," Curran told him. "But be prepared, I may have follow-up questions."

"Fantastic to know." But he let the detective lead the way and paused only long enough to say, "It was a pleasure, doctor."

Tony shook her dark head. Her braid slid over her shoulder. "Death is rarely a pleasure."

"Depends on who is dying."

Her brows lifted once more. "You are an unusual man."

"I get that a lot."

Curran pushed him toward the door. Aiden Warner assessed him, then stepped aside so that Royal and Curran could pass. And as Royal walked into the waiting corridor...

"Well, hello, beautiful," Royal crooned. He extended his hand toward the German Shepherd who waited with perfect patience for her human. "Banshee, isn't it? Your reputation has proceeded you." As if he wouldn't recognize the doctor of the dead's dog.

Banshee delicately sniffed him. Stared up with her deep and gorgeous eyes. And patiently continued to wait for Tony.

"How the hell do you know the dog's name?" Curran asked.

"I know because Banshee is Tony's partner. If Tony came here looking for the dead, then no way would she leave Banshee behind." He could have sworn the dog smiled at him.

But Curran kept urging him forward so Royal didn't get to linger.

"You are running too many games," Curran whispered.

Royal laughed softly. "Like you aren't, my friend?"

"Oh, cut the shit. It's me and it's you right now." But he cut a quick, worried glance over his shoulder before focusing on Royal once more. "You had to know the cops and Feds were watching you and that I'd be pushed to tail your crazy ass. What was I supposed to do? Let you shoot the prick in the face?"

That would have been an option. "Where is Violet?" He kept walking down the hallway with Curran.

"I'm taking you to her now. Jeez, breathe a minute, would you? I have her in my office. She had to go through the grilling process just like you. And, FYI, she's still as freaking protective of you as she was the first time I met her."

His chest ached. "You shouldn't still have her at the station."

"Oh, yeah, please, tell me more about how to do my job. Love that shit."

Royal stopped. Glared.

"I get it." An inhale from Curran. "You want to kick my ass. Rip my head off. Chop me up and feed me to the alligators you used to talk about so much that lived in the swamps of Louisiana."

"I need Violet."

Curran faced off with him. "I had a job to do. Believe it or not, I was helping your fool ass. You are welcome."

"*Violet.*" Curran was in his path. Either the guy would move or Royal would move him.

"All right, slow your roll. Just one damn thing first,

okay?" Curran glanced around, then back at Royal. "No marks."

"What?"

"Your Violet said she tased her attacker. Stabbed him and tased him."

"Micah *had* a stab wound."

"Yeah, and we had to take him to the hospital to get it stitched up. He's still at the damn hospital—with guards— but you know what he *doesn't* have? Marks from a taser."

So what? "Maybe the taser didn't make contact. He *has* the knife wound." That should be enough.

"And he says someone ran up and stabbed him! I'm just warning you—all the pieces don't fit. They *don't*."

They rarely ever fit perfectly. "While you were trailing me, did you see anyone else at that service station?"

Curran shook his head.

"So either Micah is the bad guy...or someone else is. Someone who got away. That's what you're telling me. The perp could still be out there." Royal assessed possibilities even as his gaze swept over Curran. "Unless it was you, old friend."

"What?" Shock rippled across Curran's face.

"You were there. Lurking about in the darkness. Watching everything. Are you hiding any wounds I might need to know about? Can't say for sure how deeply Violet stabbed her attacker." He took a step closer to Curran. "You were at the scene. Maybe you ditched the mask in the dark. Switched clothes. Maybe it was *you*."

Curran's chin whipped up. "Now you think I'm a killer?"

"Only fair, isn't it?" he returned with a shrug. "You think I'm one. You think—"

"*Royal!*"

Violet's voice. Violet's voice pouring over him, and he shouldered past the detective. Violet rushed from the end of the hallway. She wore soft gray sweats and a t-shirt that was far too big for her. Her hair spilled down her back. Her face was too pale. And her eyes—her eyes lit up when they locked on Royal.

"Just watch her," Curran advised, voice grim. "I don't think this is over."

It won't be over until you let me put her attacker six feet under.

Royal reached for Violet, and she threw herself against him. Immediately, his arms closed around her. He lifted her up against him, and Royal knew he held her too tightly. He should ease his grip. He should.

He didn't. He buried his face in the fall of her hair and inhaled her sweet scent. Lilacs for his Violet. "Sweetheart..."

"I told them you had saved me. I told them that Simone called me and asked me to come meet her. That you warned me it was a trap, but I convinced you to go with me anyway." She shuddered against him. "Simone is dead. They told me she died—that she never spoke again." Violet pulled back. When she looked at him, there were tears gleaming in her eyes. "I told all the cops that she said Micah's name. She *told* me that he was the one to attack her." A tear spilled down her cheek. "There was so much blood on her. *Everywhere.* And she's dead. That could have been me. It *would* have been me. Without you."

"It will *never* be you." Over *his* dead body. "Let's get the hell out of here."

"Reporters are out front," Curran warned.

Fine. "Then we'll go out back."

"Out that way, too."

Figured they were.

"But your buddy Beau has a limo waiting at the curb for you," Curran added with a wave of his hand. "I'll get you a police escort to it."

Right. Sure. A police escort as he wore prison orange. Whatever. Like he gave a damn. There would be no more standing in the shadows. Not now. The world had seen him. Some would think he was a villain. The cops and Feds did. But others would think he was more. Because of Violet.

Minutes later, they were rushing through the crowd of reporters who did, in fact, wait outside. Royal curled his body closely around Violet's and didn't let anyone else get near enough to touch her. Reporters hurled questions at them, but Royal didn't stop to answer anything. He just wanted to get Violet away.

He recognized the man standing near the back of the limo. Kai. A friend of his and Beau's. Hell, technically Kai was Beau's right-hand man at LeBlanc's. But, like Royal, Kai knew all about getting his hands dirty.

Kai was also the guy that Royal had recently hired to keep an extra eye on Violet. When you had something precious, you needed someone you trusted to be close in case of an emergency.

He trusted Kai. Kai was the kind of man who would walk through fire for a friend. Literally. *Kai had been there and done that before.*

Kai dipped his head toward Royal. "Was starting to think you were enjoying the time at the station too much."

Royal grunted. "You know me. I do love spending time with cops." He urged Violet inside the limo. "Take us home," he told Kai.

"Gladly."

Royal ducked inside and yanked the door closed behind

him. The shouted questions were immediately muted, and he found himself sitting across from Violet as the limo swiftly drove from the scene.

Violet's breath shuddered in and out. "Is it...over?"

He didn't move.

"They have Micah. Simone identified him. I *stabbed* him." Her hands twisted in her lap. "They're not going to let him go, are they? It's over? I'm safe?"

"You're safe, sweetheart." *I will keep you safe. I swear it.* But...

Curran's words whispered through his mind and made Royal's gut knot. *All the pieces don't fit. They don't.*

Chapter Eighteen

EVEN AS THE LIMO DROVE DOWN THE ROAD, VIOLET launched herself at Royal. She held him tightly and did not want to let go. "I told the cops that you saved me. I told them and the federal agent to let you go." She'd told them over and over. "You aren't the bad guy, I *told them that*."

His hands came up and curled around the wrists she'd locked behind his neck. Slowly, carefully, he pulled her hands down. She was sprawled on top of his lap. She should move. But she didn't.

His gaze seemed so intense. His expression hard and unreadable.

"I didn't tell them about the night at the winery." He needed to understand that. "I promised you that I'd keep your secrets, and I will."

His mouth took hers. Not soft. Hard with need and passion and a burning desire that had hunger and lust flooding through her. She'd barely held her control during all of those long hours at the station. And when Curran had quietly told her that Simone had died...

I was the one to shatter. Just like glass, she'd felt herself breaking apart on the inside. She'd wanted to save Simone. No matter what else might have happened between her and her friend, the last thing she'd wanted was for Simone to die.

Then Violet had been kept from Royal. Though she'd asked to see him again and again.

His mouth pulled from hers.

She wanted it back.

"They kept us separated," he growled against her lips. "Because they thought one of us would break."

Not one of them. Her. "They think I'm the weak link."

"Sweetheart, you're fucking steel beneath silk. Without you, I'm the one who is weak." Royal kissed her again. A deep, drugging kiss. His hands still held her wrists, but she fought that grip because she needed to touch *him*.

Desperation and desire warred inside of her. Her body seemed to be ripping apart. Her heart raced. Her breath heaved, and her legs had fallen open so that she straddled him. The thick length of his dick pushed against her, and her hips arched and rocked hard against him.

Oblivion. That was what she wanted.

She wanted to stop seeing Simone's bloody body when she closed her eyes.

And when her eyes were open.

She wanted to stop seeing the bastard in the night vision goggles as he ran toward her. And that knife...that big, sharp knife...

"Fuck me," she whispered to Royal.

Right then. Right there.

She didn't care if it was wrong. Everything was wrong around her. She needed to feel him and the pleasure he gave her. Her body was too tight and tense and everything was shattering around her. "Royal, *fuck me." Make the pain stop. Take it all away. Please.*

"Like you have to ask." A savage growl against her mouth. He lifted her up. Just for a moment. She twisted onto the seat near him and kicked off the borrowed sweats, her underwear, and shoes. Still with the donated t-shirt covering her upper body, she climbed back on him.

Royal had shoved his garish orange pants down. When she straddled him again, she pushed eagerly toward the cock that shoved up against her.

"Baby, slow..."

"No." No *slow.* She pushed down *hard.*

He sank in completely.

Her body fought him at first. One quick flash of pain as he stretched her.

"You weren't ready...*fuck.*"

Her breath came faster. His hands were fierce clamps around her waist, preventing her from rising and arching against him. He held her prisoner, and she was acutely conscious of every thick inch of him within her.

Every thick, bare inch of him.

They both seemed to have that realization at once. *Bare.*

His head whipped up. He stared straight into her eyes. His nostrils flared. The gold in his gaze seemed to swallow the green and brown. His face went even more savage. "Tell me to stop."

"Fuck me," she said instead.

"*Violet...*"

She squirmed against his hold, but he held her too tightly. "Fuck. Me."

"Shouldn't..." Royal gritted.

"Yes." He most definitely should. She kissed him. Stroked her tongue against his. "I want you. This way. Any way." Violet needed this. *Him*. Didn't he understand? "Royal, don't make me beg."

"*Never.*"

And he was lifting her up. Pulling her down. Driving his heavy cock into her and making her moan and thrash against him. He kissed her and took her and the pounding of their bodies was wild and hard.

One of his strong hands remained locked on her hip. The other slid between them. Demanding, he stroked her clit. Pushed her straight to her orgasm even as his cock shoved ever deeper into her.

A wild cry broke from her but was swallowed by his mouth. The release blew through every cell in Violet's body, and then she felt him coming. Powerful jets inside of her that just seemed to make her own release stretch and stretch as her core contracted greedily around him.

His mouth broke from hers.

Her heart drummed. Her head dipped forward.

His lips feathered over her forehead.

Then...down her cheeks.

Because she was crying. She hadn't even realized the tears were trailing down her cheeks, not until she felt Royal kissing them away.

"Did I hurt you?" Gruff. "I'm sorry. I never meant—"

"You didn't." The release had sent all of her emotions crashing into her. The feelings she'd tried to keep in check? Ha. There was no check. Pain and grief and fear battled within her. "I wanted to be strong like you. I wanted to hunt him. But I was so scared."

His head lifted. "It's because of me."

"It's because of *me*." He was still in her. Getting bigger by the second. "I wanted to be able to stop him. I wanted to make the fear I felt end, but when I was in that garage, I was absolutely terrified."

"Violet..."

"And I didn't save her." She didn't want to keep seeing Simone's bloody image. "Make it stop," she pleaded.

"Baby?"

"Can you make the pain stop? And the fear? Just make it go away. Tell me it's over." Her hands dropped to his waist. She pushed her body up. Sank back down on him. "Make it go away." Because it had gone away. In that blinding moment of release, she'd known only him.

She wanted that reckless release again. Pleasure swept away everything else, and in the moment of climax, she could be absolutely mindless. No fear. No sadness. No pain.

Nothing but Royal.

Them.

Nothing but...

"The damn car is slowing down," he growled. Both of his hands had returned to her waist. "We're at my place, sweetheart, and in a few minutes, Kai is going to be opening the back door. I'm not really in the mood to give him a show." His eyes still glittered at her. "For future reference, I'm the only one who ever gets a show from you."

Reality washed over her in a hard, cold wave.

What am I doing?

She'd jumped on him. In the back of a limo. With his friend driving in the front. With *no* protection. Simone's body was in the morgue. Micah had been taken away by the cops in an ambulance.

She and Royal had spent so many hours at the police station.

And as soon as they were alone. She was...they were...

She scrambled off him.

He winced.

Violet grabbed for her clothes. Put the borrowed gear on as quickly as she could even as she was far, far too aware of the wetness between her thighs. "We shouldn't...I shouldn't..." Her eyes squeezed shut. "What is wrong with me?"

"*Nothing.*" Savage.

Her eyes flew open.

He'd already adjusted his clothes.

"Not a damn thing is wrong with you. Don't sit there and feel guilty for taking pleasure."

She was. Feeling guilty for having an orgasm that shook her bones in the back of a limo while Simone was cold on a slab.

"You're alive. I'm alive. You needed to be reminded of that. Sex is basic. It's primal. With you, it's fucking life affirming. And I've told you before, but I'm telling you again. *Nothing about you is wrong.*"

The limo had stopped.

She shoved back her hair.

"Reporters are here," he muttered as he peered out the tinted window. "Swarming around my house. You don't have to talk to them. I'll get you inside, and we'll shut out the rest of the world."

But that pack of reporters told her it wasn't going to be so easy to shut things out.

The screen that separated them from the front of the limo lowered with a whir of sound. "You two ready for this?" Kai—the driver—asked.

Good thing he hadn't rolled that screen down about three minutes ago. Heat stained her cheeks as Violet realized he probably knew exactly what they'd been doing.

"I can take you someplace else," he offered. "Say the word, Royal."

Royal peered through the window once more. "I think my low profile has been shot to hell and back." A reckless smile curved his lips. "So much for hunting in the shadows."

"Royal?" Violet said his name softly.

He reached for her hand. "No one else will touch you."

She wasn't afraid of the reporters. She was afraid of the man in the mask. *Micah. All along, it was him?*

It made sense, though. A twisted sense. He would have been able to stay late at the theater on the night of her abduction. He would have known her routine.

He would have also been able to get Simone to leave and go just about anywhere with him. Because Simone would have trusted him. Right up until the moment he plunged his knife into her.

"Ready?" Royal asked.

Violet didn't speak. She was lost staring at the crowd.

"Can't get closer," Kai said. "The reporters are blocking the drive. Dick move, one that they're doing deliberately."

"Yeah, I figured that," Royal said. "Thanks for the lift, Kai."

"You know I'm coming in with you. I'll be watching your back. I'll leave the car out here. Not like anyone would dare tow it. And, fair warning? Beau is already inside."

"Yeah. Saw his car." Royal's thumb stroked over Violet's knuckles. "My brother has a key."

Brother. She hadn't even called her brothers. Everything had been so crazy, and she knew that Dawson must have seen the stories on the news. With Parker being deployed, he probably hadn't heard about the attack last night.

But Dawson would be a different story, and he would be freaking out.

Where is my phone? She didn't even have her phone. Had she left it at the police station? If Dawson had tried to call her, he would have just gotten voicemail. She'd have to contact him as soon as she got inside.

And they were going to head inside. Kai had already raised the screen back up and was coming around to open the limo door. But Royal didn't move. He just stared at her and waited.

Oh, right. He'd asked if she was ready. She had to give some kind of agreement. Her head inclined toward him.

He leaned forward, and Royal's mouth pressed lightly to hers. "Focus on me. Not them."

She was going to focus on putting one foot in front of the other.

The back door opened.

The questions roared at them. Just as before, Royal wrapped his arms around her. He tucked her against his body as they hurried through the crowd.

"Back up!" The bellow came from Kai as he trailed them. "And you guys know the drill—you don't step foot on private property, so stay off—"

He said something else, but she didn't hear the words because a man had just rushed toward her.

"Violet!" he yelled her name even as he grabbed for her. Hard. One of his hands closed around her arm and he pulled her—

Royal drove his fist into the guy's face. A fast hit that sent the other man crashing to the ground.

"You don't touch her!" Royal thundered.

And...

The cameras got everything. The reporters greedily recorded the scene.

The man on the ground groaned. He lifted his head and rubbed his jaw. "Violet?" Dawson croaked.

Yep, her brother Dawson. In that frantic flash—with all of the other bodies around them—she hadn't gotten a look at his face when he grabbed her.

"Violet, what the hell?" Dawson demanded. He pushed to his feet and took a step toward her.

Then he was blocked by the wall that was Royal.

"Royal!" She curled her hand around his shoulder. "That's my brother!"

"Yeah, I know who the hell he is."

He knew? Had he known before or after he'd slugged Dawson?

"Let him come in the house," she said. Her gaze darted around to the reporters. *Madness. Chaos.* "We can talk there."

"Violet! Violet!" A woman shoved close. "Is it true that you were having an affair with Micah Wright?"

"What?" Her head whipped toward the reporter. "No, absolutely not!"

"Violet is involved with me," Royal said flatly. "No one else." Then his arm was curling around her again. "House," he breathed into her ear. "Now."

"Did *you* attack Micah Wright in a jealous rage?" The shouted question came from another reporter.

What was this? She'd explained everything to them all last night! "Royal saved me. He stopped a killer from slicing me apart." She glared at the reporters. "Get your story straight."

Then she and Royal were on Royal's property.

The reporters stayed back, she'd give them that much. Royal ushered her into the house. His arm remained around her as they went straight to the den.

As promised by Kai, Beau was waiting. Sprawled on the couch, he raised one brow. "Well, well, seems you have attracted quite the crowd." A whistle. "Love the orange, Royal. Definitely your color."

Royal grunted. He dropped his hold on Violet and darted his gaze over her. "You okay?"

She nodded.

"Liar," he breathed.

Yes.

"*Violet!*" Dawson rushed into the den, with Kai right behind him. "What the hell is happening?" He beelined toward her with blood dripping from his lower lip and with his hands outstretched. He swiped out at her in a fast grab.

And Royal's hand flew out to curl right around Dawson's throat. Two steps, and Royal had her brother pinned against the nearest wall.

"Royal!" Beau shot off the couch.

Violet lunged for Royal. She curled her hand around his arm. "What are you doing? That is my brother!"

"Violet!" Her name emerged from Dawson as a croak. "Help!"

Royal glared at him. "You're the sonofabitch who locked Violet in a closet when she was a kid. Did you apologize for that shit? Did you tell her you were sorry?"

Her mouth dropped open. Then snapped closed.

Her brother's eyes bulged.

"And don't be so damn grabby with her," Royal fired off.

"Uh, Royal, let him go," Beau ordered.

He didn't.

"Royal, let my brother go," she whispered.

He immediately let Dawson go. "She needs an apology." His head turned toward her. His eyes blazed.

All of the moisture had dried from her mouth.

"Bro." Beau shook his head. "We need to talk. *Alone.*"

Dawson rubbed his hand over his neck. "Are you crazy?" he half-yelled. "Seriously psycho? You don't just attack someone. Jesus! Violet, let's get the hell out of here!" And Dawson reached for her again.

A growl rumbled from Royal.

Dawson's eyes turned into saucers.

Beau immediately hauled Royal away from Dawson. "We're just gonna take a minute," Beau announced to the group. "Gonna have a quick talk. You guys, uh, why don't you get something from the kitchen? I'm sure you're all hungry."

Royal's head turned toward Violet. "Do not leave this house."

"Uh, yeah, Violet." Dawson sidled toward her. "We need to leave this house. As fast as humanly possible." He grimaced. "That's the guy who has been protecting you? The one you said was so *good?* Screw that shit. He is crazy. Certifiable. Let's get away from him, now."

From the corner of her eye, she realized that Kai had moved to position his body so that in order to leave the den and go back toward the front door, they'd have to go through him.

Not that she intended to leave. Quite the opposite. "I'm *not* leaving."

Royal nodded. And he let Beau pull him toward the study that waited on the right.

"Why the hell not?" Dawson demanded.

She sighed. "Because I'm exactly where I want to be."

* * *

Beau slammed the study door and immediately took up a position in front of it. With his hands on his hips, he glowered at Royal. "Have you lost your ever-loving mind? You just wrapped your hand around her brother's throat and pinned him to the wall. In front of the woman! And I'd bet odds you're responsible for his busted lip, too!"

Royal paced in front of his desk. Back and forth. Fast, angry movements.

"I don't see Violet slugging me!" Beau continued. "Not like she tries to attack me every time our paths cross. So why in the hell would you go at him?"

"He locked her in a closet when she was a kid." Royal raked a hand down his face. "She freaking hates the dark and tight spaces now. Asshole still hasn't said sorry. He will," Royal swore.

"What. The. Hell?"

Royal's head whipped toward Beau.

"Where is your control? You're attacking her family? In front of her?"

"He locked her in a closet," Royal gritted out.

Beau took a step toward him. "This isn't you. You're in control. You always have—"

"*I'm not.*" That was the problem. "I'm not in control. Not now. Not with her." His hand dropped to his side where it fisted. "Do you know I was the one who wanted to use her? I wanted to make sure the killer was at that damn location. I went with her to meet Simone even though I knew it was a trap." He sucked in a breath. "Violet crawled under this stupid garage door. It lowered behind her. She was in there with him. *Glass* separated us. Damn glass. I could see her. I could see him. I could see the knife he had." *And I could see me losing everything that mattered.* "I had to bust my way in to her."

"That would explain all the scratches I see on your hands." Another gliding step from Beau. "You got to her. She's okay, bro."

"He came at her with his knife." The image would not get out of his head. "She saved herself. I didn't do it. I was behind the glass."

"Royal..."

He lifted his hand to ward off his brother. Because there was more that had to be said. "Curran stopped me from putting a bullet in Micah Wright's brain."

Beau swore.

"Now he's telling me that he doesn't think Micah was the killer. That I was about to shoot the wrong guy." His hand dropped. Then immediately fisted again. "Micah has a stab wound. Violet *stabbed* her attacker. Micah was at the scene. Micah was fucking Simone."

"Why doesn't Curran think Micah is the perp? Walk me through this. I'm playing catch-up since I've missed most of the game."

"Because Curran says Simone called Micah, too. That she made arrangements for him to come out to that godforsaken station and get her. And because Micah doesn't have marks from a taser on him."

Beau's brows rose.

"Violet tased her attacker," Royal explained.

"Tased and stabbed? I'm impressed. Seems she's as blood-thirsty as you are."

Royal bounded toward him.

"Whoa! Whoa!" Now Beau put his hands in the air with his palms facing Royal. "Easy, slugger. I'm not the enemy here."

"She's not like me. She's a million times better, and I should never have touched her." He stared down at his hands. Both had fisted. "But I can't seem to stop myself. I don't have control with her." A dangerous admission. He forced his gaze to rise and meet Beau's. "I don't have control."

And wasn't that what they had both always feared? That Royal would lose his control, and all of the darkness he kept chained inside would break free. "Curran is working both sides. Freaking in bed with a Fed named Teresa Duncan."

"I warned you about getting too close with cops." Beau shook his head. "People change, man. He's not the boy from years ago."

No, he was a detective out for blood. "Curran knows about Will Kelly."

Beau's expression hardened. "Just what, exactly, does he know?"

"He thinks I put a bullet in Will's brain." *And he would not be wrong.*

Beau glanced over his shoulder toward the closed study door, then back at Royal. "He had a fourteen-year-old runaway in that garage."

Yes. And Beau had been the one to get her out of there. She'd been blindfolded. Terrified.

"He was going to shoot me in the back," Beau rasped. "You stopped him. You saved my life."

"I ended his, and I didn't hesitate."

"He would have killed me. Me and the girl. You fired first. That's all. *You fired first.*"

"I fired. That's what matters." His hands were still fisted. "You watched me so closely after that because you were worried I'd do it again. That I wouldn't just tie up the predators."

"Royal..."

"I would have fired that gun at Micah even with Curran yelling at me to stop." A stark truth. "But *she* screamed."

Beau blinked.

"Violet called for me. She wanted me to help her." He swallowed. "She'd found her friend in the trunk of the car. Simone had stab wounds all over her body. Violet wanted me to help, but I knew there wasn't anything I could do. The woman was dead even as her pulse kept struggling to beat."

"Shit."

"And all I could think was…if I hadn't taken Violet out of the trunk that night, it could have been her. If I hadn't broken through the glass of the service station in time…" He had cuts all over his fisted hands and up his forearms. "It could have been her. *I* was the one who put her in danger by allowing her to go out and meet Simone. I could have stopped her."

"Oh, yeah? How?"

"Handcuffed her to my bed, if necessary."

"Really?" Beau shook his head. "You just went after her brother for leaving her in a closet. I'm supposed to buy that you'd handcuff her and walk away? Try bullshitting someone else. She blinks those golden eyes and you do whatever she wants. And if that *whatever* includes taking her to hunt a killer? Well, I guess we both know what you already *did*."

"Fuck you."

"Fuck yourself." Beau didn't miss a beat. "You're out of control because you're *scared*. I'll mark the date on my calendar because this shit doesn't happen often. It's like a special holiday. The mighty Royal has fallen. Turns out, he's just a mere mortal like the rest of us."

"Is this supposed to be helping me? Are you helping right now?"

"Yeah, I am helping you." Beau rocked forward onto the balls of his feet. "I'm telling you what you are too blind to see."

"And just what would that be?" Royal fired right back. "Enlighten me. Share the big news."

"Fine. You are in love with this woman. Absolutely *insanely* in love with her."

Royal backed up a step. "You take that shit back."

"Because it's a lie?" Beau sent him a reckless smile. "Say it. Tell me that you don't love her. Tell me that I'm wrong."

Royal opened his mouth.

And Violet opened the door.

Chapter Nineteen

Violet poked her head inside the study. Her tousled hair slid over her shoulder. "I wanted to check on you." Her golden eyes swept over both Beau and Royal. "You two good?"

Hell, no, he was not *good*. But Royal pasted a smile on his face. "Be right out, sweetheart."

She nodded.

"Has that prick brother of yours apologized yet?" Royal heard himself ask.

She bit her lip. "You...you seriously punched him because of something we did when we were kids? Because he locked me in a closet during a game of hide and seek?"

"Because that's normal," Beau murmured. "Totally normal response to a long-ago situation."

Royal cut him a disgusted glance. Then he focused on what mattered. Violet. "He shouldn't have scared you." *And I shouldn't have put you at risk. I should have handcuffed you to the bed. There's where I'd like for you to be right now.*

Handcuffed. To my bed.

"You can't go around attacking my brother." She shook

241

her head. "You do stuff like that, and Christmas will be extremely awkward for everyone." Violet turned around and closed the door softly behind her.

Christmas?

Beau whistled. "Oh, yeah. Sure. You're not hopelessly and completely in love with her. Totally. Not you. Because it's ever so normal to punch and throat-grab a guy because of hide and seek?"

"She was scared," he bit off.

"*You're* scared now. Scared that you're going to lose her. Scared that she won't accept you and all those twisted pieces you think you have inside yourself. News flash, Royal. You're not some psychopathic predator. Maybe start using those skills of yours for good. Work with the Ice Breakers. Bring closure to victims. *Help* people. You can have a normal life. Have friggin' Christmas with her." He slapped a hand around Royal's shoulder. "Be happy. Stop thinking you aren't good enough."

He stiffened. Beau had *not* just gone there.

"I know you, brother. Inside and out. I know it's burned you alive over the years—always thinking you weren't good enough and that your family tossed you away."

"They did toss me away." *Because they'd known even then that something was wrong with me?* The thought that had run through his head all his life.

My family abandoned me when I was two years old. What in the hell had a two-year-old done that was so bad his family walked away and left him on a New Orleans street?

"I am your family," Beau told him fiercely. "I will never toss you away. I will never walk away."

No, Beau would not. Beau would try to fix him, as he'd done over and over again during their lives. Beau would try to help him. Always. Even when the guy should cut his losses and walk away. "You got the doctor of the dead to come to town for me."

"Just working my usual miracles."

"She's going to find more bodies."

"Then maybe she'll find proof on those bodies that will keep that prick Micah locked up. Because so what if he doesn't have marks from a taser? Maybe it didn't leave marks. Maybe it didn't cut through his clothes. Did you actually see him go down from the charge?"

No, he hadn't. Royal gave a negative shake of his head.

"I'd do anything for you." Beau's face had gone very, very serious. "I'd help you bury a body any day of the week, you know that. Only when we bury them, even the doctor of the dead wouldn't be able to dig them back up." Beau squeezed his shoulder. "I'm your family," he said again. "And that woman out there? The woman who has those sad eyes that look like she's just seen into hell? Why don't you *try* telling her how you really feel? Because I get the feeling she already knows some of your secrets, and she's not running away. Instead, she's coming in to check on you. She's running *to* you."

Royal swallowed. "I'm not good for her."

"Then be bad for her. Be the baddest bastard in the world. Be the bastard who protects her from any and every threat. You're *good* at that kind of thing." He let Royal go. "Now shall we go back and pretend that we're civilized?"

"I'll never be civilized."

"Yeah, well, being civilized is boring as hell, so I figure it just was never for us."

"She needs someone civilized," he heard himself say. "Someone polished. Someone who'll always be a gentleman." And not fuck her in the back of a car on the way home from a police station.

"Gentleman don't get jack done." Beau laughed. "You think a gentleman would know how to handle a killer? Not likely. Besides, why are you rattling off negatives? Let's be positive. You've got money to burn, you worship the woman, and you'll break the hand of anyone who hurts her. Win, win, win." He sauntered for the door. "Pretend you have control. Even if you don't. I don't know her brother, so I don't trust him. We never show our weaknesses to those we don't trust."

Royal didn't show his weaknesses to anyone.

Just like he didn't share his deepest, darkest secrets with anyone but Beau.

Except...*I shared with Violet.*

"Tell her you love her. See what she does. I think it might surprise you." Beau's back was to him.

"I...don't."

"Ah, cute. That lie just got caught in your throat." Beau looked back. "Want to try saying the words while you stare into my eyes? Wanna try lying right to my face? Think you can pull it off?"

Royal didn't speak.

"Didn't think so," Beau muttered, satisfied. "Just like I don't think you'll be able to lie to her face."

"She'll...leave." Shit. Why the hell had that slipped out?

Beau shook his head. "When they love you back—when someone really loves you—they don't leave." A pause. "I didn't leave."

But what if she doesn't love me back?

And then, from the darkest part of himself...*Why would she love me?*

* * *

"WHAT IN THE hell is happening here?" Micah yanked at the handcuff around his right wrist. The cuff attached to the railing on the side of his hospital bed. "I'm a victim! Victim! I should be treated with care and respect, and I shouldn't have my ass handcuffed!" He yanked at the cuff again.

"Easy." FBI Agent Teresa Duncan edged closer to the bed.

The detective—Curran Barlow—was right behind her. They'd arrived in Micah's room moments ago.

"We have some follow-up questions for you," Teresa said.

"Fuck your follow-ups!" Spittle flew from his mouth. "I need more pain meds." Where was the button for the nurse? A damn uniformed cop had been watching him for hours. He'd been trapped in the hospital bed, and Micah wanted *out*. "They had to stitch me up! Do you know that? I have like, six or seven stitches because the damn blade sliced me so badly!"

"I am aware," Teresa replied as if it were no big deal at all.

His life. No big deal. "This is bullshit. I want the cuff *off*. I told you—over and over—that I had nothing to do with the attack on Simone!"

"Not just an attack. We're talking about the matter of Simone Wilmont's murder," Curran inserted.

Murder. Simone is dead. He stopped yanking on the handcuff. "I got a call from her. She told me she needed a ride. I went to help." His same story. He wasn't changing his tune. He'd told the cops this crap before. "I arrived and some guy in a black mask and funny glasses ran at me."

"Funny glasses?" Curran prompted.

"Night vision BS, okay? He ran at me. Stabbed me. Then the next thing I know, I'm bleeding, I'm hurting, and Violet's crazy boyfriend has a gun in my face." His stare swept toward the cop. "You know the rest. You were there." The prick had cuffed him even as Micah lay bleeding on the ground.

"We found discarded night vision goggles near the location you were discovered," Teresa informed him.

"Fantastic for you."

"No prints were on them."

"Whatever."

"You say you never saw Simone at the gas station?" Teresa's head tilted to the right.

He swallowed. His throat felt raw and achy. "That's what I said."

"What about Violet?" the detective asked him. "Did you see her out there?"

"Just her gun-crazy boyfriend," Micah groused. But… "He's the one you should be questioning. He *attacked me*. Maybe he found out that Simone let Violet be taken that first night, and he got pissed and he decided to get some revenge and he—" Micah clamped his lips shut.

Too late.

Teresa stepped closer to his bed. "How did you know that Simone saw Violet get taken from the theater?"

"She didn't just see her get taken." Soft laughter came from him. A little rusty because his throat was so dry. "I think that—once Violet was back—I think that Simone made the light fall on Violet. I think she rigged the coffin to lock on her. Simone could be one cold bitch." Something he'd admired about her. "She wanted Violet's role, and she would have done anything to get it."

Silence.

Then, from the detective, "That's one hell of a way to speak about the dead. Want to tell me again how the woman who sustained over ten deep knife wounds into her body was one 'cold bitch' as you called her?"

Shit.

"And while you're telling us about that," Teresa sent him a chilling smile, "why don't you just tell us exactly what you know about a woman named Fiona Law?"

Fiona. Fuck.

"Just like Simone, Fiona was abducted and stabbed to death." Teresa blinked her pale blue eyes at him. "What would you know about her?"

Too much.

He was gonna need a lawyer, stat. A damn good one.

* * *

"I'm sorry for locking Violet in the closet," Dawson said as soon as Royal stepped back into the den. "I was a dumb punk kid." He pressed a wet, bloody cloth to his lower lip. "I freaked out and ran when the door jammed because I didn't know what to do. I was an absolute ass, and I *never* scared my sister again like that. Never."

Violet stood beside Dawson. Her gaze darted between her brother and Royal.

"I was thrilled when she told me that she'd been cast to do a show here in Savannah. Thought it would be a great chance for us to reconnect. Our mom died a few years ago, and I *missed* my family." Dawson lowered the cloth. "Instead, some psycho abducts her. When she comes to stay with me, she's terrified and screaming in the middle of the night."

Royal hated her fear.

"And then, the next thing I know, she's telling me that she's moving in with some club owner—some guy I have heard is tied to way too much trouble—and now...*this*." Dawson's eyes—a slightly darker gold than Violet's—flared with fury. "She's almost killed? I can't get hold of her, and I'm seeing these news stories and then—then you attack me!" A shake of his head. "I don't like you, man."

"The feeling is pretty mutual," Royal agreed silkily.

"Stop it." Violet stepped between them. "You attacked him, Royal. But he just apologized to you!"

"His apology should be for you. Not me. You're the one he left in the closet."

"I went back!" Dawson cried. "I tried to pry the dang door off! But it wouldn't budge." His breath heaved. "I was a kid! Scared as hell, but I swore then that I would never just stand by while my sister was afraid again." Dawson moved to her side. "But look what I'm doing." His shoulders slumped. "Twice you've been in danger—three times if you count that mess at the theater—"

Royal did count that as an attack.

"And I haven't done anything to help you." An exhale. "I *want* to help. Come back home with me, Violet. I'll stay with you. Parker has gotten leave. He'll be flying in as soon as he can. We can keep you safe." His right hand fisted the cloth, but his left reached out to curl around Violet's fingers. "We are your family. You belong with me and Parker."

We are your family.

A blood family. One raised together. A family that had never abandoned her. She would choose to go with her brother, Royal knew that. He was just trying to figure out how to stop himself from demanding—begging?—that she stay with him.

Don't leave me. I can be better. I will be better.

Violet's gaze swept toward him.

Beau was at his side. Kai was trying to be invisible a few feet away and…Violet pulled her hand from Dawson. She walked across the room with slow, graceful steps. A dancer's steps. She stopped in front of Royal. Tilted back her head. Then reached for Royal's hand. "I'm exactly where I want to be."

The drumming of Royal's heartbeat seemed far too loud. Maybe that drumming had made him misunderstand her. He shook his head.

Pain flashed on her face. "Don't you want me to be here?"

"You're the only thing I want." Flat.

"Good." He heard the click of her swallow. "Because I'm not leaving you."

Those words seemed to tear open something inside of him. He hauled her against him. Royal's mouth took hers. Claiming and consuming and worshipping all at the same time.

"Ahem." From close by. And followed immediately by a tap on Royal's shoulder. He wanted to ignore the tap, but he knew he couldn't.

"Really need to talk about the little matter of a serial killer," Beau informed him.

Yeah. They did.

Royal eased away from Violet. To be one hundred percent sure, he asked, "You're choosing me?"

"Always."

Hell, yes.

He stepped back, but brought her hand to his mouth so he could press a kiss to her knuckles.

"I thought the cops had someone in custody." Dawson's voice was tight. "They're not letting him go, are they?

They've got the killer? If they let him go after what he's done to my sister, I will kill him myself."

Royal laughed softly. "Get in line."

Dawson paled.

"By the way, sorry for the hit." This was Violet's brother, and he certainly didn't want Christmas to be awkward. *And I want every Christmas with her.* "And for the throat grab."

"You're apologizing?" Dawson squinted suspiciously at him.

Didn't it sound like he was? "But you ever do anything to so much as hurt her feelings, and you and I will have a problem."

"Control," Beau rasped.

"What?" Royal rolled back his shoulders. "I said *sorry.*"

"But then you threatened him," Beau pointed out.

"I never claimed to be perfect." Now, to focus... "Who wants to know about the serial killer?"

* * *

FIVE HOURS LATER, Detective Curran Barlow knocked at Royal's door.

Royal saw the guy on his security monitor and figured Curran was there to do one of three things.

Option A...*He's here to arrest my ass.*

Option B...*He's here to tell me that he's arrested Micah Wright for the murder of Simone Wilmont.*

Or, Option C...*He's here to tell me that he cut Micah free.*

Royal took his time going for the door. Violet and her brother were in the kitchen cooking with Beau. As for Kai, his friend was keeping watch. Out of sight, but close enough to rush forward in an emergency.

Royal opened the door. The detective appeared extra grim, with deeper lines cutting near his mouth and eyes. "You look like shit," Royal told him.

Curran grunted. "One day, those compliments will hurt my feelings." His stare swept over Royal. "I see you ditched the prison orange."

"For the moment." A pause. "You here to critique my wardrobe? Or was there another reason for this special visit?"

Curran glanced back at the reporters who waited just beyond Royal's property line, then his gaze returned to Royal. "You gonna let me over the threshold?"

"Got a warrant?"

Curran's jaw hardened. "Like that, is it?"

"You tell me, Detective Barlow."

"Can't. Too many eyes on us." A low whisper. Then he rolled back his shoulders. His voice rose as he said, "Thought you and Violet might like to know that Micah Wright has been placed under arrest for the murder of Simone Wilmont."

Tension slid to the pit of Royal's belly. "Thought you weren't so sure he was the bad guy. What about those taser marks you mentioned?"

"Maybe the taser never connected with him. Other evidence is strong. The Feds think he fits for the crimes."

"Do tell."

"Let me into the house. Don't really want to lay out the whole case on your front porch."

Royal backed up a step.

"Thanks. Really rolling out the welcome mat, aren't you?"

"At least I didn't toss you into the back of a patrol car."

Curran winced. He also shut the door behind him.

Footsteps tapped toward them. Royal wasn't the least bit surprised to see Violet, Dawson, and Beau hurrying right for him and Curran.

"What's happening?" Violet asked. Her eyes were wide as she immediately moved to Royal's side.

Curran surveyed the group. His attention lingered a bit on Dawson. "The brother, I presume? You have her eyes. A little darker."

"What's happening?" Dawson echoed Violet.

Beau didn't ask questions. He just waited.

"An arrest has been made," Curran told them. "Came here personally to share the news that Micah Wright is being charged with Simone Wilmont's murder."

"What made you change your mind?" Royal asked.

"Never said my mind needed changing. But there were procedures to follow. We recovered a knife in the field about fifty yards from the gas station. Turns out, that bloody knife matches a set in Micah's home. Appears the bastard took his butcher knife from home to carve up Simone."

Violet sucked in a sharp breath.

"More circumstantial evidence has piled up against him, material I am not at liberty to discuss just yet. However, I believe you might find it interesting to know that Micah briefly dated Fiona Law last year. She left him and told her friends he was too controlling." His hands remained loose at his sides even as his attention shifted back to Royal. "But something tells me you already knew about his connection to Fiona, didn't you?"

Yeah, he might know about that. "If you and your new Fed friend keep digging, you'll see he frequently traveled to Atlanta. Did a lot of work with the ballet there." No emotion entered Royal's voice. He made sure of that fact. "You might even discover that he often visited the restaurant where Marcella White served as assistant manager."

Violet's shoulder bumped into his arm.

"And just *when* were you going to share that intel with me?" Curran burst out. He stepped even closer to Royal. "Or were you *not* going to share? This part of your vigilante BS? You were closing in for the kill?"

"I believe that Micah is still breathing, thanks to you, detective. As to when I was going to share intel, you're the detective. Thought you'd have intel of your own. Or at least, I would have thought your Fed buddy would." He smiled and knew the sight would hold no humor. "The news about Micah's visits to the restaurant just came to me a few hours ago. Someone I knew in Atlanta saw the news story about Simone's murder. Micah's picture—and my own—have been flashed everywhere as a result of that story. This person thought I might find the connection... pertinent."

"Yeah, it's real pertinent, all right. That person got a name? Because I'll be wanting to follow up."

"I'll be sure and send you all the contact information." He waited a beat. "Is Micah still in the hospital or has he been transferred to a holding cell?"

Curran shook his head. "Not telling you where he is right now. Just wanted you to know that he was being charged." He waved toward Violet. "It's over. You are safe now. You can go back to the life you had." His expression hardened. "I would really recommend that you go back to that life."

He means a life before me.

"Apparently, that life involved working right beside a sadistic killer," Violet returned in her cool, quiet voice. "So I think I'll try something different in the future." She did not move from Royal's side.

"Ah, excuse me." Dawson barreled forward. "Why won't you tell us where he is? If this guy is after my sister, I damn well would like to know if he's in some hospital bed with minimum security or if he's locked in a cell. I *really, really* want his ass locked away."

"I'm not saying for Micah's safety."

"For *his* safety?" Dawson's jaw nearly hit the floor. "You kidding me?"

Curran returned his dark stare to Royal. "No, I'm not kidding you. He'll get a real judge and jury to decide his fate. I don't want him dead before arraignment." An incline of his head. "We'll be talking soon, Royal."

"Can't wait, buddy."

Curran left. Royal shut and bolted the door behind him. Beau crept close to him. "Might want to secure everything in the house," Beau murmured. A murmur meant for Royal alone. "In case any cops decide they do want to come back here with a warrant."

Yeah, he'd be taking care of things.

"Need a hand with that?" Beau asked.

Royal gave a slight nod.

"On it." Beau walked away, whistling as if he didn't have a care in the world.

Some family members were absolutely priceless.

"*What is happening?*" Dawson seemed to practically vibrate. "Why is a cop acting like you're a breath away from committing murder or something?" He stared at Royal as if Royal was...yeah, the monster.

Some family members are gonna be a pain in my ass. "Probably shouldn't ask questions if you don't truly want to hear the answers."

"Hell." Dawson swallowed. His Adam's apple clicked. "Hell," he repeated.

Violet stepped between Dawson and Royal. She stared straight up at Royal, and he could see the hope in her eyes. "The cops aren't letting Micah go."

Not unless some dumbass judge gave him a bail that Micah could meet. And in that case...*I may have to hunt again.* Instead of saying that, though, because her brother already looked close enough to fainting, Royal responded, "My gut tells me that the doctor of the dead is going to turn up more evidence." He'd told Violet all about Tony's arrival.

"You mean she'll turn up more victims."

He dipped his head toward her. "If the cops and Feds get enough proof, Micah will never see the light of a free day again." His hand rose, and his fingers curled carefully under her chin. "You are safe."

And I will keep you that way.

Chapter Twenty

THREE DAYS LATER...

THE BALLET HAD BEEN CANCELED. How could it not be canceled? The artistic director was in jail, charged with murdering one of the dancers. And, according to the authorities, Micah Wright was a person of interest in the deaths of three other women.

Violet stood on the stage and stared out at all the empty seats. The theater felt huge. Cavernous. There was no music. No applause. No dancers gliding across the stage as they tried to create some magic for the attendees.

There wasn't any magic in the theater. Standing on that stage just made her feel sad.

"Violet?"

She jerked at the call of her name. Her head turned to the right, and a man stepped from the shadows on the stage.

"Violet Murphy." He advanced slowly. "I don't think we've formally met." He wore khakis, a crisp, white shirt, and a blue blazer. "I'm Leo Barnes." His hand extended toward her. "Dr. Barnes. I've been, uh, hired to help the crew during this time of upheaval and grief."

Dr. Barnes. The name clicked for her as she automatically extended her hand. "You're the psychiatrist."

The backers behind the show had given the cast and crew a compensation package—and they were also encouraging everyone to get counseling. *Because when your boss turns out to be a killer who murders one of your castmates, that could leave a psychological mark or two on your psyche.*

Violet didn't want to think too much about her battered psyche. She wanted to just keep putting one foot in front of the other. If she thought too much about everything that had happened—about Simone—she was afraid that she might start crying and not stop.

His fingers lightly squeezed hers, and then he let her go. "Yes." A nod of his head. The light hit on his brown hair. His warm, green eyes studied her with a hint of sympathy. "I'm the psychiatrist. I heard a lot of the crew were here, cleaning out dressing rooms and lockers, and I just wanted to see if I could be of any assistance to anyone."

There were plenty of others in the theater—not out front, in the seats. But backstage. Picking up the remains of a show that would never be.

"You haven't scheduled an appointment with me," he noted carefully.

"No, I haven't." She looked back at the empty seats.

"I don't bite."

Her gaze cut to him.

He sent her a quick, friendly smile. "I'm sure the other dancers can attest to the fact that I'm a very good listener." Again, sympathy flashed in his eyes. "Of everyone here, you're the one who should be getting the most attention."

"I'm fine."

"Are you? Or do you just tell people that so they won't realize how close you are to the edge?"

Her sweaty palms pressed to the front of her jeans. Had he felt the sweat when they shook hands?

"It's okay not to be *fine*, Violet. It's okay to feel guilty that you're alive."

She flinched.

"Survivor's guilt." He nodded. "Completely natural. It's okay to feel that guilt. It's okay to feel angry. To feel vengeful. It's okay to want to scream and cry and rage at the world." He didn't move any closer to her. "I can be your safe space. You need to talk with someone."

"Micah told me to go and see you." He'd even given her the doctor's card. Violet was pretty sure she'd lost it.

He winced. "Well, I can get where that would hardly be a ringing endorsement for me."

She crossed her arms over her chest.

"If you would prefer to talk with someone else, I have the names of several colleagues I could recommend for you," Leo offered. "There are some wonderful counselors in the area. I just—I truly want to help. I've been a long supporter of the arts here in Savannah." And this time, his gaze darted to the theater seats. Or rather, to the boxed seats in the right corner. "My late wife loved the show. We always had season tickets. Coming here still reminds me of her."

His late wife? "I'm sorry for your loss."

His stare lingered on the box. "Grief hits us all in different ways. Sometimes, we think we're in control." His green gaze slid back to her. "But then the pain will sneak up on us at the oddest times. It's impossible to be strong every moment." His lips curled down. "You don't have to face the darkness alone."

"She's not alone." Royal's strong voice. He came from stage left, emerging from the shadow of the red curtains there, and Violet wondered just how long he had been watching and listening.

The wooden stage creaked lightly beneath his steps as he crossed to them.

Leo's eyes widened. "Royal Boudreaux. The hero of the hour." He extended his hand to Royal. "I've seen the news stories on you."

"Don't like that title at all." Royal stared at the offered hand, then slowly took it. "I didn't do anything. Violet saved herself. She's the one who stabbed the asshole."

"Well, from what I saw Violet tell the media, she views you as quite the hero. I'm Dr. Leo Barnes, by the way. Don't think our paths have crossed before."

"Violet knows exactly what I am. And what I'm not." He released Leo's hand and his attention shifted to Violet. "Kai put the stuff from your dressing room in the car. We're ready whenever you are."

Right. She'd asked for a few moments so she could just say goodbye to the stage. No, not the stage. *To Simone.* To the life Violet had known before. Was that weird? Did it even matter if it was?

"Take as long as you need, sweetheart," Royal added. "There's no rush."

He'd been at her side for the last few days. Watching. Worrying. But the threat had passed. She was safe. She knew he couldn't stay by her side all the time. He had his businesses. His life.

She had hers.

They hadn't talked about the future yet. What would

the future look like? He'd offered her protection, but she didn't need that any longer.

I still need him, though. Violet thought that she just might always need him.

"I was offering my services to Violet," Leo explained when the silence stretched a little too long. "I'm a psychiatrist. I'm helping to counsel some of the other cast members. Thought Violet might need someone to talk with."

"She's got me," Royal returned, voice flat.

Leo laughed softly. "I'm sure she does. But a significant other can't always provide the assistance that a trained psychiatrist can. When nightmares come, when the flashbacks won't stop, Violet might like to speak with someone who has professional expertise."

The nightmares still come. Last night, she'd woken up screaming. Convinced that she was in the trunk of the sedan once again.

"Surely, you would permit Violet to seek the help she needs?"

"I don't *permit* Violet do to anything. She does whatever the hell she wants. Always. I'm just there to make sure no one hurts her *while* she's doing what makes her happy."

"That's an excellent response," Leo praised. "So good to have a supportive partner."

Royal grunted. "I've seen your face before."

Violet caught the flash of surprise in the doctor's eyes.

"Excuse me?" Then Leo smiled again. "Well, I have been trying to help the other—"

"It was the night I danced with Violet. The charity dance. You were there."

"Uh, yes, yes, I was." A bob of Leo's head. "I donate quite substantially to the ballet in Savannah. My wife was a dancer in her youth, until a bike riding accident ended her career when she was just seventeen. She'd always dreamed of dancing on a stage, with the lights all around her. Since that dream couldn't come true, Vanessa worked diligently to make sure that dream could be possible for others." A soft sigh. "We both always supported the arts as much as possible."

"His wife passed away," Violet said.

"I know," Royal returned.

Not really the expected response. He was right at her side now, so she elbowed him. *When you hear that someone has lost a loved one, you're supposed to offer condolences.*

After her poke, Royal added, "I heard you talking to the blonde who was at your side the night of the charity dance. She was speaking about your wife."

"You have a very good memory," Leo noted.

"I do."

"And you don't really care about the polite conventions of society at all, do you?"

"Not at all."

Violet elbowed him again.

Brows raising, Royal peered at her. "Is that your sign that you're ready to go?"

Heat flushed in her cheeks. "Sure, yes." Whatever. "Nice to meet you, doctor."

"Let me give you my card. In case you change your mind about my help." He reached into his blazer and pulled out a business card. He extended it toward her.

Violet took the card. Their fingers brushed.

"You don't have to be afraid," Leo told her. "I can keep your secrets." His gaze slid to Royal. "I can keep secrets for both of you." He straightened his already straight blazer. "Be careful when you leave. The reporters just won't give up, will they? Saw them out front and out back." He turned on his heel and strode back toward the side of the stage.

"Royal," she began, voice low, "you're supposed to say *sorry*."

"Why? I didn't kill his wife."

Her eyes widened. Her hand flew up—the hand not holding the business card—and she pressed her fingers over his mouth. *"Don't!"*

He stared at her.

Then his tongue slid out and licked her palm.

She immediately snatched her hand back. "You...you were doing all that deliberately. Being difficult."

"Difficult?" Royal seemed to taste the word. "Probably." A nod. "Definitely."

"His wife *died*."

"I saw him at the charity dance."

"Yes, you said that already—"

"I saw him when you first appeared on the staircase that night."

Something about his tone had her tensing.

"He looked like he could eat you alive."

Her mouth fell open. Then snapped closed. "You're wrong."

"No. I understood his expression because I knew that I was looking at you the same way. Didn't like the prick from that moment onward."

"I—" She tried to regain control of the conversation. She also glanced to the side, and, dammit, Leo was still close enough that he'd probably overheard. Mostly because Royal had made no attempt to lower his voice. "You're wrong, I'm sure."

Royal shrugged. "Don't think so."

She shoved the business card into her pocket.

"Don't like him sniffing around you."

"He was offering help." Her eyes narrowed. "You're in a mood, aren't you?"

"A mood?" Royal seemed to choke on those words.

"Yeah, you've been extra growly and dark all day. Ever since I said I needed to come by the theater and pack up. Look, the show isn't running—everyone agrees it's basically cursed. I had to pack up so I could leave—"

His growl broke through her words.

"Leave," she repeated, deliberately.

He growled again.

Her eyes widened. "Is...is that what this is about? You're worried about me leaving?"

"You have to leave town, sooner or later. Just didn't realize you were planning to go so soon." He took a step away from her. "I think I want to have another word with the good doctor."

She grabbed his arm. "I'm not planning to leave town yet. The ballet's board of directors actually indicated they might want me staying on to potentially help direct the next production." Her heart was suddenly racing. And not just at the idea of getting a chance to organize and direct a show. Again, choosing her words deliberately, she told him, "I'm not planning to leave *you*." Did he want her gone? The thought had her stomach knotting.

Royal turned to steel beneath her touch. "Probably not the place to have this discussion."

He was—probably—right. But she'd started and couldn't seem to stop. "You saved my life here."

"And you saved mine in that fucking winery." Low, just for her.

"Wh-what?" Violet shook her head. He was wrong. "I didn't. You were the one rescuing me."

"All depends on how you look at it." And, suddenly, he was looking straight at her. Seeming to look into her. "I was headed straight to hell, sweetheart, and I knew it."

No. "Royal…"

"Then I met you. Touched a piece of heaven." His knuckles skimmed down her cheek. "But the devil isn't meant to keep heaven with him, is he?"

Her hand grabbed his wrist. Held tightly. "You aren't the devil."

"Then who the hell am I?"

This was simple. "You're mine."

His long, dark lashes flickered.

"Just like I'm yours." She edged closer to him. Her head tilted back as she stared up at him. "You were right. This probably isn't the place for this talk."

A muscle jerked along his jaw. "You done here?"

"For now."

His hand twisted, fell, and then he was holding *her* hand clasped within his much stronger grip as he led her off the stage. Not down the front steps, but through the curtain and through the snaking, twisting halls in the back. They didn't stop at her dressing room. Though she had a sudden, vivid memory of the two of them in there, together. He kept going, never slowing, and soon they were right in front of the rear theater door.

"Ignore any reporters," he told her gruffly. "Doesn't matter what they say. We keep going. Bastards have been digging into my past, and they're going to throw a ton of BS our way. I can explain everything they say about me. I *will* explain everything."

"Or you don't have to explain a single thing."

His head wrenched toward her.

"I trust you," she told him simply. The total truth.

"Why?" Ragged.

Oh, that was simple, too. Her lips parted to reply.

"No, dammit, I'm getting you out of here. If you say something sweet and sexy, I'll go crazy and try to fuck you right here." He sucked in a breath. "I've been trying to be *good* the last few days. You were grieving. You needed care. You still need it."

"I need you."

A jerky nod. "You're gonna get me."

Finally.

He shoved open the door. Sure enough, plenty of reporters were waiting. The theater had extra guards on hand, but some of the other dancers didn't seem to mind the reporters. In fact, plenty of people were talking eagerly with the press.

Royal guided her past Dante, and she heard her former co-star tell a redhead with a microphone, "Yes, yes, I was there when the light came toppling down on the stage." He shuddered. "Horrifying. But not nearly as horrifying as learning that Simone was killed by Micah. We *trusted* him." A sigh. "You just can't ever know someone, can you?"

Violet's steps hurried forward.

But the reporters had noticed her. And Royal.

"Royal!" A shout from a man on the right.

"Boudreaux!" From a woman in dark blue.

"Is it true that you were questioned in conjunction with the murder of Will—" The question was cut off, mostly because so many other voices were suddenly blasting over the reporter's voice.

"Violet, Violet!" The woman who'd been interviewing Dante dashed toward her. "Were you aware that your hero was suspected of murder?"

She could see the limo. Kai was already out of the

vehicle. Glaring at the crowd. She'd talked to Kai more in the last few days. He'd moved to Savannah from Hawaii a few years before, gotten a job with Beau and become tight with both Beau and Royal. He was quiet, unless he was ragging on his two best friends, and the man had been a steady—and intimidating—guard since the world had come crashing down on Violet.

"Violet!" Another reporter had his phone up and on her. The phone partially blocked his face as he filmed. "Is it true that you and Micah had a sexual relationship?"

That question had come often in the past few days. She'd denied it, over and over again.

Now, she just pushed forward.

"Royal!" A man stepped into her path. Gray suit. Sunglasses that threw Violet's reflection back at her. "Royal, I need to talk with you about your family!"

She heard Royal's rumbling growl behind her.

This man wasn't filming. No microphone. No phone clutched tightly in his hand. Instead, he was just standing there.

"Get out of the way," Royal snapped at him.

"*Your family wants to see you.*"

Her heart lurched in her chest even as she staggered to a stop. His family? The family that had abandoned Royal all those years ago? She glanced back. "Royal?"

Fury marked every line and plane of his face. "I'm not dealing with bullshit. Get out of the way or I move you," he told the man.

Her head whipped back around.

The stranger stepped to the side. Probably a wise choice.

Kai grabbed Violet's hand and hauled her forward. He

tucked her into the back of the limo even as she looked back and saw Royal lean in close to the stranger.

What is happening?

* * *

"I'M NOT DEALING WITH BULLSHIT," Royal told the stranger, completely aware that his voice had gone low and lethal.

Sweat trickled down the man's cheek. "I-I was sent by your family."

Royal laughed. "Do you know how many of my *family* members have reached out to me in the last few days?" He knew others would pick up his words, and he didn't care. "Not in the mood for the scam today. Go try your luck somewhere else."

"But—"

But nothing. Royal strode away.

"My employer isn't the kind of person you tell no."

What the hell was that? A threat? Laughter spilled from Royal as he whirled back to face the older man. "No," he said clearly. "You can quote me on that to your employer." Then he climbed into the limo. Kai slammed the door behind him.

Chapter Twenty-One

Royal's hands fisted at his sides. He sat on the leather seat and stared straight ahead at the woman he did consider part of his family. Only he hadn't gotten around to actually telling her that fact. Mostly because he didn't know how, and he was very, very worried he'd screw things to hell and back when he tried.

Hey, Violet, so...Beau was right about me. I'm an idiot who completely loves you. Any chance you want to give me a shot at convincing you to stay with me? Always?

When she'd been standing on that stage, when he'd realized she was saying goodbye to the show, he'd understood that there would be another town for her. Another production. She'd only been in Savannah for a temporary period. She'd hit the road again. It was only a matter of time.

And what was he supposed to do then?

The screen between the front and rear of the limo lowered. "Those jokers just won't leave you alone, will they?" Kai sounded disgusted. "Knew you'd been getting phone calls and texts since your story went national. Some people have no damn shame."

"I'm not buying the lies about my long-lost family." He wasn't some green idiot. "Don't worry about me."

"Good." Kai had driven them away from the theater. "Don't know what's worse. The reporters or the people suddenly pretending to be family. I got your back, know it. I'll make sure the creep in the gray suit doesn't get close again."

"Thanks, man."

"Know it," Kai repeated. The screen rose back into place.

Royal looked over at Violet. So beautiful. Staring at her took his breath away. She wore red again. An oversized, red blouse that seemed to be made of silk. It fell lightly over her shoulders. It reminded him of the dress she'd worn the first time they'd danced.

"Where are we headed?" Violet asked.

"Punishment." He cleared his throat. "Got a few things I need to take care of there." Some files that he had to make sure remained hidden. The cops hadn't come to search his home or businesses yet, but it paid to be careful. "Don't you want to ask me some questions?"

"Do you have something you want to tell me?" Her hands were on her lap. She wore faded blue jeans. Black flats on her feet.

He swallowed. "Kai made sure the limo was clear. No listening devices."

"Uh, is that something we have to worry about? Listening devices being stashed in one of your rides?"

Unfortunately, yes. "Some of the Feds want to lock me up for murder."

She just waited.

"Will Kelly." Saying the name had his mouth tightening with distaste. "He was a bastard who got off on hurting young girls. Hurting them. Killing them."

She nodded. "He's someone you hunted and left for the cops to find?"

Okay. This part was going to be hard. And he almost didn't want to look into her eyes as he revealed the truth. Almost? Hell. He might have traded part of his soul not to tell her this. But if he was going to ask her to stay with him, then she had to know everything. "He's a man I killed."

She didn't blanch. Didn't draw back in horror. She just watched him and waited.

"Sweetheart." He found himself leaning toward her. "Shouldn't you be getting scared right now?"

Her hand rose to touch his cheek. He'd shaved cleanly that morning, and her palm pressed to his skin. "Sweetheart," Violet said softly, huskily, "why do you look at me like you're the one who is scared?"

Because I don't want you to hate me. I don't want you to leave me. And I'm scared you will go running. Sooner or later, didn't everyone run? "They're not my family," he said. Hell. Talk about a conversational jump.

She went right on touching him. Staring at him with those gorgeous eyes that seemed to see right into his soul.

"Some reporter dug up my past. Found out that I was dumped in New Orleans. No family to ever claim me. And that same reporter knows I have money to burn these days." His lips twisted. "So the orphan boy who is suddenly a hero..." *Or a villain, depending on who told the story.* "He's got people coming out of the woodwork, claiming to be family."

"Like the man behind the theater. The guy in the gray suit."

"Yeah, like him," Royal agreed. "Only that jackass and the people like him aren't my real family. They're just after some cash." Opportunists who'd come rushing for a potential payday. "My family abandoned me long ago, and they never looked back." A stark truth.

"Did you ever look for them?"

He sucked in a breath.

"You're such a good hunter," she added as her soft palm pressed against him. "Did you hunt for them? You must have."

She did know him well. He'd looked. Not because he wanted them to take him back with open arms and tear-stained cheeks, but because he'd wanted to know who the hell they were. "There wasn't anything to find. I was thrown away. Left like garbage. No one came for me while I was growing up. Just Beau. He was there." The brother that fate had given to him. "I did look some, when I was older, but there was nothing to find. It was like I'd never existed before that day." *Tell her. Tell. Her.* "I used to think I was thrown away because my family knew that I wasn't good enough for them."

"Royal..."

"I killed Will Kelly." Flat. "The cops aren't ever going to find enough evidence to convict me, but I did it. I pulled the trigger, and I ended his life."

She...moved forward. Hugged him.

His hands hovered in the air above her. Afraid to touch her, in case he'd break her. "Violet?"

"Hug me back," she ordered him.

He did. "I just told you I killed a man." She shouldn't ask him to hug her in response.

"You told me that, yes. And yet you didn't kill the other two predators. You left them alive. That means something happened with Will that was different," she said into his shirtfront. "Did he attack you? Was he about to kill another girl? Who did you save?"

"Beau." Raspy. Rusty. "Will was going to shoot at Beau. Beau came to try and stop me from doing something stupid." A broken laugh escaped him. "Story of our lives. And there was a young girl there. Beau was getting her out, Will got a gun, and he was going to shoot my brother." *My family.* "I couldn't let it happen."

"So you fired your gun."

"Yes."

"Did you leave any evidence behind?"

Another laugh. "Baby, I told you, they won't ever be able pin that on me. They have suspicions, but nothing will stick." The gun he'd used was long gone. No one would ever recover it. He knew how to cover his tracks.

She eased back. Peered up at him. "You're that good?"

No, I'm that bad. "You will run from me."

"Why are you so certain of that?"

"Because you deserve better than me."

"Stop it." Anger roughened her voice.

Surprise had him blinking.

"Don't you *dare* talk that way about the man I love, do you understand me?"

He did not speak. Mostly because he couldn't.

"This is some absolute bullshit," she fired back. "You are great. You've saved me. Over and over, you've been there for me. Listen up, Royal. I want to be with you. Now. Always. I want you to take me to New Orleans, and I want you to show me why the city is so beautiful to you. I want you to make me jambalaya, and I want to dance with you while jazz music plays in the air around us. I want to be with you." Her gaze searched his. "It's you. Don't you get that? For me, it's just *you*."

The loud drumming of his heartbeat filled Royal's ears. "Did you just say that you love me?"

"Yes, that is exactly what I said. And don't tell me it's too soon. Don't tell me it's some crazy hero-worship crap. I know what I feel. I know that when I'm scared, I want you with me. I know that when I'm happy, you're beside me. I know that when I think of the future, I think of one with you. Me. Us." Her hand lowered from his cheek. "And I know that in that future, I see a family. *Our* family. Where everyone belongs. Where everyone is wanted. And loved so much."

He had to swallow. Twice. "I didn't use protection the other day." In this limo. Nearly in this exact same spot.

"I didn't want you to use protection. I happen to think a mini-Royal would be pretty wonderful."

"A mini-Violet would be even better."

She blinked quickly. "Royal…"

"I'm scared." Stark. Rough.

Another blink. "Why?"

"Because I shouldn't want you so much. Because you are too good for me, and I know it. But I don't want to let you go. I want to put the entire world at your feet. Anything you want, you whisper it to me, and it's yours. I would fight, lie, and kill for you in an instant." Now that he'd started, he couldn't stop. "I'm not even sure this is love. It's darker than I thought love would be. Consuming." On the verge of obsession. "I just know that when I think of my life, I think of you. *You* are life for me, Violet. I don't want to let you go."

Her mouth came close to his. "Then don't. Don't ever let go."

His lips pressed to hers.

But...Sweetheart, there is more I have to tell you.

"Royal?"

"Trouble's coming." He could all but feel it. His instincts screamed at him. "And we need to be ready." He reached into his pocket and pulled out the new switchblade he'd bought for her. He tucked it into her palm.

"You always give me the best presents."

* * *

"This is bullshit," Micah growled. He was out of the hospital. Still freaking in pain and with stitches in his side, and he was at the police station. In an interrogation room with his stuffy lawyer sitting at his side. "I've told you a million times, I did not kill Simone."

"But you were fucking her," FBI Agent Teresa Duncan pointed out.

"Yes," he hissed. "But fucking isn't a crime."

Teresa and the detective shared a long look. Then Teresa glanced back at Micah. He did not like the smirk on her face.

"We recovered a butcher knife at the scene. It was covered in Simone's blood. Violet had mentioned her attacker had a knife, but in the struggle with him, she thought the knife fell. It wasn't recovered inside the old gas station, but our crime techs did find the weapon about fifty yards away."

"Okay, great. Then you can run it for prints." He straightened. The stitches pulled. "And when you get the real killer, I expect you to apologize to me. A nice, public apology because you have trashed my reputation." Fury boiled within him. "They canceled my show. Can you believe that? I had dancers and crew members counting on me. We'd had freaking sold out shows booked."

"A woman died," Detective Curran Barlow reminded him.

Micah cut a glance at his lawyer. The old guy glared at him. "Yeah, yeah, and I'm grieving for Simone," Micah rushed to say. "But I didn't *kill* her."

"Then why were your prints on the knife?" Teresa asked in fake confusion. She blinked her beady eyes at him. "To be specific, a thumb print. Right on the inside of the handle."

As if on cue, the door opened. A uniformed cop walked inside. He held a big, plastic bag. And inside that bag? One big-ass butcher knife.

Oh, shit.

It looked just like the knife that he had in his kitchen. In his knife block.

"We searched your house," Curran told him even as the uniform put the plastic bag down right in the middle of the table and then walked out. "You have a nice knife block in your kitchen. Very fancy. Very high-end."

Sweat trickled down Micah's back.

"Weird thing, though," Curran continued as he scratched his chin. "One knife was missing from that block. Want to guess which one?"

He stared through the plastic. He could have sworn that he saw dried blood on the blade. Simone's blood?

"Don't say a word," his lawyer instructed. He clamped a hand on Micah's shoulder.

Micah shoved that hand away. Don't say a word? Was the guy crazy? "I'm being framed!"

"Oh, yeah? Who's framing you?" Curran wanted to know.

"The real killer!" Clearly. "Someone stole my knife."

"So it *is* your knife?" Teresa pushed.

"I—"

"My client has nothing to say," the lawyer interrupted fiercely. "Not like my client can look at some random knife and know who it belongs to!"

"Not random." Teresa's response was cool. "That knife is the murder weapon."

"Not a word," his lawyer bit out. "You don't have anything to say to them, Micah."

Wrong. He had plenty to say. He wasn't going to be locked away. He was *not*. "Someone stole the knife! It probably has my print on it because it was mine, but the real killer must have worn gloves, so he didn't leave his prints on the damn thing." His breath heaved out. "I was *stabbed*. He stabbed me."

The lawyer cleared his throat. Loudly. "Have you received the results from the examination of the switchblade?"

"The blade that Violet used on her attacker?" Teresa flickered a glance the lawyer's way. "We're still searching for that weapon."

"You haven't *found* it?" Micah exploded. "Hello! Isn't that a giant red flag? The killer obviously took it from the scene. He is setting me up!"

"Did this mysterious killer also date Fiona Law?" Teresa wanted to know.

Shit. "That was a brief hookup," he gritted. "A friend introduced us."

"Uh, huh." Curran crossed his arms over his chest. "And does this friend have a name?"

"*I am not a killer!*"

Curran opened his mouth to reply.

And the door to the interrogation room opened again. It was the same young cop who'd come in a few moments before. The kid's face appeared tense. "The doctor...she found more."

More? And what doctor?

Teresa rose. She hurried toward the cop. Whispered with him.

More sweat trickled down Micah's back.

"Don't say another word," the lawyer groused.

Teresa turned back toward them. "I didn't realize that your great-uncle was the owner of the Freemont Winery."

"Uh, yeah."

"You didn't mention that fact before," Teresa said. "I actually discovered it last night after doing a ton of research on several shell companies."

"My, um, great-uncle used to own a lot of property." He raked a hand through his hair. "A lot has been sold off." Mentioning that he went out there every now and then to tend to some grapevines didn't seem like a good idea. Was it a fucking crime that he'd always enjoyed making some wine? Probably, in the eyes of the cops. "His ex-wife manages things. She sells stuff to help provide for his medical care. Guy lost his mind. Doesn't know what's happening around him."

Teresa's heels tapped across the floor. "Violet Murphy was abducted and taken to that winery, and you saw no need to mention your great-uncle owned the place?"

His lips clamped together.

"Thought it might make you look guilty, huh?" Curran asked.

Yeah, actually, he had thought that.

"Not. A. Word." From the lawyer.

Was that all the over-priced prick could say?

"We have an expert who has been searching the winery." Teresa peered down at Micah. "The cop just came in to inform me that our expert has made a startling discovery. At least two bodies are buried at the winery."

Oh, fuck. He shook his head.

Teresa had returned to her side of the table. But she didn't sit. She stared straight at him. "Guess that spot was special for you, huh? Those your first kills?"

"I haven't killed anyone!"

"First kills are usually sloppy," she told him. "So I'm looking forward to finding the evidence you left behind." She slapped her hands on the table and leaned toward him. "And then I will nail your ass to the wall."

He leapt to his feet. "It wasn't me! It's a setup! Can't you see that?" He lunged for her.

And the uniformed cop who was still in the room grabbed him and slammed Micah face-first into the table. He thrashed against the cop's hold. "Look, dammit! Fine, fine—I made the light fall on stage! I did that shit. I just—I wanted the publicity! If Violet got a few scratches, I knew it would be one hell of a story. *But I'm not a killer!* I'm not!"

His lawyer was yelling, but Micah didn't care. He fought the young cop. Twisted so he could at least see—Curran. The detective was frowning at him. "It's a setup!" Spittle flew from Micah's mouth. "Someone lured me out to that godforsaken gas station! When Simone called me, she told me that she knew what I'd done. That I had to come or she'd go to the cops." A snarl broke from him. "Don't you see? Someone wanted me to be at that place! Someone wants me to pay for all these crimes. But I didn't do it! I swear, I didn't kill anyone!"

* * *

THE LAST TIME she'd been in Punishment, it had been filled with dancers. Music. Laughter. The lights had rolled over the crowd. Concealing. Revealing.

She'd danced on the floor with Royal. They'd started their pretend relationship on the dance floor so that others would see them and believe they'd fallen hard for each other.

Simone was here. She was worried and didn't want to leave me on my own.

"I'll stay out front," Kai announced. "If you need me, just shout."

His voice pulled Violet out of the memory. Her head turned in time to catch Kai giving a little salute as he stepped back outside.

The club wouldn't open for hours. It was just her and Royal inside. And he was heading for the spiral staircase. Or, he had been. He'd stopped and extended his hand toward her.

Royal said he loved me.

Then they'd arrived at Punishment, and she hadn't been given the chance to say anything else to him. They'd kissed in the limo. She could still taste him. Could feel the heat of his mouth seeming to linger against her own.

She hurried toward him and took his offered hand. The stairs squeaked a little beneath their steps, and then, a few moments later, they were on the second floor. He unlocked his door. Ushered her inside and turned on the lights.

Her gaze darted to his desk.

He went down on me right here.

Why did that seem so long ago?

"What is causing that blush, sweetheart?" Royal murmured. "Reliving the past? Or thinking about the future?"

A little bit of both.

He hurried around the desk. Then to the wall. An abstract piece of artwork hung on that wall. Reds and blacks on the white canvas. He lifted it up to reveal a wall safe. She watched in silence as he turned the dial and then entered a code. He even scanned his retina.

High-tech.

The safe opened. "Got most things out already. Just needed to get one more item." His hand swept inside. Royal pocketed something so small she could barely even see it. "A drive with some important files," he told her as he turned back her way. "I like to have a backup." He shut the safe. Put the canvas back into place.

Then he turned toward her.

And when he turned toward her, horror flashed on his handsome face. Horror, wiped away immediately by blinding rage.

She tensed. "Royal?"

That was when she felt the flutter on her shoulder. A light, soft touch.

And then the blade of a knife pressed to her throat.

Chapter Twenty-Two

"GET HIM OUT OF MY SIGHT!" TERESA BLASTED.

The uniform hauled Micah away from the table.

Blood covered the lower right side of the guy's shirt, red staining the garish orange. Dammit. "He tore open his stitches," Curran said. What a pain in the ass. The last thing they needed was this guy saying he'd been roughhoused into an injury. *If he's our killer, this case needs to be airtight. No walking. No doubt on anything. And no accusations that cops are getting too physical.*

"Infirmary first," Teresa directed the uniform, "then back in a cell."

But Micah kept fighting. "I didn't do it! I'm being set up! It wasn't *me!*"

The uniform got him out of the room. The overpriced lawyer hustled out after them. Teresa shook her head even as her hands went to her hips. "Always the same line from perps like him. Even when you have them dead to rights."

Yeah, the evidence was all lined up. Maybe too lined up? Curran's gaze slid to the bagged knife. "Tied up with a pretty bow."

"What?"

His gaze rose even as his jaw clenched. "If I hadn't followed Royal, Micah would be dead right now." Because Royal would have pulled that trigger.

"Georgia has the death penalty. Let a judge and jury decide if that's his fate." She scooped up the bagged knife.

"There wouldn't be questions." His voice was low. "It would have been tied up. Royal wouldn't have cooperated worth a damn with investigators. Violet would have said she stabbed her attacker—"

"She *did* stab him. That's the wound the prick just broke open when he charged at me."

"Royal would have killed him," Curran muttered. "The suspected serial killer would be cold in the morgue. No more questions..." His voice trailed away.

"Uh, Detective Barlow? You with me?"

He didn't speak.

A long sigh escaped her. "I get that this is your first big case, so I'll explain things to you. This is what we call a win. The evidence is piling up, and Micah Wright is going to be convicted of multiple murders. I don't know about you, but I'm going out to celebrate tonight." She swung on her heel and headed for the door.

He didn't follow. His mind wouldn't stop spinning.

Everything was a little too neat.

Tied up with a freaking bow.

If he hadn't been there that night, if he hadn't stopped Royal...

Maybe I wasn't meant to stop him. Maybe Royal was supposed to kill Micah, and Micah would have taken the fall for everything. Not like a dead man could proclaim his innocence.

And if that had been the case, if Royal had ended

Micah, then no one—not even Royal—would still be looking for the man who'd abducted Violet.

The man who'd also killed Marcella White, Bailey Brown, and Fiona Law.

And the other vics that the doctor of the dead had unearthed at the winery? Would they have ever been recovered? Or would the case have ended with Micah's dead body?

Did someone want it all to end with him? With Simone's dying breath, she'd said Micah's name. But had that been because Micah was guilty of her murder? Or had Simone been trying to tell them something else?

The pieces all just did not *fit*.

"Fuck." Curran yanked out his phone and called Royal. But the line just rang and rang and rang.

* * *

"Hello, Dr. Barnes," Royal said, his voice as smooth as silk. The rage had vanished from his expression. No emotion showed on his face at all.

"Surprised?" Leo Barnes asked. His breath blew over the shell of Violet's ear as he urged her forward. She heard him kick the door shut behind them. No soft click following the closing, though. He hadn't locked the door.

"I'm not particularly surprised." Royal shrugged. "I know Micah wasn't the killer."

"Oh?"

"Some things didn't add—"

Royal's phone started to ring.

"Turn it off and put it on the desk," Leo snarled, "or I will cut her throat open and you can watch her bleed out right in front of you."

Violet sucked in a breath. And her right hand slid down her body. She dipped it beneath the flowing edge of her oversized blouse. Slid her fingers into her pocket.

Royal turned off his phone and tossed it face down onto his desk. "Happy?"

"You realized it was me."

Leo stood right behind her. His body pressed against her back, and that damn knife lingered at her throat.

"I saw it in your eyes, at the theater. You were suspicious of me," Leo accused. "Realized I had to follow you here. I did plan on a different ending, but you made me change things. What's happening here is on you."

Violet's heart drummed in a double-time rhythm.

But Royal looked as cool as could be as he studied the killer. After a tense, silent moment, Royal said, "You planned for me to kill Micah Wright. You're the one who lured him to the station, aren't you? Did you make Simone call both him and Violet?"

"Guilty," Leo confessed. And he sounded proud of himself.

Royal's lips twisted. His eyes glinted. "You thought he'd take the fall for all of your crimes, and with me killing him, the cops would have to tie me to the vigilante hunts. Micah would be gone, and so would I. He'd be in a grave. I'd be in a cell."

Soft laughter rang from behind her. "I wondered if I was on your radar. First you took out Owen Bell, then the Slasher, Everett Thomas. Got to say, I was fascinated by your work. Hunting predators? How devious and delightful. I would have so liked to pick your brain in a session."

"That shit wouldn't ever happen."

"When I realized someone was taking out killers, I tried to be extra careful. But when you stole my Violet from me, well, I knew for certain I was being hunted." The laughter had faded away. "I don't like being hunted."

Royal shrugged. He stood behind the desk, still close to the painting on the wall. "Too damn bad," Royal told him.

"Oh, you misunderstand. Things aren't bad for me. They're bad for you."

Royal wasn't looking at her. Her eyes were on him, but he stared straight at the man behind her. Her hand had slipped out of her pocket. Leo didn't seem at all aware of her small movements.

"The cops know nothing about me," Leo boasted. "They never will. I considered letting you live, just so you understand. If you'd killed Micah like I'd planned, then we could have both walked away. And lived to hunt another day," he finished, voice mocking.

"You hate Micah," Violet realized. There was something about the way he said Micah's name.

"Of course, I do. He fucked my wife. I took that personally. I loved my wife. *She. Was. Mine.*"

"That why you've been killing her over and over again?" Royal asked. "Because you loved her so much?"

Leo's left hand held the knife to her throat and his right hand—his right hand suddenly flew up in front of her. And that hand held a gun.

"No!" Violet screamed.

"Curl your fingers around the fucking gun grip," Leo blasted. The knife bit into her.

She shook her head. The blade sliced deeper.

"Do it, Violet," Royal urged her. "It's okay."

No, it was *not* okay.

The blade bit into her. She did not lift her hand. "You want me holding the gun while you shoot Royal. *Not* happening." The hell she'd do that.

Royal's nostrils flared. He edged closer to the desk. "Trying to get gunshot residue on her hand? What's the end game now? Gonna make it look like a murder-suicide?"

Her breath froze in her throat.

"Yes." Leo kept the gun on Royal. "That's exactly what I'm going to do. Thought it would be extra fun for her to hold the weapon while I shot you."

The knife dug deeper.

She refused to put her hand on the gun. She also refused to cry out in pain.

"But I can always just shoot you now, and then, after I'm done carving up Violet, I'll curl her fingers around the gun and fire again—"

"Or I'll carve you," she said softly. Then she drove her right elbow back as hard as she could.

You were the man in the garage. You, not Micah. And I stabbed you right here.

He screamed in pain. As he screamed, she uncurled her hand. The new switchblade Royal had given her rested in her palm. She hit the button, and the blade appeared. As hard as she could, Violet drove that blade into Leo's upper thigh. Then she wrenched it to the side.

He howled. He also let go of her. She sprang forward, still desperately gripping her switchblade, and ran straight for Royal. He grabbed her and shoved her behind his body.

Boom.

The gunshot seemed to echo around her. And, honestly, for a beat after that blast, she could hear nothing but the frantic drumming of her own heart. "Royal!" He'd been hit? Had Royal been hit? Leo must have fired. She spun back around. Her frantic gaze swept over Royal.

She saw that Royal had his arm out and up. A gun was still in his hand. Her stare whipped from his hand to Leo.

Leo had stumbled back against the closed door. The knife had fallen from his left hand. His right still gripped his gun. He was trying to raise it up.

Royal shot him in the shoulder. The gun dropped from Leo's fingers as he screamed in pain.

"Soundproof room," Royal murmured. "You can scream as loudly as you want, and no one will come." He looked back at Violet. "Stay behind me," he told her. "Please, baby." His gaze dropped to her throat. For just a moment, his rage broke loose. She saw it flare in his eyes.

"Royal?" Violet inched closer to him.

"Good job with the knife, sweetheart. Told you in the limo that I thought trouble was coming." He looked back at the man who was bleeding by the door. "You counted on it being soundproofed in here, didn't you? That's why you followed us from the theater. You came in the back. Probably been to Punishment a few times, haven't you? Scoping out the place. *Hunting me.*"

Hate twisted Leo's face. "You should have...fucking left...my Violet—"

"I would never leave Violet." He took a step closer to Leo. "Violet, sweetheart, there is another gun in the top drawer of my desk. Get it, will you?"

She got it. The drawer was open. She put down her switchblade, and her sweaty fingers grabbed for the gun. Then she immediately took aim at Leo, too.

"You were going to shoot me. Make it look as if I'd attacked Violet and she had no choice but to kill me in order to survive." Royal shook his head. "But you were going to make sure she died, right? That she fell victim to all the terrible wounds I gave her before she could end me."

Leo had one hand slapped against his thigh. The other

hand was moving toward his blazer. Did he have another weapon?

"Royal..." Violet warned.

"It was the mention of your wife that made me suspicious at the theater," Royal said. "All my instincts were screaming when I talked to you on that stage. And, yeah, I planned to immediately do a deep dive on your dead wife. I'll still do that dive. I'm guessing that when I research her, I'll find that she looked just like Violet?"

Leo's gaze whipped to Violet. "Mirror...image..."

Violet swallowed.

"So Micah fucked your wife," Royal snapped out. "And you—what? Caught them together? Went crazy? Killed her?"

"Robbery...gone wrong. Guy tried to take her purse. S-sliced her open." A shudder shook Leo's form. "So much blood..." He licked his lips. "She was beautiful covered in blood."

"Robbery, my ass," Royal threw at him. "You killed her. Staged the scene to *look* like a robbery, huh? And you got a taste for all that blood and violence."

"Always hear...the darkest parts of my patients...their lives." His hand lifted a little higher toward his blazer. "They never knew...I was worse than all of them."

She should grab Royal's phone. Call the cops. Instead, Violet found she was rooted to the spot. The gun in her grip trembled.

"Gonna...pull the trigger, sweet Violet?" Leo asked her. He smiled. "Bet you're not...can't shoot...unarmed man."

"I can," Royal said. And he did. Boom.

Violet flinched.

The bullet slammed into Leo's already injured left leg, and the psychiatrist hit the floor. He howled in agony.

Violet's stare flew back and forth between Leo and a stone-faced Royal.

"She's...seeing you..." Leo gasped out. "Just...as bad...as..." He slumped on the floor. His body had gone still.

Royal stared down at him. His weapon was still aimed.

"You're not like him," Violet whispered.

"I know." He waited.

Violet took a step forward.

Royal shook his head.

And Leo surged forward. He hurtled across the floor even as his hand flew out. He grabbed for the gun he'd dropped moments before.

A guttural scream broke from Leo as he lifted the weapon and aimed it at Royal.

Violet fired.

So did Royal.

Which one had fired first?

Did it matter?

Leo went down and pieces of him went everywhere. Her eyes squeezed shut at the horrible sight.

Time passed in excruciating silence. *Boom. Boom. Boom.* That was her heart racing, but the sound was like gunshots.

"Violet? Sweetheart?" Royal took the gun from her. "Can you look at me?"

Her eyes opened just as the door to his office flew inward.

"Royal, you are not going to believe this shit," Kai announced dramatically. "But you have got to take a look at —*sonofabitch. What is happening here?*"

Her head jerked toward Kai's shocked voice. He stood in the doorway and gaped at the body that had slumped right in front of him.

Only Kai wasn't alone. There was someone else with him. A man with dark blond hair. Wide shoulders. A man who edged closer and peered down at the blood and chaos with zero expression on his face.

A face that was almost an exact mirror copy of Royal's.

The stranger looked up even as Kai dropped to his knees to search for a pulse at Leo's throat.

"Not gonna find one." Royal had moved to stand protectively before Violet. She had to crane her head to see around him. And to blink a few times because surely...surely, she was having some sort of hallucination. Maybe one brought on by shock or trauma. There were not two Royals in the room.

If only she had a good psychiatrist to ask about the problem.

A wild bubble of laughter escaped her.

Is this what happens when the stress breaks you?

The stranger stared back at Royal.

Not an exact copy of Royal's face. Older. Harder. With a long scar that stretched across his right cheek and over his lip.

"Who the fuck are you?" Royal breathed.

"I'm your brother," the stranger replied. His stare dropped to the body once more. "Some sins sure do run in a family."

And what did *that* mean?

"You gonna need help burying the body?" the man asked.

Violet blanched. "It was self-defense."

The man with Royal's face smiled. "Right."

Royal picked up his phone. His fingers swiped across the screen. Her breath heaved in and out and then she heard him say, "Curran? Yeah. Sorry, got a little busy." A pause. "Calm down. Calm down. Jeez. Did you get all that? Most of it, at least?"

Wait, had he answered the call? Before he'd tossed it down, had he turned the phone *on*? It had looked as if he turned off the phone, but as he talked, she realized that he hadn't.

"Good," Royal praised. "Was really hoping you'd say that. I'm gonna need you to come over with some of your buddies in blue. Seems I have a killer for you. Is he tied up with a red bow?" His gaze drifted to the body. "There is plenty of red, so I guess you could say that." Then that gaze shifted to Violet as he turned his back on the man in the doorway and on Kai. Royal's focus drifted to her throat. His jaw hardened. "Get EMTs here. Violet is hurt. Where are we? I'm at my freaking club. Did you not trace the location yet? Man, don't be sloppy."

She touched her neck. Felt the sticky wetness of her blood. "Scratch."

His eyes glittered.

"It's a scratch," she repeated. But that didn't make the fury in his gaze lessen any. She could feel his rage filling the room. Unable to help herself, Violet surged for Royal. She pressed onto her toes and caught the back of his head. Ignoring the phone, she tugged him close to her. So close that she could hear the thunder of Curran's voice as he barked out questions.

"I love you," Violet told Royal.

Then she kissed him.

With a dead body just a few feet away.

With a long lost...brother close by?

With her whole world imploding, she kissed Royal. And when the cops did come bursting in—the cops and the

EMTs and a whole cavalry, she was still with Royal. Still right at his side.

And when Curran looked at the still-warm body, then at her and Royal, Violet lifted her chin.

"What in the hell happened here?" Curran demanded.

Hadn't he heard everything on the phone? Maybe he just needed confirmation for the record. She could explain things. "He tried to kill us," Violet began.

"So we killed him," Royal finished.

Their hands were linked together. They were linked. Nothing was going to break them apart. Nothing.

"Sonofabitch," Curran growled.

"Self-defense," Royal corrected. "I do believe what you meant to say was...*self-defense*."

Chapter Twenty-Three

"I don't need to go to the hospital," Violet insisted. She was currently sitting on a gurney, in the back of an ambulance, and a white bandage covered her neck. "I want to stay with you."

"Sweetheart, for my sanity, go to the hospital."

"It's a *scratch*."

No, it had been a knife to the throat. That was what it had been. A new image for his nightmare highlight reel. Royal put his forehead against hers. "You want me to beg? In front of all these gawking people?" He'd shoved his way into the ambulance after she'd been bandaged up.

"No. I never want you to beg." Her breath whispered out. "Don't you dare get locked into a cell while I'm gone, you hear me?"

"Yes, ma'am." He thought everyone within a thirty-foot radius might have heard her.

"Don't be a smartass, either." Then she was kissing him. Quick. Desperate. "And don't forget that *I love you*."

He'd remember her love until his dying day. There were

some things that could never be erased. "And you remember that you're the center of my world."

Then he made himself back away. Hop out of the ambulance. His gaze met hers. "Kai," he said to his friend who was close by. Just that. His name.

Kai climbed in the ambulance. He knew what to do. "She'll have a guard every minute. Damn, but I sure hope we encounter some hot nurses. The last time I was in the hospital, there was one woman that was absolutely out of this world."

The doors slammed shut. The ambulance pulled away.

Then Royal turned to the detective who was waiting. Not that Curran was alone. Curran's new federal agent buddy was right beside him. Both looked pissed. Fair enough, Royal felt pretty pissed, too.

I killed him. And if I had it to do all over again, I'd still pull that trigger.

"Forensics are working in your office. We'd really like for you to walk us through the shooting once more." Teresa's hands were on her hips. The pose pulled back her suit coat and showed both her badge and her weapon. "How about we go down to the station so that we can talk?"

Ah, and here Violet had just asked him not to get locked away. But in this case, he could oblige his lady. He would not be spending time in a cell. "Absolutely. Happy to cooperate. If there is one thing I love to do, it's cooperate with law enforcement. I'll make sure I call my lawyer to sit in on the cooperation bout with me, but first..." He marched right up to Curran. "You were calling me about something?" A perfectly timed call.

Curran nodded. "Micah kept singing that he'd been set up. I believed him and wanted to warn you."

"Aw, detective, be careful, or I'll think you care about me."

"You bastard." Curran threw his arms around Royal and hauled him close. "Thought you were dead. Shit. I heard the guns going off in the background. I heard Violet scream."

"You do care."

Curran eased back and glared at him. "You and Beau saved my ass when I was seventeen. You dragged me out of that fucking gang and gave me a life. Hell, yes, I care. Now you stop doing dumb shit."

"I didn't do anything dumb. An upstanding officer of the law heard every word I said—and every word the killer said. I'm hoping you put the call on speaker." He glanced toward the watchful Teresa. "So that the whole team could hear? Did you hear, Agent Duncan?"

"I heard," she affirmed.

"Great. Then our visit to the police station should be blessedly short. The dead man upstairs is the serial killer you're after. He also murdered his wife—and whoever the unfortunate victims are at the winery. I'm guessing they were probably homeless women. Maybe prostitutes who resembled his dead wife. Women who'd been taken when he was still learning. Someone he hoped no one would miss." So Leo had preyed on the weakest members of society first. *Burn in hell, you piece of shit. Burn.* "He used the winery probably because his good friend Micah told him about the place once—and Leo really hated Micah." *He played the long game, always intending to frame Micah for the crimes. But then I came along and screwed things to hell for him.*

"What did he mean," Teresa advanced with her head

cocked and her expression suspicious, "when he said you were *hunting him*?"

"Hunting?" He let his brows rise. "Oh, didn't I mention it? I've started working with the Ice Breakers. I'm helping them solve some cold cases." He *would* be helping them so it was just a twist on the truth, not a full lie. "I'm gonna be working up close and personal with the doctor of the dead." He'd finally take the leap and do something that Beau had been pushing him to do. Change up his hobby...work with a team...but still bring down the bad guys.

Since he was planning for a future—with Violet and kids and the whole wild *family* dream that he'd almost been too afraid to have—Royal was willing to change.

For Violet, he'd do anything.

His head tilted back, and he looked up at the second floor of Punishment. The body hadn't been brought out yet. But it would be. Sooner or later. Bagged and tagged and then buried in a pit in the ground.

No one would mourn Leo Barnes.

But some would be celebrating his death. *I'm gonna celebrate.*

Reporters were sneaking closer. He knew they would have picked up the story on the police scanner. More headlines. More people crawling out of the woodwork, pretending to know him and be his long-lost family.

Except...

His head turned to the right. He'd felt the stare on him the whole time. Ever since he'd followed Violet to the ambulance.

The stranger stood with his back against the nearby brick wall. Sure enough, his eyes were locked on Royal.

"Who the hell is he?" Curran asked softly.

Excellent question. "That is something I intend to discover."

The stranger tipped his head to Royal.

Curran pointed out, "He's got your face."

"Not exactly." But damn close enough. Close enough that if Royal hadn't just sent a man to hell, he might be freaking the shit out. However, he preferred to focus on one crisis at a time.

The stranger turned and walked away. He headed in the opposite direction of the approaching reporters.

"Want me to stop him?" Curran took a step after the guy.

"Yeah." He actually did.

"Material witness. He's not going anywhere." Curran took off after the stranger. "Hey, buddy! Buddy, *stop!*"

It paid to have cops who were your friends. Sometimes, those do-gooders would stop you from making a fatal mistake.

And sometimes, they'd be the perfect alibi you needed when you sent a man to hell. *Heard every word, didn't you, Curran? You and everyone near you at the station.*

The minute Leo had put the knife to Violet's throat, he'd been a dead man. But having a whole team of cops hear his confession and the chaos that had played over the phone...*Don't worry, Violet. There's no way I'll be seeing the inside of a cell.*

Instead, he'd be spending his days and nights with her. For the rest of his life.

Provided, of course, that she wanted forever with him.

* * *

ANOTHER DAY, another interrogation room.

Only this time, Royal was the one going in with the questions.

"Are you sure about this?" Violet asked. She stood at Royal's side. Night had fallen. The hours had swirled by in a blur. As soon as the cops and Feds had cleared him, he'd rushed to the hospital to be with her.

A white bandage still covered her throat. Her eyes were huge. Her skin too pale. And she looked like absolute perfection to him. She always would, no matter what.

"You don't have to walk into that room," Violet added. "You don't have to look back."

"Sweetheart, you're worried?"

"Yes."

"We took out the killer. We're still standing." He motioned toward the closed interrogation room door. "What could be worse than that?"

She reached for his hand. Her fingers squeezed his. "You might not like your past."

Oh, he pretty much hated it, no doubt.

"That man in there isn't your family. I don't care if he has your face. *Beau* is your family."

Beau was waiting for him in Curran's office.

"*I'm* your family," Violet told him fiercely. "If there is pain waiting for you in there, then I say just forget it. Look forward, not back."

His lips brushed over hers. "I like the way you protect me."

"And I like the way you're ready to kill for me," she murmured in return. "I like the way you fight for me, and know that I will always fight for you, too."

He knew it. Something else he knew with all of his being? "I fucking love you."

She kissed him again. Soft. Promising.

And part of him did want to just grab Violet. To turn away. To run with her and just keep going toward the beautiful new life that waited. But some chapters needed to be closed before you could look forward. This one chapter had haunted Royal his entire life. Time to shut the door on it.

"Doesn't matter what you hear in there." Violet's lilac scent teased him and reassured him. "You're strong. You're sexy. You're brilliant. You're mine."

He was also dangerous and manipulative and predatory, but he liked that she focused on the positives.

"I'll be with you. Every second." Her gaze searched his. "I'm not going to leave."

She kept saying those words. Did she realize that, to him, they were just as special as when she told him, *I love you?*

It was time to face the past. Time to put another monster to rest. He opened the interrogation room door. Two men waited inside at the narrow table.

Curran.

And the stranger with Royal's face.

The stranger glanced down at the watch—a Rolex—on his wrist. "About time. I thought you were going to let me die of boredom in here."

Well, well. Someone thought he was funny. "Had the little matter of a dead body to handle."

The stranger grunted. He rose from the table and turned to fully face Royal. Royal hadn't entered the room yet. He stood on the threshold with Violet just behind him.

He weighed the stranger.

The stranger weighed him.

Royal had about an inch on the guy in height. Similar builds. Similar features. Eyes the same swirling hazel.

The scar was different, of course.

And while Royal was wearing his battered jeans and a black t-shirt—items that Beau had brought him because Royal's other clothes had been stained with blood and perhaps some brain matter—the man before Royal wore an expensive suit.

Like money could hide a monster.

"Can Violet and I have a chat with him?" Royal asked as his attention shifted to Curran. "One that the rest of the police station doesn't hear?"

Curran nodded and headed for Royal. He waved a hand toward the one-way mirror. "I'll be on the other side. Just me." He paused in front of Royal. "His name's Declan Flynn. No criminal background."

That could just mean he'd gotten away with his crimes.

"He's from Chicago," Curran added. "Runs some sort of tech company up there."

Vague curiosity stirred within Royal.

"He's also a bit of an asshole," Curran disclosed. "Just so you're aware."

"More than a bit," Declan admitted. "It's been a lifelong problem."

Good to know.

Royal moved to the side. Then he advanced into the interrogation room, but his gaze cut back to the detective.

Curran skimmed his stare over Violet. "You sure you want to be here?"

"I'm with Royal."

"Yeah, thought you'd say something like that. Protective." Shaking his head, he eased past her. "Number one necessary trait in a mate." He exited.

Violet shut the door behind the detective. Then she moved to Royal's side.

"Guess you two are a package deal, huh?" Declan crossed his arms over his chest. "So, which of you killed the guy in the club? Who pulled the trigger that ended his life?"

"Does it matter?" Violet asked. Her voice was carefully flat.

"It was me," Royal said. Like he'd ever let Violet carry any unnecessary weight on her shoulders.

Her head whipped toward him.

"My bullet went in his head, baby." Exactly where he'd aimed. "Yours went in the wall about a foot to the side." The crime scene techs had already dug out the bullet from the wall. "But you did slice one beautiful hole in the guy's thigh with your knife." A knife that had been taken into evidence. No worries, he would just get her another.

"Do you often eliminate serial killers?" Declan asked in the tone one would use to inquire about the weather.

"Everyone needs a hobby." Royal faced the man he'd never expected to see. "Guessing that prick at the back of the theater—the one in the expensive gray suit—was acting on your behalf?"

An incline of Declan's head. His hair was little shorter than Royal's. "Thought we could set up a meeting. All civilized-like."

"I don't really do civilized," Royal informed him.

"I did notice that." A faint smile teased Declan's lips but was gone in a blink. "I followed you to the club. I was talking to the guard at your door, convincing him that I needed to be let inside." An exhale. "I owe you both an apology. If I hadn't been distracting him, then your serial killer wouldn't have gotten around the building and slipped inside. The day could have ended differently."

Royal doubted much would have been different. Leo Barnes had needed to die. But Violet getting hurt? Violet being at risk for even a single second? Yeah, that shit should have been different.

"Saw your story on the news." Declan rolled back his shoulders. Seemed as comfortable and casual as could be. As if he lingered in interrogation rooms all the time. "Actually, my guy James saw it. James was the suit at the theater, by the way. One look, and he knew who you were."

"I'm Royal Boudreaux." He knew exactly who he was.

Declan's Adam's apple bobbed. Maybe he wasn't as comfortable as he appeared. "Once upon a time, you were Garrison Flynn."

Royal took a step back.

Instantly, Violet's hand was around his. Squeezing.

His stare flew to her. "I'm Royal Boudreaux," he said again.

"You're Royal Boudreaux," she repeated. "You're the man I love."

He sucked in a breath. His hand twisted so that he was holding hers. He looked back at Declan, only to find Declan's gaze on Royal and Violet's joined hands. What could have been a flash of envy came and went on Declan's face.

But then there was no emotion. Like Declan had just locked down all his feelings. "Royal Boudreaux." A nod. "I think I like that name better." He pulled in a deep breath. Released it out slowly. "We can do the whole DNA routine, but I believe the result is gonna show that I'm your brother. Older by four years."

Brother. Brother. "I have a brother already." Beau.

Declan's Adam's apple bobbed once more. "Good for you." His gaze cut to the one-way mirror. Then back to Royal. "I had a brother, too. *You.* A lifetime ago. A little guy that I fought to remember. A kid that would sing off-key and always ask for more stories at night."

"I don't sing," Royal groused.

"Our mom would read the stories to us. We shared a room. Me and my brother. She'd read to us over and over again."

A tremble shook Royal's body. "How the fuck did I wind up tossed away like garbage?" The question that had haunted him forever.

Declan didn't answer.

"Hey." Violet's voice. Soft. Husky. Tender. Her left hand rose to slide against Royal's cheek.

Immediately, he looked at her. He saw *her*.

"Never garbage." Not so husky. Fierce. "Don't talk that way again about the man I love, got it? Doesn't happen. Not from you. Not from anyone."

And a weight seemed to lift. The family he'd always sought was right there. Not the man named Declan but Violet. His Violet.

She'd saved his whole soul. Did she know that?

"Our mother was...trying to get away." Declan's voice came out haltingly. "She took you first. She was going to hide you. Then come back for me. Or at least, that's what I've been able to piece together."

Royal's gaze pulled away from Violet. But he kept holding her hand, tightly.

"Our father was a bastard." Declan's hand scraped over the scar on his cheek. "Believe me when I say, you were better off not knowing him."

Royal's body tensed even more.

"She ran with you. And I *believe* she was coming back for me. But something happened. She didn't make it back. I was actually told you were both dead. Fiery car crash. No survivors. I don't know how you wound up on that street, but I am damn glad you weren't in the car with her. Maybe she left you there because she knew danger was closing in. Maybe she was trying to save you. But she wasn't able to save herself."

Dead. Royal's heart slammed into his chest. "And your father?"

"Our father?" A cold smile twisted Declan's lips. "Dead and buried, too. So I'm sorry to say it's just me."

Royal didn't speak.

"I have money to burn. An inheritance. Half will go to you, so I'm not here trying to—"

"I don't need your money."

"No. Right." Declan exhaled. "You don't need anything from me, do you? You have a life. A different brother. A woman who looks at you like you freaking hang the moon. And you look at her like she's your world."

"She is," he affirmed. There would never be any doubt on that note.

"Must be fucking nice." Declan nodded. "We'll do the DNA tests. Lawyers will need that stuff. Whether you want the family money or not, it's yours. Put it in a trust for your kids. After the paperwork is settled, I won't bother you again. Just came because I..." His lashes flickered. "I always hoped you were alive. Don't know how the hell you got to New Orleans when you were two. But I'm glad you did. I'm glad you are still breathing." He motioned toward Violet. "And I'm glad you have a chance to be really happy." Declan squared his shoulders. "Hope you have a good life... Royal." He headed for the door.

Violet squeezed Royal's hand.

Royal stepped into Declan's path.

He stared at the face so like his own. "I don't remember you."

"Yeah, well, you were two the last time you saw me."

"I can't sing for shit."

A half-smile. "You couldn't when you were two, either."

"You walked in, saw me over a dead man, and offered to help me bury the body."

Declan's brows rose. "What else would a good brother do?"

Royal's chest burned. "Who killed our father?" *Our.*

"I did." Flat. "He was an abusive bastard who deserved exactly what he got. No charges were ever filed against me. I was sixteen at the time, so most of the records are sealed. If you want the whole bloody story, I'll give it to you. But it's not pretty."

Royal didn't look at the scar on Declan's cheek, not again. "And our mother?"

"I think he might have hired someone to go after her. Still trying to piece that all together. Trying to find out who is responsible for taking her from us."

Royal nodded. "You want some help with that?"

Hope lit Declan's eyes. "You offering?"

"Maybe. And maybe I know some people who are pretty good when it comes to stirring up cold cases." Could the Ice Breakers help? He sure as hell hoped so. To finally close a mystery that had haunted him forever—damn, that would be something. *My mother.* And his father...no, no, he wasn't ready to go there, not yet.

If he was a monster...

"You're not him," Violet said, as if reading his mind.

Royal flinched.

"You're not your father. You will never be," Violet told him, her voice fierce. "You're my Royal."

He inhaled. Exhaled. He stared into Declan's eyes.

"I'm not like the bastard, either," Declan told him. "I work every single day not to be like him." A pause. "We can be more than he ever was." Declan ducked his head. "I'll just, uh, make my exit. Your detective buddy knows where to find me." His stare slid to Violet. "You'll take care of him?"

"I think we'll take care of each other," she replied softly.

"Sounds like a plan." Declan cleared his throat. "Lucky bastard."

Royal stepped to the side. Declan headed out. Royal watched him go.

"Really?" From Violet. "You want something your whole life. It's right there, and you just let it walk away?"

His breath sawed in and out.

"You have me. You have Beau. You have a family. What does he have?"

Lucky bastard. Declan's words rang in his ears.

Declan was heading down the narrow station corridor. Beau suddenly appeared in his path. He barely glanced at Declan, though. His focus was on Royal. A wide smile split Beau's lips. "About time!" he called out. "Bro, are you ready to get the hell out of here?"

Declan stumbled, then straightened quickly.

"Almost." Keeping his hold on Violet's hand and tugging her with him, he advanced. "Declan."

Declan whirled toward him.

Beau blinked in confusion.

"Beau, there's someone I think you should meet."

Declan and Beau were pretty much standing side by side. They filled that hallway. Royal and Violet advanced toward them. As he closed in on the other two men, they both faced him and Royal said, "Beau always told me that we can choose our families."

Declan's chin lifted. The garish light in the hallway hit the scar on his face.

"Declan, this is my brother, Beau."

Declan's eyes glittered as he cast a sideways glance at Beau.

And Beau was finally *looking* at the guy. "What in the hell...?" Beau began.

"And Beau, this is Declan. He's my—"

"Yeah, I can figure that shit out." Suspicion darkened Beau's face. "Are you here to hurt or to help?"

Well, as to that... "He's already offered to bury a body for me."

Beau's eyes widened. "Dammit, man!" Beau exploded on Royal. "How many times do I have to tell you...don't say stuff like that *in a police station?*"

Declan appeared frozen in place.

"There are no bodies to bury!" Beau announced loudly. "None. The doctor of the dead is *raising bodies*. It's a misunderstanding. She's digging them up. Nothing to see here. Jeez." He glowered. "You know what, how about we take this *out* of the station? Who wants a drink? I say we all hit LeBlanc's."

LeBlanc's. Beau's prized bar. "They have the best whiskey in town." Royal wasn't sure if Declan was aware of that pertinent fact. "We can talk there."

Declan released a long breath. "I'd like that."

Talking...step one.

Tearing the past apart...step two.

Moving the hell on to the future with Violet at his side... *end game.*

His head turned toward her. A faint smile tilted her

lips. She'd stopped him from letting Declan walk away. Oh, hell, it was more than that. She'd stopped Royal the very first night. She'd kept him from going over the edge and straight into the darkness that waited.

He'd meant what he told her before. She might think that he'd saved her when he found Violet in the trunk of that car, but the truth was that she'd saved him.

She glanced his way. Her lashes fluttered as a little furrow appeared between her delicate brows. "Royal?"

"Thank you," he told her.

"For what?"

His mouth pressed to hers. She kissed him back with no hesitation. Just with joy and need and love.

Thank you.

As to her question...

Thank you for loving the devil, sweetheart. Because I would be lost without you.

Epilogue

THE BRASS BAND DANCED EVEN AS THEIR MUSIC FILLED the air. Laughter and cheers followed the music...and the second line cascaded down the New Orleans street. Colorful umbrellas swirled in the air, and attendees waved blue handkerchiefs. The groom held the bride's hand tightly within his grip. Her white dress twirled around her legs as she danced with him. Friends followed. Strong men in dark suits. Women in soft blue dresses holding flowers and laughing the night away. Tourists stopped to wave and cheer.

The wedding had taken place in the St. Louis Cathedral, and Royal still couldn't quite believe it.

She's mine.

I'm hers.

In the cathedral that he used to sneak into as a child... well, he'd gone in as a man and married the love of his life. And when Violet had walked down that aisle toward him— with her brothers at her side, she'd been smiling the whole time. Staring at him like he was the best thing she'd ever seen.

She looked at him like he mattered.

Like he was special.

Like he was a hero when she knew so much better.

And Royal knew he looked at her like she was everything...because she was.

Six months had passed since the attack in Punishment. He'd tried to court Violet. Tried to take his time so she could be sure of him.

And then she'd just popped the question one night in his club. They'd been dancing—God, he loved to dance with her—and she'd asked him to marry her.

Was he a fucking fool? He'd said yes immediately and went to work. He'd pulled every string he had and gotten the wedding set up three weeks later.

The brass band kept playing. The trumpet let out a joyous cry. The second line was going strong as tourists joined at the tail and the party kept moving. New Orleans was full of life and hope and love.

Royal Street waited not too far away. They'd go down that street. The place where his life had seemed to start so long ago. But his *new* life...

Oh, that life had started when he opened the trunk of a car and found an angel waiting for him.

You saved me. He told her that often, but he wasn't sure Violet believed him. She should.

He scooped her into his arms. Kissed her with all the love and devotion he had.

His friends cheered. His brothers—Beau and Declan— slapped him on the back. There wasn't any fear in New Orleans right then. No pain. No anger. No hate for what could have been.

Just hope.

He lifted Violet into the air and swung her around so

that her dress streamed behind her. Her hands pressed to his shoulders as she smiled down at him.

Hope.

Life.

Love.

"I love you, sweetheart," he told her. "I. Love. You."

In the mood for another romantic suspense? Be sure and check out WHEN HE PROTECTS, coming in October 2024 from Cynthia Eden.

He knew she was trouble from the moment they met.

Esme Laurent is a con artist. An accomplished liar. A world-class thief. And probably the most beautiful and intriguing woman that Tyler Barrett has ever met. Sure, he has to arrest her at their first meeting, and she absolutely hates him, but...well, he has a job to do. And Spencer *always* gets the job done.

Turns out, she *is* the new job.

The people in charge want to use Esme to bring down a very dangerous criminal operation. And in order to do that, Esme has to stay in the land of the living. She needs protection, she needs a new identity, and she needs to disappear, immediately. Because Esme has more than a bit of power, she makes her own deal...her protection needs to come in the ever-so-gorgeous, ever-so-dangerous, and ever-so-law-abiding form of U.S. Marshal Tyler Barrett.

They'll disappear into Small Town, USA. And they'll pretend to be newlyweds who just can't keep their hands off each other.

No, absolutely, this cannot be happening. But no matter how much Tyler protests, the new job is, in fact, happening. He's being sent to Asylum, Alabama, with the delectable Esme. He's supposed to be her husband—a role that will give him twenty-four, seven access in order to protect her. He needs that access in order to make sure that Esme doesn't run from the authorities *and* that she stays alive. But what Tyler doesn't count on is the consuming desire he feels for a woman who should be off-limits.

She'll test every limit that he has...

Esme doesn't expect her attraction to the rule-following Tyler. He's big, he's buttoned-down, and he's absolutely... delicious. She also suspects that he may be carefully controlling a wild side—one that she would love to see erupt. *Oh, if only.*

When danger comes calling, Tyler is more than ready to handle any threat. Who knew that falling for the good guy could be so tempting? And so very...heart-breaking. Because there was no way a guy like Tyler would want to stay around once they stop pretending. Everyone knows the bad girl never gets to keep the good guy, especially when she's still working a very long con.

Author's Note: Are you in the mood for a strong hero who makes "protecting and defending" his life code? Tyler is big, fierce, and more than ready to step into the line of fire in order to protect his charge. He's also falling fast under the spell of a woman he should not trust. Everything with Esme is just pretend...everything, except the desire they feel for each other. And the very, very real danger that stalks her. A danger that may wind up costing Tyler more than he ever expected. WHEN HE PROTECTS, Tyler gives his all, and when he loves...he will fight like hell for the woman who stole his heart.

Learn more about WHEN HE PROTECTS.

Author's Note

Thank you so much for reading Brutal Ice! I hope that you enjoyed Royal and Violet's story. I am such a cold case addict—and I am thrilled that I had the chance to write the Ice Breaker books.

If you have time, please consider leaving a review. Reviews help readers to discover new books—and authors certainly appreciate them!

If you'd like to stay updated on my releases and sales, please join my newsletter list.

I'm also active on social media. You can find me on Instagram and Facebook.

Again, thank you for reading BRUTAL ICE.

Best,

Cynthia Eden

cynthiaeden.com

More Books By Cynthia Eden

Ice Breaker Cold Case Romance
- Frozen In Ice (Book 1)
- Falling For The Ice Queen (Book 2)
- Ice Cold Saint (Book 3)
- Touched By Ice (Book 4)
- Trapped In Ice (Book 5)
- Forged From Ice (Book 6)
- Buried Under Ice (Book 7)
- Ice Cold Kiss (Book 8)
- Locked In Ice (Book 9)
- Savage Ice (Book 10)

Wilde Ways
- Protecting Piper (Book 1)
- Guarding Gwen (Book 2)
- Before Ben (Book 3)
- The Heart You Break (Book 4)
- Fighting For Her (Book 5)
- Ghost Of A Chance (Book 6)
- Crossing The Line (Book 7)

- Counting On Cole (Book 8)
- Chase After Me (Book 9)
- Say I Do (Book 10)
- Roman Will Fall (Book 11)
- The One Who Got Away (Book 12)
- Pretend You Want Me (Book 13)
- Cross My Heart (Book 14)
- The Bodyguard Next Door (Book 15)
- Ex Marks The Perfect Spot (Book 16)
- The Thief Who Loved Me (Book 17)

Wilde Ways: Gone Rogue
- How To Protect A Princess (Book 1)
- How To Heal A Heartbreak (Book 2)
- How To Con A Crime Boss (Book 3)

Night Watch Paranormal Romance
- Hunt Me Down (Book 1)
- Slay My Name (Book 2)
- Face Your Demon (Book 3)

Trouble For Hire
- No Escape From War (Book 1)
- Don't Play With Odin (Book 2)
- Jinx, You're It (Book 3)
- Remember Ramsey (Book 4)

Death and Moonlight Mystery
- Step Into My Web (Book 1)
- Save Me From The Dark (Book 2)

Phoenix Fury
- Hot Enough To Burn (Book 1)

- Slow Burn (Book 2)
- Burn It Down (Book 3)

Dark Sins
- Don't Trust A Killer (Book 1)
- Don't Love A Liar (Book 2)

Lazarus Rising
- Never Let Go (Book One)
- Keep Me Close (Book Two)
- Stay With Me (Book Three)
- Run To Me (Book Four)
- Lie Close To Me (Book Five)
- Hold On Tight (Book Six)

Bad Things
- The Devil In Disguise (Book 1)
- On The Prowl (Book 2)
- Undead Or Alive (Book 3)
- Broken Angel (Book 4)
- Heart Of Stone (Book 5)
- Tempted By Fate (Book 6)
- Wicked And Wild (Book 7)
- Saint Or Sinner (Book 8)

Bite Series
- Forbidden Bite (Bite Book 1)
- Mating Bite (Bite Book 2)

Blood and Moonlight Series
- Bite The Dust (Book 1)
- Better Off Undead (Book 2)
- Bitter Blood (Book 3)

Mine Series

- Mine To Take (Book 1)
- Mine To Keep (Book 2)
- Mine To Hold (Book 3)
- Mine To Crave (Book 4)
- Mine To Have (Book 5)
- Mine To Protect (Book 6)

Dark Obsession Series

- Watch Me (Book 1)
- Want Me (Book 2)
- Need Me (Book 3)
- Beware Of Me (Book 4)

Purgatory Series

- The Wolf Within (Book 1)
- Marked By The Vampire (Book 2)
- Charming The Beast (Book 3)
- Deal with the Devil (Book 4)

Bound Series

- Bound By Blood (Book 1)
- Bound In Darkness (Book 2)
- Bound In Sin (Book 3)
- Bound By The Night (Book 4)
- Bound in Death (Book 5)

Stand-Alone Romantic Suspense

- Waiting For Christmas
- Monster Without Mercy
- Kiss Me This Christmas
- It's A Wonderful Werewolf
- Never Cry Werewolf

- Immortal Danger
- Deck The Halls
- Come Back To Me
- Put A Spell On Me
- Never Gonna Happen
- One Hot Holiday
- Slay All Day
- Midnight Bite
- Secret Admirer
- Christmas With A Spy
- Femme Fatale
- Until Death
- Sinful Secrets
- First Taste of Darkness
- A Vampire's Christmas Carol

About the Author

Cynthia Eden loves romance books, chocolate, and going on semi-lazy adventures. She is a *New York Times*, *USA Today*, *Digital Book World*, and *IndieReader* best-seller. She writes romantic suspense, paranormal romance, and fun contemporary novels. You can find out more about her work at www.cynthiaeden.com.

If you want to stay updated on her new releases and books deals, be sure to join her newsletter group: cynthiaeden. com/newsletter.